The Frathole

DEVON McCORMACK

PEACH STATE FRATBROS, BOOK 2

THE FRATHOLE (PEACH STATE FRATBROS #2)

ALSO IN THE PEACH STATE UNIVERSE

PEACH STATE STEPBROS

The Step Bet (Peach State Stepbros #1)

The Step Don't (Peach State Stepbros #2)

The Step Dare (Peach State Stepbros #3)

PEACH STATE FRATBROS

Frat Around and Find Out (Peach State Fratbros #1)

1

Ryan

TONIGHT'S MY LUCKY night.

I've barely unlocked the door before the Phi Lambda brunette charges me, her lips locking with mine, her sweet lavender smell filling my nostrils. I push her back against the wall, unfastening her skirt and sliding my hand beneath her panties. As I find her clit, she gasps, and her blonde Phi Lambda sister turns my head toward her, taking her own kiss as I continue to work her friend. She has more of a vanilla scent—I figure her conditioner or maybe a hair product.

I've seen these girls around at events, but tonight, at the Alpha Theta Mu party, was the first time we've chatted each other up. I could hardly believe it when they both expressed interest—and even better, impatience—about getting up to my room.

The music was loud, but I think the brunette said her name was Dani. She leans against the wall, arching her back as she moans. The blonde—pretty sure I heard her say Em (yeah, we'll go with that)—breaks our kiss and says, "Seems like you know what you're doing."

"Just wait till you get a feel for yourself," Dani assures her.

Pride swells in my chest. "You're making me cocky as hell."

"I can tell it's not your first time with two girls," Dani says.

"Two is easy. Things get complicated at four, but I'm ambitious."

"I'm starting to get a little jealous," Em says, moving closer.

"We can't have that," I say, still thumbing Dani. "There's one rule of messing around like this, and that's that no one gets left out."

With my free hand, I pop the button on Em's jeans and slide the zipper down, then reach into her panties. Moving slowly, I trace the outline of her as she backs up to the wall, now side by side with her sorority sister. As Dani moans, I start toying with Em.

Her body trembles, and she whispers, "The hell, Dani, you weren't kidding. Guess I should've expected as much from a linebacker for Peach State."

"We're only getting started," I tell her, offering a kiss. I speed up my movements until she's moaning into my mouth. "Mmmm…" I breathe, feeling how worked up Dani is.

"Your friend's getting real wet for me," I mumble into Em's mouth before turning my attention to Dani. While we kiss, Em joins in, and I can taste them both. I've just discovered how perfectly lavender and vanilla complement each other.

"Okay, you need to stop, or you're gonna make me come too soon," Dani warns.

"We wouldn't want that." I'm not thrilled at the idea of putting on the brakes, so I give Em a little more attention as Dani blinks a few times, as though she's coming to her senses from a haze of pleasure.

Damn right that's how good I am.

"You deserve a reward for that," Dani says, working my fly. In no time, she has my jeans at my ankles, my cock in her grip as she settles on her knees. But then she shifts into slow motion.

Dani runs her tongue along the underside of my shaft, up to the head. She's torturing me, but I'm not teasing Em anymore. I'm playing her the way I've learned she enjoys in this brief exploratory phase. I can tell she likes a firmer touch than Dani—only slightly, but damn, it's got her calling out my name again.

"You're being real good to my bestie," Dani says. "So I guess I have to be nice to you too." She slides her lips over my cock, gliding down.

"Oh, fucking hell," I mutter as she demonstrates how she can work that mouth. As she pleasures me, I lean close to Em for a kiss. She's still practically humming from how worked up I'm getting her.

"I'm gonna move my hand," I whisper into her mouth. "But only because we have to get out of these clothes for the real fun."

"Fuck," she says like it pains her, which only makes me that much harder in Dani's eager mouth.

I give Em one last sweep of my thumb before pulling back and sliding her panties and jeans down her thighs. After I get them off, she tosses her shirt, and I unfasten her bra from the back, noticing a tattoo of a rose at the base of her neck.

"You're good at that," she tells me.

Dani pulls off my dick. "Practice makes perfect?" she jokes as she pushes to her feet.

"That should be my line," I insist.

"You have two beautiful girls willing to make your night," Dani says. "I think you should let us have whatever the fuck we want, including your lines."

I nod. "Fair point."

The girls exchange a look. They seem even more excited than when we got to the room—like they've realized how lucky they are to be with a man who knows what he's doing in the bedroom.

Dani helps me with my shirt while I step out of my jeans. Em and I help Dani strip down, and we've only barely gotten her out of her clothes before the girls gang up and toss me onto my roomie Marty's bed.

"Fuck," I say, distracted for a moment as I glance at my air mattress on the floor by the door.

Usually I have my own room, but after Omega Psi's failed glitter-bomb prank resulted in the Sigma Alpha fire last semester, the guys at Alpha Theta Mu agreed to let us stay here. It was a preferred alternative to splitting up to stay at different hotels across town. That would have defeated the purpose of joining a fraternity.

But this solution hasn't been the best for my sex life.

I've already gotten hell from Marty a few times for breaking the rule about only hooking up in my own bed. And I know I should say something now, but surely Marty will understand that I can't make these girls have a threesome on an air mattress.

And given how horny I've gotten them, it'd be rude to stop—mean, even.

After a moment, it's easy to forget the issue when Dani and Em go feral. I get lost in their kisses, and soon it's hard to tell who's even got my cock because of how they're switching off. But I'm starting to learn that Em has a lighter grip, not as confident as Dani's, which is pretty damn adorable.

"Fuck, where are the condoms?" Em asks. "I want to sit on that dick."

I have some in my bag on the floor, but I don't want to kill the vibe, so I reach into Marty's nightstand instead, searching around until I discover the package that was in plastic wrap until I opened it during one of my previous sessions. I also grab the lube.

I tear the condom wrapper open, and Dani seizes it. "Come on, babe," she tells Em. "I'll get him in for you." She turns back to me. "That got you turned on, didn't it?"

Sparks are going off in my chest. "Fuck, you girls are wild."

And they prove just how wild as we go at it.

Dani and Em are attentive to each other as they swap turns on my cock. Em rides me to completion first, and then I fuck Dani on her back, putting in the work like I'm running drills.

"Almost there," Dani whispers.

Em stops kissing me and drops down, using her mouth and finger to take Dani to the end. Dani throws her head back as her body twists, her breasts bouncing as she releases. I keep up my pace as she rides out her orgasm, and as her body settles, Em pulls away and I steady my hips.

"So where do you ladies want me to come?" I ask.

I'm a gentleman, after all.

"Oh, suddenly we're ladies?" Dani asks, and they both crack up.

"I kind of want him to come on my chest," Em says, looking at Dani for confirmation.

Dani wears a mischievous expression. "You think you can shoot across us both?"

I nod. "After all that, I'm sure I've got plenty stored up." I pull out and slip off the condom as they kneel before me.

I rise up, standing on the mattress, jerking myself.

"It was so hot watching you both enjoy my cock," I tell them. "And seeing how generous you were with each other. Time for me to give you a reward."

"I think you deserve a reward too," Dani says, resting her hand on my ass. She slides her fingers back, rubbing until she's rimming me.

"Christ," I mutter as a burst of energy pulses through me. "This is too fucking much."

Em follows with her own hand around my ass, finger sliding up against me too.

"Reward us," Em says.

They pull the cum right from me as I shoot a powerful explosion, hitting Em's chest first, then quickly turning to mark Dani too.

But I'm not finished, and another burst escapes. I roll my head back, shouting as it rips right through me, my muscles locking up as I finally manage to spend it all. I can barely see straight, the climax still rocking me as I'm left with the scent of lavender and vanilla mixed with my sweat.

"Wow," Dani says, sounding impressed as hell.

I glance down. "You beauties look like satisfied customers."

They look at one another before Em says, "More than satisfied, but you made a mess."

I examine the sheets, noticing how much cum I got on them. "Fuck," I mutter as I think about the rule I violated.

"What?"

"Um, well…"

Before I have a chance to explain, I hear the lock turn behind me, and the door opens. Marty stands in the doorway, his face red as I've ever seen it, giving me a death glare. "Are you fucking kidding me right now?"

I chuckle nervously. "Hey there, roomie."

2

Marty

"I'VE FUCKING HAD it up to here with this guy," I say to the group I've gathered in Lance's room for the emergency meeting.

Lance is Alpha Theta Mu's sitting president, my best friend, and the guy I'm hoping can find a solution for our Ryan problem. He sits at his desk while his boyfriend and Sigma Alpha's president, Ty, stands at his side.

"Me?" Ryan says. "You should get penalized for how rude you were to my guests."

"How was I rude? I took you in the hall to fuss, let them get dressed and leave, before dragging your ass down here to sort this out."

I had just finished up at the party. Had a great time and was ready to head to bed. If Ryan had so much as left the door hanger out so I would've known what was going on in my room, at least I wouldn't have barged in unannounced. Although, now that I know what he was doing on my bed, I'm glad I did. These past few weeks

Ryan's proven he has no interest in following the house rules, and at this point I'm absolutely seething.

For the most part, since the Sigma Alpha fire, sharing space with them at Alpha Theta Mu has worked out. Everyone except Ryan has been easy enough to get along with, but if he can't get his act together, he has no right to stay under our roof.

Keegan searches around uncomfortably. He's Ryan's Sigma Alpha buddy and only joined this emergency meeting because we ran into him as I was urging Ryan toward Lance's room.

"Maybe you should have gotten dressed with your friends," Keegan says as he passes Ryan a pillow from Lance's bed.

Since I was busy fussing at Ryan about his transgression before hauling his ass across the house, he didn't really have time to get dressed, so he just stands there, in the buff, though like when he's hanging around my room, he's not self-conscious about it. If I were a football player stacked with muscle like Ryan, I probably wouldn't be either.

As Ryan obstructs the view of his dick with the pillow, Lance cringes. "Wait, he's gonna get his cum on my pillow."

"Now you know how I feel since this guy soaked my duvet with his jizz," I snap.

"We could've swapped our covers out for the rest of

the night, dude," Ryan says.

"Yeah, because I'm sure the one on your air mattress is *so* sanitary and semen-free?"

"My semen's always free," he quips.

"Oh, you're real funny tonight, aren't ya? Doesn't even matter. I have a spare duvet—as you know from the last time this happened." I'm so pissed, I can feel the heat radiating from my face, down my neck.

Ryan's got this twinkle in his eyes, clearly enjoying goading me. "It's so cute how jealous you are that I was fucking around with two beautiful women while you were thinking about the next wank you were gonna get in."

It's like he stuck a hot poker in my chest. I step up to him, which is comical since the guy's, like, four inches taller than me, and even if he wasn't, with a body like his, he could effortlessly squash me like a bug. "Not everyone aspires to be the biggest manwhore in the house."

"But if there was a competition, I'd probably win. Well, maybe aside from Dax."

Dax is a Sigma Alpha who has plenty of fun but is at least cool and considerate of our rules.

"Yeah, definitely not hitting it as much as Dax," Keegan assures him.

I'm not surprised to see one of his own making light of all this, but I'm not backing down either. "Lance…" I press.

"Okay, okay," Lance says, obviously still struggling against the number of drinks he's had, while simultaneously trying to fulfill his obligations as Alpha Theta Mu's prez. "Why don't you two calm the hell down so we can get to bed. I'm tipsy and wanna pass out."

Ty adds, "And the longer you guys keep fighting, the more you're keeping me from cuddling up with my man, so let's wrap this up." He's only talking about cuddling, but his tone sounds like he's threatening us…because I do know Lance's man loves his cuddle time with my fratbro.

Lance groans. I'm sure he hates being put in the middle since the offender is his boyfriend Ty's best buddy. But being the best friend to our president's boyfriend and a player on the Peach State football team doesn't entitle Ryan to continue violating the rules Alpha Theta Mu set forth when the Sigma Alphas came to stay with us.

"Okay," Lance says. "To confirm, Ryan, you had girls over in Marty's bed?"

Ryan huffs. "Of course I did. I didn't want to be rude and have a threesome on a fucking air mattress."

"He has a very good point there," Keegan says, and upon earning glares, raises his hands in a defensive stance. "Just saying."

"Come on," Ryan pleads. "It's a dumb rule. What was I supposed to do?"

"To have sex in your own bed," I insist. "And if you didn't want to fuck on an air mattress, you could have hooked up with them at their sorority."

"Would have killed the mood to have to walk all the way there."

"See!" I exclaim. "*This* is the issue. You were only thinking about yourself and your raging hard-on."

"What about their horny pussies?" Ryan asks. "Ty, come on. Back me up here."

Ty grits his teeth. "Marty's not wrong." I'm surprised to see him calling out one of his own. If anything, that only shows how bad Ryan's behavior has been. "You've been breaking rules, and we haven't been here for even a month yet."

"Breaking rules?" Ryan says. "You make it sound like I'm running around fucking shit up."

"There was the time you fucked in Marty's bed the week we moved in here," Ty says. "Then you broke the coffee table from dancing on it—"

"I paid to replace that."

"You were having a four-way in the weight room during operating hours."

"Ash and Colin mess around in there too."

I'm not gonna stand for him bringing my friends into this. "Ash and Colin were reprimanded when they were caught in there during *off* hours."

Ty continues, "And then there was the time you ate

all of Payton's protein bars in, like, a day—"

"Okay, I ran out of mine, and those are hard to find," Ryan interjects. "I also don't need a blow by blow. I broke a few stupid rules. I'm not denying that."

"Really? Because I have more if you need them," I add.

Ryan glares at me. "Are you keeping tabs on every rule I break? Can't stop thinking about me, huh?" He relaxes the pillow to his side as he steps toward me, that fat cock shifting about.

"Just annoyed by you," I say.

"Well, you look really sexy when you get annoyed as fuck."

A pulse of rage shoots through me. Fuck, this guy loves getting under my skin. I don't even really know why that comment would bother me so much—probably because he's the one saying it.

"Enough!" Lance says. "Ryan, you've admitted to breaking the rule, so there are consequences."

"A few guys can't make decisions about this," Ryan objects. "You have to call a meeting with the whole house."

"Wrong," Ty says. "We already had a meeting about your behavior, and if you recall, we decided that the next infraction, we would put you on probation."

Ryan chews on his bottom lip, his confidence clearly waning. "Eh…but I get, like, a final warning or something?"

"That *was* your final warning," Lance says through his teeth, pressing his hand against his head like he's already getting a hangover.

"What does probation even mean?" Ryan asks.

"It means any more slips with the rules," I explain, "and your ass is out."

"Where would I go?"

"Maybe you can find a sorority that would adopt you."

He takes a moment, as though he's seriously considering it, so I have to interrupt any fantasy he might be entertaining. "That would be against *their* rules, so that's not happening either. I don't know, get an apartment. Find a roomie or several. But you won't be able to stay at Alpha Theta Mu."

Ryan looks to Ty.

"Don't look at me like I haven't had your back." Ty's obviously frustrated, and I feel for him since I know he's gone out on a limb for Ryan. "I have been here from day one, defending your ass, and I love you, but you keep pulling shit like this. And these guys don't have to let us stay here. This is a favor. I'm sorry, but your reckless behavior is messing this up, not only for you, but for the rest of us."

"So what does this mean?" Ryan asks.

"Probation lasts six weeks," Lance explains. "During

that time, no slipups or you know the consequence."

"And after six weeks?"

"You'll receive one warning before being back on probation, and as time goes on, you will earn back the right to have warnings."

"Hopefully we won't even be here by then," Ryan says with a pout.

"Ry, don't kid yourself," Ty says. "Between insurance and getting contractors together, Sigma Alpha's house won't be up and running until next fall, after we've both graduated, and that's if everything goes well."

The room falls silent, and I notice Ryan's never put the pillow back in front of his cock, so it's just dangling there, that fat menace between his legs.

"Okay," Lance says. "Now, please, everyone get back to their rooms. We can finalize this tomorrow, but I need to get some Tylenol and head to bed."

"You heard my boyfriend," Ty says. "Out!"

Like the protective partner he is, he ushers us out of Lance's room, and I can feel the animosity from Keegan and Ryan.

Ryan's miraculously quiet all the way back to our room.

"Will you at least help me with getting a new duvet cover on?" I ask. "I'll need to wash the comforter too, but I can do that tomorrow."

"Depends. Will I be violating any rules if I don't?"

"Never mind. I'll do it myself." I retrieve the spare duvet from the closet while Ryan stands there, baring it all, his arms folded.

"I don't get it," he says, scratching at his blond locks that somehow manage to look messy, like a model's on an Abercrombie billboard. "Everyone likes me but you."

I set the spare on the window seat and pull my duvet off the bed. "Some people think the whole clowning-around bit is cute. I don't."

"Mr. Goody-goody."

That's a fact. I've always been the rule follower of Alpha Theta Mu. I know it annoys some of the guys, but I'm not ashamed that I care about the frat and want to ensure that everyone's safe. And no one, not even Ryan, will make me feel bad about that.

"Yes, that's me, Ryan. I'm the prick who keeps things in order around the house. I'm sorry it's taken you this long to get that. And on top of finishing my BA and working part-time at the registrar's office, I didn't sign up to babysit your ass."

"You're a risk management major. You should consider me an internship."

I don't even acknowledge the remark, but he's not wrong: Having Ryan in this house is certainly prepping me for the future.

As I'm pulling the comforter from the duvet, I feel something cool and slick on the back of my hand. "Oh

God. It's your cum. I'm gonna have to cut this hand off, aren't I?"

Ryan laughs. "Don't worry. From my experience, it's not infectious."

I roll my eyes and take the duvet off the comforter, and there's some jizz on it too, but I'll just have to live with it tonight.

Ryan sighs. "Maybe we figure something else out. Tomorrow, we can swap rooms with some other guys."

"So you can torture another guy with your bullshit?"

"So I won't be on probation with the biggest asshat in the house, is what I was thinking. If I stay in here with your prude ass, I'm definitely getting thrown out."

"You can ask, but it's not happening."

"Why?"

"For the same reason I let you room with me to begin with. I want to keep an eye on you. I'm gonna watch you like a goddamn hawk, and if you so much as step up to the line of a rule, I'm getting your ass kicked out of here."

By now, I'm trying to get the fresh duvet over my comforter, but it's not easy by myself, and even less so when I'm so worked up.

"Give me that," Ryan says, grabbing the other side and helping me. "All this because you're mad I get laid more than you do," he mumbles.

I can't pretend I don't envy how effortlessly Ryan

gets together with girls while I fail at nearly every attempt.

"Do I need to leave you some time to jerk off from now on? Maybe need me to make sure you get milked once a day to keep you chill?"

There's that sting in my chest that he so easily elicits. "You're vile."

"And you're a grumpy prude."

Grumpy prude? Are we ten? "Oh, you're really hurting my feelings."

"I'm so sorry. How about we kiss and make up?" He's not holding back with the sarcasm, and when I turn to him, his lips are only a few inches from my face, puckered up.

I step away, stretching the duvet so I can adjust the comforter in it. We spread it across the bed, and as I zip up the duvet, I say, "Thank you for the help, but this changes nothing between us. I don't know how anyone can be attracted to an asshole like you."

"And I understand why you're like a citronella candle that repels girls. Any progress with Angie, by the way?"

He really struck a nerve with that one. Yes, I'm fucking into Lance's friend Angie, who's always coming over these days, and I don't doubt how obvious I am about it. Or that Ryan's picked up on it.

"To think, this isn't even our worst fight," I observe.

"It's really not," he says with a smile, making me groan.

"Okay, I'm getting to sleep. Please do me a favor and go pick up a girl and bring her back here so I can get you out tonight. Save this whole frat the trouble."

I rush to the en suite and wash Ryan's cum off my hands. By the time I'm in bed, Ryan's on his air mattress. And I'm still reeling from how he's been needling me all night, especially bringing my crush into it. What a low blow.

I must admit, it's even worse knowing he was getting so much pleasure in this bed while I'm fucking stewing. The only saving grace is that knowing Ryan, I'm not gonna have to suffer much longer.

3

Ryan

"HOW WAS YOUR weekend?" my boss, Troy, asks as we work together in the pit, replacing suspension brakes on a Nissan Sentra.

I started at the auto shop the summer before last, after hearing from one of my teammates that a position had opened up. It was a great opportunity with flexible hours that, unlike most jobs, worked with my schedule for training and games during the season. I didn't realize how much I'd enjoy it, but it's kind of like football—I'm a natural. I like working with my hands, figuring out what's wrong with whatever car I'm working on. And Troy, who recently became part owner of the place, is a great boss. Really taken me under his wing. It helps that he played football in high school, so even when we don't have much to talk about, we can always talk about our favorite teams. He also has great sports analogies for when shit goes wrong in a car to help me understand what's going on.

"My weekend?" I ask. "Hmmm. How do I put this? Hot until it wasn't."

Troy fidgets with the brake line. "Uh-oh. That doesn't sound good."

"You ever go on probation at your frat?"

Troy's an Alpha Theta Mu alum, though I don't hold it against him…much.

He stops what he's doing and turns to me. "No, and how the hell am I only now hearing about this? What did you do this time?"

"Already assuming it was my bad?" At his glare, I confess, "It involves a couple of girls and Marty." His eyebrows flare, and I quickly add, "Not like, us all together. A four-way with Marty? Fuck, I can't even imagine."

As I cringe at the thought, Troy bursts into a laugh. "That wasn't where my mind went at all. I thought it was odd, the idea of you two fighting over girls."

I snicker just thinking about Marty trying to hit on girls. "Not at all. You should see him with Lance's friend Angie. He can barely get words out whenever she's around. Although, it's fun watching him get all flustered."

When she's over, he's quiet, attentive…and I'm not even sure he's noticing anyone else. Adorable.

Maybe not adorable.

That's a weird thing to think about a guy I don't

even like.

"Can't tell if she picks up on it, but it's hard to believe she doesn't with how obvious he is."

"Yeah, Marty's a great guy, but I don't think I've ever seen him with a girlfriend. But your night sounds like it was better if a couple of girls were involved."

"It was until Marty came in."

Troy's brow rises. "I have a feeling you're not totally innocent in this story."

"Whose side are you on?"

"Alpha Theta Mu for life," he teases with a wink.

Of course that's where his allegiance would lie.

"Now hand me another C-clamp," he says.

I pass one over, and while he affixes it, I go on, "That guy does not like me, and the feeling is mutual. He wanted me out of the house the day we came to stay over there. That's why he was so insistent on me staying in his room. So he could watch over me and wait for me to fuck up. And now I feel like if I so much as don't change the toilet paper roll, I'm outta there."

My fate depends on Marty, so I wasn't doing myself any favors by continuing to argue with him even after I was put on probation, but I can't help it. We're fire and gasoline, and I guess I'm the gasoline because it seems like everywhere I go, the flames are chasing me.

"Marty's a good guy," Troy says. "He can be prickly, but he's also very considerate, and loyal as hell when you get to know him."

"Doesn't account for why the guy's whole personality revolves around being such a stick-in-the-mud. You know he's a lifeguard at a community pool over the summer? I can only imagine him chasing those poor kids around, sounding the whistle every time there's a splash."

"You realize he's really just trying to keep everyone safe."

"Maybe that applies to the rest of the guys, but that's not how it is with me. He doesn't like me, and I honestly can't think of anyone who bugs me more than him."

Troy smiles, a sparkle in his eyes.

"What?" I press.

"I had a guy like that in my life. Real prick. Always annoying the hell out of me, keeping me on edge. To think how many times I wanted to sock him one."

"What happened?"

"We're considering getting a dog." He beams, making me laugh.

That's when it hits me. "Dude, you're talking about your boyfriend? Seriously? You really got me with that one. I was thinking you were gonna say you kicked his ass or something."

"Nah, kicking isn't what I do with him."

We share another laugh.

"Now he's fucking branded you, dude," I say, indicating the tat of Atlas's name on his wrist.

I used to see his boyfriend/stepbro around campus, and since he graduated, I mostly see him through Troy. He's a cool guy who does a lot of good work for a nonprofit in Peachtree Springs. When they're together, they're totally obsessed, which isn't surprising given they have each other's name tattooed on their bodies.

"The animosity between Mart and me is different," I explain. "You and Atlas give each other hell, but it's always like roasting, there's something friendly behind it. That's the way I am with most of the guys in the house."

"It wasn't always like that. Atlas used to know how to pick at my sorest spots. Guy could get me from zero to a hundred with one snide comment. Not saying you and Marty are destined to be boyfriends, though."

I huff. "I can just imagine Marty as a boyfriend. He'd be exhausting. Always stressed. I keep thinking if he got laid, then maybe he'd be less of an ass. Someone needs to give it to him so that maybe he can chill the fuck out. Actually, on second thought, maybe it would work out because that might match my sex drive."

Troy eyes me, his expression twisted up.

"What?" I ask.

"You realize you just went on a tangent about messing around with him, right?"

"No, I was saying *someone* should. Not me. Don't make it weird."

He glares playfully. "You already did."

"Whatever, dude."

My phone buzzes in my back pocket, and when I pull it out, I see Mom's calling. Not whom I was expecting, since Dad's pretty much been nonstop lately due to the Combine week coming up. Maybe he got Mom to call on his behalf since I haven't responded yet. Although, he knows I'm working.

"Interesting," I say.

"That you're taking calls while you're on the job?"

"Oh, fuck." I quickly tuck my phone back in my pocket.

"I'm only giving you hell, man. You think I never pulled that stuff on the job? Just don't do it while you're messing with shit."

"Thanks, Troy. I appreciate your not reporting this back to the frat." Troy laughs, but I have this tension in my gut. "Ugh. Dad's so excited about next week."

"It's exciting," Troy insists. "This is what you've been doing all this for, right?"

It should be. I've been incredibly fortunate when it comes to football.

But it's been more than that. Since I was a kid, Dad and I have been a team, building me up, training constantly, working with the right trainers for this moment to happen. Now here it is, and…this is not how I thought I'd feel.

Troy must sense my hesitation because he says, "Ry?"

I scratch the back of my neck.

He stops what he's doing and folds his arms. "Okay. I've noticed you get like this whenever I talk about the draft lately. What's up?"

I hesitate. It's not something I've talked to anyone about, but Troy has experience with all this. From what I've heard through guys on the team, he was a sure pick for a few colleges before his injury in high school.

"Maybe I'm just getting in my head too much, but…kind of having second thoughts about pro."

"Really?"

"That was always the dream, and Dad threw his life into prepping me for it. Always supporting me a thousand percent. All hands on deck. But as much fun as it's been playing for Peach State, I'm wondering if maybe I've done it and there are other parts of my life I want to explore."

"I hear that. It was different for me since I was forced to step back from it, but I was on the same track. And life had other plans for me, I guess. Just know, if you're wondering if there is a life besides football, I can assure you, there definitely is. And it can be really beautiful and a lot more chill."

"Chill sounds nice right now," I blurt out.

For my entire college career, it's been go-go-go, training and traveling for games. When my life isn't about winning and making "the dream" come true, I've been working toward my BS in exercise science or squeezing in fun with my fratbros. Now…working with my agent, and Dad being all gung-ho about what my options'll be, I'm not as excited about the idea as I once was. Although, I'm scared to even say that out loud. Like I'm betraying the kid who wanted that and my dad who gave so much so I could live this dream.

"Could be the stress of next week," Troy says. "Just get through the Combine and then see how you feel. Maybe you'll get your spark back once you see who wants to draft you."

"You could be right. And that's another thing that concerns me. Because on the other side of it, there's a chance I make a huge fuckup and wreck my life."

"Eh, knowing you, you'll probably fuck it up either way."

As I laugh, Troy pats my arm. "If you ever want to talk about it more, I'm here, man."

Given that I've been struggling with this on my own, it's nice that Troy's willing to hear me out.

I finish the rest of my shift, then head to the break room. I figure Mom and Dad are in the middle of dinner, so I call Mom since she's always more likely to have her phone nearby.

"Hey, Ma. What's up?"

"Oh, hey, sweetie." I hear what sounds like a crowd in the background, which throws me.

"Did you guys go out to eat?" I ask, surprised since I can't remember the last time they went to a restaurant.

"Oh, with who? Your dad?"

"Who else would it be with?"

She laughs. "No one. I'm having cocktails with friends."

"Well, I can just call him. He's overdue for a chat. He home?"

"Um…" She hesitates in a way that, again, throws me. "Yeah, I'm sure."

"Everything okay?"

"Why would you ask that?"

"You called me, and now you're out with friends and don't know where Dad is."

"I just—I'm sorry, I can't really think straight. It's been a week. I wanted to catch up with you a little. I know you must be excited about next week. But now's not a great time. Let's try and make something happen before your flight, though."

I grit my teeth. Troy's probably right. It's only nerves. This is what I've wanted most of my life. I can't fuck this up now. "Of course," I tell Mom, then exchange I-love-yous before hanging up.

I'm surprised Mom was out. She's usually working or at home with Dad. And both are more likely to stay home than go out, so it's nice she's getting to spend time with friends.

I consider calling Dad, but I don't really want to hear the "Hey, champ," and asking me about my workouts this week. Besides, I'll see him plenty next week.

Tonight, I just want to head back to the house, do my homework, and get to bed without causing any controversy that might get me in trouble with Marty.

4

Marty

"AND ONE-TWO-THREE, ONE-TWO-THREE," my tango instructor, Jenni, says as I work with my partner, moving in a circle around the classroom.

"Tango would be a great way to help you learn to let go," my therapist said.

"It'll get you out of your comfort zone."

"You could make some new friends."

She might've been right about all that, but going with the flow isn't really my thing, and when I fuck up again during my Sunday afternoon class at the student center, I halt in place, trying to remember which foot I need to start with to get going again.

"We're supposed to keep moving," my partner says, sounding annoyed because this isn't the first time I've messed up during this song…or the first time she's been paired with me.

"I just need a second."

One of the other pairs, an older couple who said on

the first day that they joined to reignite the spark in their relationship, passes by.

"Keep moving, Marty!" Jenni calls out. "You were doing fine!"

"Okay, okay," I say, forcing myself to continue, fumbling my way through the basic steps we're learning, then move on for a few more steps.

Tango is not exactly effortless for a guy as uptight as I am, but I'm such a ball of anxiety, I'll try anything if it might help me out.

Meditation.

Yoga.

Cognitive behavioral therapy.

Dialectical behavioral therapy.

All my attempts the past few years have helped, but I'm a work in progress. That's what my therapist says, at least.

After class wraps up, Jenni pulls me aside. "Hey, Marty, how are you feeling so far about the class?"

"Eh, it's okay."

"I would encourage you to practice at home a little more."

"Practice would be a lot easier if I didn't have a roommate." Several times now Ryan's stormed in when I've been in the middle of working on my steps. Guy really gets a kick out of that. *"Oh, no, please. Keep going. I gotta see this."*

That goddamn frathole.

"Maybe your roommate could help you," Jenni says.

If only she knew how pissed Ryan has been at me the past week, she'd realize he's not helping me with much of anything right now.

"Just try to relax. That's what tango's all about. Going with the flow. Easing up. And if you mess up—"

"I know, keep going. Easier said than done."

She grins. "You're doing fine. I don't mean to single you out. I can tell by the way you're doing it that you're in your head, trying to get it right, and that's not how tango works. Be easy on yourself."

Jenni doesn't know I'm here at the recommendation of my therapist, and I don't see a reason to point it out, so I thank her for her suggestion before grabbing my bag and heading out.

When I get out to the courtyard, I consider giving my brother a call.

You just talked to him yesterday. He's doing fine.

My younger brother, Aiden, is in high school right now, and he's suddenly too cool to talk to his big bro, so I try to give him his space.

I return to the house to find Angie, Ty, and Lance hanging out in the living area.

Angie Williams looks like a goddess, sitting on the sofa, her brown hair practically sparkling in the afternoon light that filters in through the blinds. She laughs at something Lance says, rolling her head back, all teeth as she cherishes the moment. Simply seeing her so at ease relaxes the muscles I tensed up through most of my class earlier.

As she recovers from her laugh, she spots me, her eyes lighting up, only it's the same way they light up when she sees Lance. Like she's seeing a friend. Of all the guys Angie could pick to go out with, I know Marty McGovern is very far down her list.

"How was tango class?" she asks.

"Uh…"

When I first signed up, I figured this would be something I did without anyone knowing, but between Lance's chatty mouth and Ryan being a douche, the secret's out.

"Class was fine," I lie.

I gravitate to Angie, settling on the couch beside her.

She moves closer to me and takes a whiff. "Oh, Marty, I always love your cologne. I could smell it all day."

My cheeks warm, and I giggle—at least the closest thing I do to a giggle—and it even takes her by surprise.

"You gonna teach me any moves?" she teases.

"How about once I've had more than two classes?"

"I think Lance should take some dance classes," Ty says from the love seat he and Lance sit on.

"Tango?" Lance asks.

"Maybe pole dancing," Ty jokes.

Lance practically crawls onto Ty. "I bet you'd like that."

Lance and Ty are so into each other, and I must admit, I'm a little envious of the amount of time Lance spends with Ty now. Before he partnered up, it was Lance and me, and before that it was Lance, Ash, and me, but now that Lance has Ty and Ash has Colin, I'm the only one flying solo. Not that I don't want Lance to be happy. I love how good his Sigma Alpha guy is to him, but it used to be us hanging out on Sunday evenings, not him sitting in his boyfriend's lap.

"It'd be fun to learn to pole dance and then maybe make a set list to play for you," Lance says, then kisses Ty—way too intimately for a public kiss.

"Ash and Colin may have rubbed off on you guys," I say. Not that Lance and Ty are into exhibitionism. At least, not that I know of.

"I'm pretty sure they would have mentioned a four-way to me," Angie jokes, which gets the guys laughing.

"Ew, gross," I say.

"What's gross?" Dax asks as he heads through the door. I'd say Dax is Sigma Alpha's most charming frat. He's earned a reputation for seducing more than a few of my peers out of the closet. Seems to have a talent for it, and even the guys who don't want to get in his pants, want to hang with him.

He's just cool…the opposite of me, basically.

Ryan heads in right behind him, and I clench my fists. Fucking A.

I couldn't go an afternoon without seeing that prick? Is it not enough that I have to see him every night before I go to bed? And every morning when I wake up?

"Our four-way with Ash and Colin," Ty replies, which has Lance in stitches.

Dax's brows tug closer together. "I don't get why that's amusing. That sounds hot as hell."

I retch. "Now I'm gonna have that image stuck in my head."

Dax shrugs as he and Ryan approach the couch.

Ryan gets right in front of Angie, resting his hand on his hip, his lips curling into a smirk. Why is he so close to her? He stands there, posing in a way that shows off his body in his tank top, his muscles really popping. Sure, he talks to her sometimes, but this seems different, and I'm suspicious of his motives. Would Ryan be a dick enough to flirt with her to get back at me for getting him placed on probation?

I already know the answer.

"I'm guessing you guys were at the gym," I say through my teeth.

"Yeah," Ryan says. "Met with my trainer for drills this morning, then headed over to get my pump. Gotta stay in shape for next week."

"Oh, that's right," Angie says. "You gotta show off your skills, and then the teams are gonna be fighting to see who you'll sign with for the NFL."

The way she says it, she's clearly trying to flatter him, but he tenses up, which is strange for him. I would have thought that would hit his ego in the sweet spot. It's almost like the guy's nervous or something, which I've never seen him be about football.

"Yeah, sure," Ryan says. "That's how the Combine should go, I guess. But what's up with you, Ang?"

"It's Angie," I correct.

"It's fine. I like Ang," she says as she drinks him in, and that's definitely not the way she looks at me or Lance.

I've noticed her sneaking looks Ryan's way every once in a while. And if she bones the enemy…I'm gonna lose my goddamn mind.

Not that I have any say in who she sleeps with, but dear God, please let it not be Ryan-fucking-Lorde.

"I swung by to spend some time with the guys," she says. "We're waiting for Payton, and then we were gonna head out to get some pizza at Junkie's. You guys want to come with?"

"I'd like that," Ryan says. "But if you're hungry, I can grab you a little something from the kitchen."

"I don't know that you can offer up any of Payton's protein bars, but I'm craving some peanut butter and chocolate right now."

Ryan buys his own of these protein bars, but he's notorious for digging into Payton's stash when he runs out.

"I grabbed my own earlier this week," he says. "They're fucking addicting, right?"

"They really are."

He moves closer to Angie, and I can't help myself. "Kitchen's over there," I say, pointing it out, earning looks from everyone.

Funny to think I felt so good when I saw Angie was here, only for it to be ruined by Ryan.

"Mart, you didn't offer her something already?" he asks. "Why are you being rude to our guest?"

"I just got here," I grumble.

"Be right back." He winks at her before heading into the kitchen.

"Speaking of which, I could use a drink," I say.

"I can get it," Ryan calls.

"Nah, I'm right behind you."

Ryan moves his slow ass toward the pantry, so I sidle up beside him.

"What the hell do you think you're doing?" I whisper.

He side-eyes me. "What's your problem?"

"I don't like the fact that you're pretending to be into Angie so that you can get back at me."

He flinches. "Angie? I'm trying to be nice. But if I weren't, as far as I'm aware, there aren't any rules against flirting with girls Marty McGovern likes."

Fuck him to hell and back. "Last I checked, the asshole jock isn't really her type."

"From general observation, she doesn't seem too cool with the uptight asshole either."

As we reach the pantry, I jump in front of it, commanding his attention. "Stop this," I insist.

"There's nothing to stop, Mart, but if there was, what would you do? Punch me? Nah, 'cause that's against the rules." He really drives that last part in, stressing why he's so angry with me.

I'm not the kind to throw punches, but if I were, I'm certain I already would have with this prick.

"Now," he says, "if you'll excuse me, I was getting Angie a protein bar."

He steps around me before spinning back toward me and whispering, "You smell real nice today, by the way. Wear that for Ang?" He snatches a bar.

The hairs on the back of my neck stand on end. I stifle a groan as I grab a cup from the cabinet and get some water from the fridge filter. When I return to the living room, I discover Dax sitting on one side of Angie, with Ryan having helped himself to my spot. Should've seen that one coming. And he's glowing, like this couldn't have worked more perfectly if he'd planned it.

"Doesn't seem like you were messing around at the gym," Angie says, admiring the way his biceps stretch the sleeves of his tank.

"Oh, you like that?" He sits up, flexing. "Go ahead, cop a feel." Angie helps herself—I don't know that my face could be much hotter right now. "Honestly, it's more about paying attention to the tris. Kill those as much as I can."

"Is she the only one who gets a feel?" Dax asks, green with envy.

"I want to feel," Lance adds.

"Hey!" Ty says. "You have tris right here."

"I can feel on those later."

"Get over here, guys." Ryan's invitation has Lance and Dax joining Angie, and Ty looks about as annoyed as me. As much as we both know Ryan's no threat to Ty, we also know Ty's protective as hell. Lance is his guy, and everyone in the house knows it.

"Yeah, yeah, feel up Sigma Alpha's secret weapon for the TaskFrat challenges," Ty says.

Lance shoots him a look, smirking.

The TaskFrat challenges are a series of task-based competitions between all the frats of Peach State. They happen throughout the year, and right now, Sigma Alpha's in the lead, and Lance is determined to make sure that's not for very long. Even as a couple, they still enjoy their infamous TaskFrat rivalry.

"If you think that's good," Ryan says as everyone continues appreciating his tris, "you should see what I've been doing for my upper abs."

As he stands, he tears off his shirt, like a fucking stripper for the mini bachelorette party that surrounds him, everyone getting a feel.

"During the season," he says, "I have to keep my bulk a little more, so it's been nice to lean down." Angie places her hand on his abs, stroking, and the guys follow her lead.

My face is hot with envy.

"Oh, wow!" she says. "So firm."

"Jesus Christ," Dax follows. "You can crush a man with these."

Even hating his goddamn guts right now, it's hard not to be impressed by his physique. Ryan doesn't fuck around at the gym. The guy doesn't even look human—more like some demigod from Greek myths. As much as I don't like him, feels like it'd be a waste not to make a statue of this guy.

Ryan continues entertaining his adoring audience before saying, "Mart, you want to get a feel too? You're looking a little left out."

"Maybe you can show me later, before bed," I tease.

"Got some other muscles that could use some attention before bed."

"I would think an exercise science guy would know

that's not a muscle."

"I said other muscles, which a cock does, in fact, contain, so why don't you stick with risk management, and I can show you what I'm talking about during our regular scheduled time later."

This comment catches Angie's attention, so I feel the need to add, "We don't ever do anything like that."

"Stop being a homophobe, Mart," Ryan says.

"What? That's not… I was just…" Can't exactly say that I just want it to be totally clear to Angie that I am free and not messing around with anyone. What would be the point? She's not gonna mess with me anyway.

"Look at his face," Ryan teases. "You wish I would let you jerk my meat."

"When you make everything sound that sexy, how can I resist?" I bite back.

Fortunately, I notice Payton heading down the stairs, so I'm hoping that'll put an end to the gun show. But it still takes too long for Ryan to put his goddamn shirt back on, with Angie basically ogling him the whole time. That only makes me hate Ryan even more, which I didn't think was possible.

We greet Payton and head out to Junkie's.

I try to work it out so I can sit next to Angie, but Lance winds up on one side of her, and Ryan—who's operating so smoothly, it'd be weird as hell for me to make a big deal about it in front of the group—sits on her other side. Now he's totally ignoring me, dedicating all his attention to Angie.

I'm starting to adjust to the heat searing my chest. I can hate on him all I want, but the guy has a way of making even what he's gonna order sound sexy as he jokes his way through the menu with her. Once he's really got her laughing, he turns to me, as though he wants to rub his victory in my face. "Did you need anything, Mart? Maybe a kids' menu or a high chair?"

"Ooh, what has crawled up your ass today?" Ty asks, overhearing the comment.

"Ah, I'm just teasing my roomie." Ryan drapes his arm over my shoulders, pulling me closer.

"Hands off."

Despite how much he's enjoying this, he must hear the rage in my tone because he releases me and turns his attention back to Angie.

This has to be the worst dinner of my entire college career, and it only gets worse as Ryan continues doting and complimenting, making Angie laugh her ass off in that way that normally has me enchanted but now I'm seething.

When we finish, we return to the house, and I head up to my room to get away from him for a minute. Unfortunately, it doesn't take him long to join me.

"You never mentioned how tango went," he says, stripping off his shirt, then dropping his pants and underwear and just leaving them beside his air mattress as he plops down on it, that fucking dick of his dropping to one side. Given his weight, I'm surprised the mattress hasn't popped.

"What are you doing?" I ask.

"Getting comfortable."

"That's not what I was talking about, and you know it."

"What were you talking about, then?" He actually sounds oblivious.

"Angie." I can't even say her name now without my face catching fire. "She's a nice girl, lovely, even. Don't put her in the middle of this thing between us."

"Relax. We were just talking."

Like I believe that. "As much of an asshole as you are, it'd be even more of an asshole move to mess around with her to get back at me."

His jaw tenses, and he pushes to his feet. That fat thing between his legs sways as he approaches me.

"First off," he says, "it's not a crime to make friends with a girl who hangs around the house, and who, as far as I can tell, has zero—and I do mean zero—interest in you."

He gets right up in my face, and I can feel his hot breath pricking my lips, the scent of the mint he grabbed from Junkie's filling my nostrils.

He sizes me up. "And second, you're real cute when

you're all worked up like this."

I ball my fists as my rage surges through me.

"We can still kiss and make up." He puckers his lips and moves like he's about to take a kiss, so I lean back, and he laughs. "Relax, man. I wasn't actually gonna kiss you. Although, all this tension's really getting me worked up."

"You fucking a-hole," I say before noticing that his cock's longer than normal. "Um…why is that…?"

"Huh. I don't know. Maybe it's just that fun giving you hell." He winks before spinning around and heading back to his air mattress, collapsing onto it, cock up as he grabs his laptop and earbuds. "I imagine you didn't want to help me out with this," he says.

"Disgusting."

"Fine. Guess I need to crank one out in the bathroom real quick." He pops up and heads for the bathroom door, then stops, turning back to me. "Unless this is violating any of the rules. No? Cool. Maybe you should take care of yourself too. You seem way too stressed." He heads in and closes the door.

I'd growl if he wouldn't hear me, but instead I fall onto my mattress and bash my fist against it a few times.

One slipup. That's all I need. And then.

He.

Is.

Out.

5

Ryan

"THIS IS IT, big guy," Dad says as he sits across from me in the Waffle House booth. "This is what we've been waiting for."

We flew into Indianapolis for the Combine, and today was my big day. Physically, mentally, and emotionally draining, since this didn't only test my physical abilities. The whole thing's a spectacle, equipped with film crews, press, so you're putting on a show and then also interviewing with the different teams. It definitely felt like one of the moments I'd been training for my entire life.

And it couldn't have gone better. I crushed my 40-yard dash, benched like a champ, and looked like I was soaring through the agility drills. It was the sort of success I could read all over the coaches' faces. I knew I was good, but now they knew it too. I should be thrilled.

So why aren't I?

Fortunately, the way Dad's glowing, his eyes practically glistening under the overhead fluorescents, it's clear he's basking in the victory, so at least one of us is thoroughly enjoying it. Although, that also twists at something in me—that conversation I had with Troy, the thing that's been eating at me for some time.

On the one hand, all through the day, it was evident how good I fucking am at this stuff. I was built to do this and have been training for it for over half my life. On the other hand, what may be in my body isn't in my heart. Not the way it was when I first set out to make this my dream at ten years old. And the biggest problem is, it's Dad's dream too, and I hate the thought of tearing this from him.

Yet if anything, today, seeing all the flashing lights and glitz of the Combine only reminded me of what a production it all is. It's not just hanging with my buddies on the team and having a good time. It's an empire.

Dad sneaks a peek at his phone and smirks.

"That Mom?" I ask.

We already called her when we finished at the stadium, caught her up on my success, but I figure they might be texting.

"What?" He cringes. "No, it's Rachel."

Rachel's my agent, who linked up with me sophomore year after seeing my stats and coming to one of Peach State's games. She called today her Super Bowl, and she acted like it as she made the rounds for her clients. She gave me the heads-up on coaches and gave me pointers for conversations during interviews.

"She's nearby and asked if she could drop in," Dad adds.

"On our Waffle House time?"

Not that I don't enjoy Rachel, but this is our thing. When I was a kid, we'd go to a Waffle House every time I won a game, and eventually we used it to incentivize me with training and career milestones, hence why we're here tonight. It's a Dad-and-me thing...not Dad, me, and my agent.

"This is the last time you'll see her before we head back," he says. "Come on. She just wants to sing your praises, so let her. Besides, she'll have all the gossip about how the coaches are raving about you."

I can tell he really wants this, so I shrug. "Yeah, sure."

He doesn't text her back, so I assume he already told her she could come.

As much as I'm trying to keep the questions about my future at bay, it's hard to see Dad looking like a kid at his birthday party with everything weighing on my mind. Dad played football in high school but didn't make the cut for a college career. And it's always meant a lot to him that I did.

When I finish my chili, I move on to the pecan pie with a scoop of ice cream—the kind of stuff I haven't been able to eat while gearing up for the Combine. I lose myself in my pie, and Rachel arrives not ten minutes later—I figure because this place isn't far from the hotel.

She looks as eager as Dad. "How are you two feeling after the big day?" she asks as Dad makes room for her on his side of the booth.

"Hungry," I say, but I take a break from devouring my pie since I don't want to be rude.

"I thought I would come over and tell you in person how everyone's chatting about you. You didn't just come in and perform. You came in and *sold*. I don't know that I've ever seen anyone charm these guys like you, Ryan Lorde."

I try to keep from cringing as I'm reminded why Rachel is so enthusiastic. Because this will earn her a good chunk of money if and when I sign with one of these teams. That never really bothered me before, but now, while I'm running back through this all in my head, I just don't feel it.

Rachel flinches, as if sensing I'm not as thrilled as I should be, then shakes her head. "Sorry, I forget how exhausted you must be after today. I'm really surprised I was even able to catch you. Some of the other guys I rep went right back to the hotel for room service."

"This is our thing," Dad reveals. "Back when he was a little guy, if he did good during a game, this was his treat."

"That's so precious. That's the sort of thing you should remember to tell the media throughout all the press you're gonna get after you're drafted, which I think after today, is going to be a huge deal. You know I was talking to Ted Rocker with the Eagles and Morgan Kennley with the Chiefs and…"

Rachel gets into industry chatter, which always gets Dad going, but I zone out. As she discusses who could get their pick of me, I keep thinking how much nicer it feels to work with Troy in the shop. How nice it'd be not to be in Indianapolis, but back at the frat house with my Sigma Alpha crew.

Hell, I'm even missing heading to bed and getting shit from Marty. Although, I'm sure if I were actually there, I'd realize how little I really want that, especially while Mr. Rule Follower is waiting for me to do something and fuck it all up. He'll probably wind up making something up, like this wild idea he got into his head that I was flirting with Angie. Not that I made that any better by chatting with her after, but I'll be damned if he thinks he gets to decide who I talk to just because he's insecure.

"Anyway," Rachel says, "I should get to bed because my work is only beginning. But you two have a great night, and, Ryan, I will definitely be reaching out with updates."

Dad and I thank her, and after she leaves, I finish my

pie and we return to the hotel.

As we're settling into our queen beds—which really look more like fulls to me—Dad slides under the covers, whispering, "It's the big time for you now, buddy." He pulls the covers over him, his face still locked in a smile because of how the day went, and I realize, if I were left on my own to make this call, and wasn't thinking about Dad's feelings at all, I wouldn't want any of this.

I simply don't want it anymore.

And I fucking hate myself for that.

6

Marty

"HOW YOU GETTING along with that jerk?" Dad asks as we plant peas in a box in the garden. I've been complaining about Ryan the last few times we talked.

"*Jerk* is such a nice word for what he is," I say, making Dad chuckle.

My Advanced Risk Modeling teacher canceled class this afternoon, so spring break started earlier than expected. My family's only forty minutes from campus, so it'll be nice to spend the time with them, catching up with everyone, especially Aiden.

"He's trying to annoy the crap out of me. Been listening to stuff on his phone or laptop without earbuds and leaving protein bar wrappers and clothes around the place." Anything to grate on my nerves.

"Anything you can do about it?"

"I'm documenting everything. He thinks he's outsmarting me, but he's become a nuisance, so as soon as I have enough, I'm taking it to the guys and getting him hauled out."

Dad cringes. "Maybe you should get his friends to talk to him. They might be able to convince him he needs to do better if he wants to continue living at your frat."

"It's hard to imagine Ryan stepping in line for anyone. He does whatever the hell he wants."

"Mart…"

I roll my eyes. "The *heck* he wants. Wait, am I not old enough to say that?"

"Sorry, Aiden's been getting too loose with it recently, and there are a lot of F-bombs, so your mom and I have been trying to stay on top of it."

The mention of Aiden reminds me how excited I am to spend the next week with my bro. "Speaking of, I haven't heard much from him. Everything okay?"

Dad focuses on smoothing out soil around a few of the pea plants he's positioned in his freshly dug holes. "He's been busy with school and friends. You know how he can be."

"It's been worse this year."

Aiden and I did everything together as kids, and after his accident, for a couple of years, we were inseparable. Even once he started getting back into the swing of things, we would talk on the phone all the time. But since he's become a senior, it's like he doesn't have time to talk to me anymore.

Dad studies my face, surely sensing my uneasiness. "He loves his big brother as much as ever. I know you have a lot of worries floating around in that smart head of yours, but that's not one you need to have."

My parents have always known I was prone to anxiety. They noticed it from early on, since pretty much anything would make me cry as a baby. They assumed I'd grow out of it, but after I learned to talk, it only seemed to help me communicate my fears of the world. It's interesting because, given how young I was when I exhibited this behavior, one might've expected Mom or Dad to be that way too, but they're pretty chill. Grandad on Dad's side is like this, though, so maybe it skipped a generation.

"I just miss him, ya know?" I tell Dad. "Feels like not talking to my best friend."

"Aiden's been busier than he used to be, which is a good thing. And you're both attending the same school next year, so I'm sure you'll be spending too much time together once that happens."

He's right. I've already been accepted to the grad program for risk management, and Aiden's received his acceptance letter to Peach State. It's not like we won't have time to hang, yet how he's acting makes me think he might not even want to be around me when he's on campus.

I use the garden shovel to create another hole and place another plant before checking the time on my phone. "Well, if I want to get to Aiden's rec game, I better go."

"I appreciate the help while you're here," Dad says before I head out.

At the rec center, I find Aiden on the basketball court with several kids I recognize as his friends from school. I came at a good time because he's flying down the court, the guys on his tail. He spins his wheelchair, faking a move, but his opponent recovers quickly, blocking the shot. Aiden tosses the ball to a teammate, who dribbles toward the goal. The opposing players abandon Aiden and swarm their new target, leaving my bro wide open. Aiden's teammate takes full advantage of the opportunity, returning the ball, and Aiden sinks one into the net.

His team cheers him on before he spins around, and when he sees me, he gives a dramatic bow before receiving high fives and fist bumps. Reminds me what a social guy he's always been. That's one of the many differences between Aiden and me. Not that I avoid people, but part of what I enjoy about the frat is that it forces me to push myself into talking to people, making friends, because if I were on my own, I would just squirrel myself away.

I sit in the bleachers and watch the rest of the game, noticing how effortlessly he soars across the court. Easy as he makes it seem, I know life is so much harder for him than it's ever been for most of the other kids he plays with, or me. But he makes the adjustments he's had to make since the accident look like second nature. Proud as I am of him, it's still difficult when I know it shouldn't be this way. It's the sort of thought that—like so many of my thoughts—I try to push away, but it sits there, always in the back of my mind.

Survivor's guilt, my therapist calls it.

Aiden's team wins the game, and he's sweaty as hell after he finishes up, the dark brown bangs we both get from Dad soaked through.

"Did you see me kicking their asses?"

"I did. You shouldn't have hogged the ball like that, though."

He laughs as he slips past me toward the car.

"How's stuff going?" I ask.

"Pretty good. Did Mom and Dad tell you I got into the play?"

"Wait, what? They definitely did not." I'm kind of pissed at them for not mentioning it as soon as I got home.

"I told them I wanted to tell you," he clarifies, but I still don't know that I give them a pass.

"What is it?"

"It's a Canadian play. You know the story of that axe murderer, Lizzie Borden. Alleged, I guess."

"I'm pretty sure she can't sue you for defamation from the grave."

"It takes place after she's acquitted. She becomes an acting teacher, and her student winds up going through an exercise where she tries to get into what really happened the night of her parents' murder."

"The hell?"

"I'm the love interest Lizzie Borden kills her parents over. Well, or not. You'll have to see to find out."

"Um…"

"Yeah, weird shit, but it's cool."

"I was thinking you were gonna say *My Fair Lady* or something."

"Dude, have you heard me sing?"

"I haven't seen you act either." I glare at him, and I know him well enough to read the guilt in his wavering gaze.

"I was taking theater as an elective, and the teacher does the play. He encouraged me to audition."

"And you didn't even mention this to me?" I try to keep my cool, but I can't help but sound hurt. I like knowing what's going on in his life.

"It was an audition. I could have been shit and not gotten the part."

"And what's your excuse for *after* that?"

"I wanted to make sure they didn't get rid of me after the first few rehearsals."

"Oh, so you were planning to tell me on opening night?"

He rolls his eyes. "I was gonna tell you today. Once I had a better idea if I'd be any good at it."

"I don't know what you were worried about. Anything you put your mind to, you do fine with."

He makes a retching sound. "This is not the whole *it's a miracle, everything you do, because you poor wounded bird.*"

He couldn't sound more sarcastic if he tried. Aiden hates when people make a big deal out of anything he does. I get it, but I also think sometimes he downplays the shit he does that is genuinely awesome.

"You know that's not how I meant it."

"I'm only giving you hell, bro," he says as he rushes, slipping the wheel in front of my leg so I have to halt in place—one of his favorite games.

"You little shit. I can still kick your ass."

"Kick away," he says, pivoting so he's in front of me. "Come on. Get around me. Try."

We run through the game for a minute before I manage to psyche him out and get in front. When I reach his car, I have to stop myself from offering help, since Aiden hates that.

Right after the accident, he had a rough time coping and needed extra help. It was about two years before he started refusing a lot of the help Mom, Dad, or I would offer. But it can be hard to watch when something I take for granted takes him much longer, like even getting the door open. And I could easily help him into his seat instead of him climbing up.

"Okay, I don't have to be a hero today. You wanna put the chair in the passenger's seat?"

A rush of adrenaline rushes through me as my bro asks me for help I'm eager to give. "I got you." I place it in the seat, then head to my car, and we meet back at our parents' place, catching up before dinner.

I notice he keeps texting someone before Mom asks, "How was Amy today?"

"Amy?" I ask. "That's a name I haven't heard before." Once again, the knot in my chest twists up. Like when he brought up the play.

Aiden shoots Mom a look.

"Was I not supposed to say anything?" she asks.

"The hell, Aiden? I mean heck. First the play and now you have a girlfriend?"

"Whoa, whoa. She's not my girlfriend," he says before smiling. "Yet." He's trying to downplay it, but his lips are tight together, his eyes wide in the way he gets when he has a secret. "And speaking of surprises..." he drags out, "Steven and Roger are going to Tybee Island for the week and asked if I wanted to come with them."

"Wait, what?" I ask, disappointment coursing through me. "I thought we'd get to spend time together." Aiden wears a guilty expression as Mom and Dad exchange an uncomfortable look, but as frustrated as I am, I know I'm being selfish. "Sorry, I wanted to see you, but that sounds fun." I can tell I already made it awkward for him, though.

"Please, Mom and Dad," he asks.

And of course, it isn't much of a discussion since he's been on vacations with his crew before. I just wish I would've had a heads-up.

He must sense how disappointed I am because after they agree, he says, "It's fine, man. It's all good. You're still my amazing big bro."

I notice the sympathy in Mom's and Dad's expressions, like they know this is not the way we are, but I try to remind myself he's growing up. He's always been his own guy and done whatever the hell he's wanted to. And I've tried to support him at every turn. Still, it's a tough blow.

"You want to throw the ball around after dinner?" he asks. "You got a better arm than Dad, and I need to keep my throw in good shape for the team next year."

I can tell he's trying to cheer me up, and I manage to get in a better mood as we play around in the backyard, but there's still this lingering discomfort because, even though I know my bro's got his own life, I don't like him pulling away from me.

7

Ryan

I'M SURE MR. Rule Follower is happy I can't bug him over spring break, when I head to Orlando with Ty and Lance. We have a good time, enjoy the rides at Universal Studios and Disney, hit the bars. It goes by too fast, and in no time we're back to class, and I'm making life annoying as hell for Marty McGovern. Anything I can think of to make his life more unpleasant. Even with him riding my ass, I've managed to keep in line with the rules. Although, the animosity I've built up has led to me finding other ways to bug Marty.

And I must admit, probably also has something to do with my frustrations about football and Dad.

On Wednesday, after I'm finished with classes, I meet the guys at the rec center for pickleball. It's a mix of frats and sororities at the indoor courts, and we play a few rounds before Ty and I swap out with Marty and our Sigma Alpha buddy Jaxon, taking seats on a nearby bench with Keegan.

"Look at the guy," I tell Ty as Marty gawks at Angie, who's playing on the court beside ours. Angie gives him a friendly wave, which Marty returns before the ball hits him in the leg.

"Man, where are you?" Lance calls out from the opposite side.

"So pathetic," I grumble.

Ty takes a sip of water from his thermos before saying, "Will you leave him the hell alone, for your own sake?"

"Not my fault he's got no moves."

Ty and Keegan eye me, but I pretend not to notice as I holler out, "Nice serve, Ang!"

"Thank you, boo," she calls back, and I've rightfully earned a glare from Marty.

She's started calling me boo since we've been back from the break, which is cute, but probably not helping with Marty thinking I'm making moves on her.

"*Ry...*" Ty says with a severe tone, the way Mom or Dad might've when I was a kid and did something wrong.

"What?"

"It's not nice what you're doing."

"What am I doing?"

"Angie...?"

I'm as thrown as when Marty got up in arms about it before the break.

"You aren't trying to get with her?" Ty asks.

"No."

His skeptical expression doesn't change.

"I know it's coming from that day before break when we went to Junkie's," I say. "I was being friendly with her like I normally am, but Marty started giving me hell like I was making moves on her, and I maybe did make sure to talk to her more than I normally would to piss him off. But not like flirting. Whatever story Marty's making up in his head is on him and not my problem."

"You really don't like that guy, do you?" Ty asks.

"*Don't like* doesn't really cover the hate I feel for that prick."

We've never gotten along, but it's been worse since probation, for sure, and as soon as we got back from break, we were right back to our usual routine. Even though I'm being a dick, he's earned it.

"Damn, Ry," Keegan says. "Give him a break. He's helped us a lot with the insurance and navigating the fire stuff."

That's the truth. After the fire, he's really stepped up, and I can't shit all over his perfectionism and obsession with rules.

"Yeah, yeah. I know he's made things easier for Sigma Alpha as a whole, but guy's gone out of his way to make my life hell since we got here."

"I imagine he'd say the same about you," Ty presses.

"Whose side are you on again?"

"My best friend's, always, man."

Another ball passes by Marty while he's exchanging a look with Angie.

"That guy has zero game, seriously," Keegan notes.

"Okay," Ty says, "I'm not gonna let you guys gang up on my boyfriend's buddy like that."

I groan. "I miss when we hated on Alpha Theta Mus."

"Yeah, can we get back to that?" Keegan teases.

"Be nice," Ty warns.

"All I have to do is be on my best behavior for the next month," I say. "Then everything will be fine."

"Really?" Keegan asks.

"Yeah…"

I look between Ty and Keegan, noting their suspicious expressions. "Why are you making those faces?"

"I just don't know you to be the kind of guy who can follow the rules," Keegan adds.

"It's been three and a half weeks, and I've been good."

"Two and a half," Ty corrects. "Spring break doesn't count. And you've been *tolerable*. Mart's already talking about how you're walking around naked in your room, listening to loud videos on your phone, hogging the bathroom so that he has to use the communal one down the hall."

"And every time he's said anything, I've put on pants and turned off the sound. And the bathroom thing…not my fault he doesn't claim it first."

"No one thing in that is against the rules, but he's documenting it because he's Marty, so all he has to do is get enough to bring to the guys and say you've become a nuisance, and then you're out."

The hell? "Nuisance? Is that a thing?"

Ty angles his head, giving me a look that tells me it definitely is.

"And you're only telling me this now? Seriously, I went on a whole trip with my president friend only for him not to warn me when I'm close to getting kicked out?"

"You didn't mention to me you were doing any of these things, and Lance just mentioned these things to me yesterday."

"Fucking hell," I mutter as tension tightens in my chest.

"Don't freak out," Ty says. "It's not enough yet, but you're really testing the waters, and it's a dangerous thing to do right now, especially if he thinks you're trying to get with the girl he's hung up on."

"That really doesn't seem like a big deal," Keegan chimes in. "Angie would never fuck around with Marty anyway."

Ty turns a stern glare on him.

"Okay, just saying. Now I'll shut up."

"What I'm trying to say," Ty goes on, "is that there are other options than living at a frat."

I can't believe I'm hearing this. "Other options? Dude, I want to be with my friends. I want to be with you two losers."

Ty smirks, but then it twists into a cringe. "I was gonna wait and talk to you about this later," he says, like one of my coaches might after a bad game, which just makes me concerned. "Keegan and I've been talking, and we don't think it would be terrible if some of you guys pitched in together for a room at an apartment complex. No one owes the frat money as long as it's unlivable, and there's that complex Troy and Atlas were at. And Brenner and Taylor."

Brenner and Taylor are Peach State alums, graduated last year, but I'm not sure why where they live should have anything to do with me.

"But *you're* gonna stay here," I say, "since you have a boyfriend. And Dax is my buddy too, and he loves the Greek life. Keeg?"

Keegan winces. "I'm enjoying saving up the money while we're here."

"But Jaxon might go with you," Ty says. "And Jonah…maybe Kline. When I talked to Lance about it, he said we might be able to find some others from Alpha Theta Mu."

I grit my teeth. "I don't love you having all these secret meetings about me with the enemy."

Ty sits down beside me, hooking his arm around me. "There's no enemy here. Just all of us trying to navigate a tough situation. And if that means you need to get a place…"

I do a double take at my best bud, studying his expression.

I was already upset, but now I'm starting to get pissed. "You guys don't think I can do it?"

"What? No, I didn't say that." But I know Ty, and this is the least sincere expression he could make.

"You wouldn't be bringing up this suggestion if you thought I could behave myself for a few more weeks. You feel that way, Keeg?"

Keegan avoids eye contact. "Honestly…?" he drags out.

"What the fuck else would I want you to be? I can't believe what I'm hearing right now. Traitors, both of you."

"Dude…"

"You don't believe in me."

I'm fuming. If there was ever a time I needed to know my friends had my back, it's when I'm considering potentially upending my life, and now there's even more uncertainty about just being around the people I love.

Although, it's not like they know. I really haven't

fully accepted it myself yet.

"That's not what either of us said," Ty insists.

"It just seems…unlikely that you'll be able to keep it together," Keegan pushes.

"You know yourself better than anyone," Ty follows. "Being a little wild is your thing. And we love you for that."

"I have some fucking self-restraint. If I need to get it together for a month, I can do that."

Ty's lips twist up. "Okay, then. A bet."

"Huh?"

"We haven't done one of those in a while, and I know my buddy is competitive as hell, so maybe we bet that you keep it together until the end of your probationary period, and we owe you a hundred dollars. And if you can't…"

I know Ty well enough to read that clever expression. "I know what you're doing here," I say.

"And what is that?" Ty asks, smirking.

"I might be slow sometimes, but you're trying to take advantage of my competitive side to see if you can inspire me to behave by turning it into a competition."

"Told you he'd figure it out," Keeg says.

And it's clear this has been their setup all along.

I must admit, it means a lot that they care enough to have weaponized this part of my personality to help me out. I can't fault them for that. Suddenly all the heated anger that built up over what felt like betrayal cools off, quickly replaced with adrenaline.

"Each?" I ask, calling them out on it.

Ty flinches. "What?"

"One hundred each?"

"Shut the fuck up!" Keegan says. "I'm not rich."

"You said you were saving all this money."

"Not to give to *you*. Fifty."

"Seventy-five. Come on. I'm an amazing friend. You should believe in me enough to put in a hundred."

Keegan's expression twists up. "But if I'm putting in an easy hundred, doesn't that mean I believe you won't be able to do it?"

"Nah, because you didn't volunteer it right away, so I know you think I can do it," I tease. "You're a good bud. Now give me your damn money. You think we can get Jaxon and Dax into this? I mean, Dax had five hundred for that bachelor auction last semester. I could walk away with a pretty penny."

Ty laughs. "We're not letting you rob Sigma Alpha. And you know a bet is definitely against the rules, so why don't you just settle for trusting your good friends with this?"

"I hate when you make a good point."

Funny to think I've been walking on eggshells, feeling so on edge the past three and a half weeks, and now I feel lighter. And I know it has nothing to do with the bet, but because Ty and Keegan were clearly scheming to find a way to keep me good through this probation, and it's not something I'll take for granted. I also have no intention of letting my bros down.

"So is it a bet?" Keeg asks.

"At a hundred each?" I confirm.

Keeg rolls his eyes. "Fine. A hundred it is."

"Damn right it's a bet."

We shake on it, and Ty says, "I'm glad you're in. Because I want to still be hanging with my buddy."

"We can't lose one of our own," Keegan adds. "Just let some of the other guys get into trouble for a minute."

I know I've been an asshole to Marty recently, but he's about to see a totally different side of Ryan Lorde. He won't even know who the fucking hell his roommate is.

"I'm gonna be so good, he won't be able to stand it," I mutter, glaring at Marty like he's my archnemesis right before he gets hit in the face with the ball.

8

Marty

I THOROUGHLY ENJOYED the break, spending the time in my old room at my parents', not having to deal with that frathole being right on top of me. And despite being disappointed with Aiden going to Tybee Island, I still got to spend a couple of days with him when he got back.

Now everything's back to normal.

Only not.

The past few days, Ryan hasn't been as bad…really, since we played pickleball with the crew. Not that he's been great, but feels like he's been laying off, not trying to make a production of annoying the crap out of me. I want to believe he's finally taking the consequences of his actions seriously, but I'm worried it's something else. That he's trying to get me to let my guard down before he surprises me with something that'll really throw me.

Any minute now, I'm sure the floor will fall right out from under me.

Sunday night, I go out with the guys to the new rock-climbing wall at the rec center. We climb for a bit before grabbing smoothies. Ash and Colin went to a queer nudist camp in South Georgia for the break, and right after, Ash went to some nerd conference, so we're only now catching up with him about the topic Lance and I are most interested in, for all the obvious reasons.

"I still can't get over your being totally fine having your junk out," I say.

Ash shrugs, and Lance pulls a face.

"We've walked in on him having sex with his boyfriend," Lance says. "How would that be the weirdest thing he's done?"

"It's different when it's just wagging around like that. You're not doing anything with it at a nudist camp."

"Uh…yeah, sure, definitely not having sex the entire time," Ash says, glancing around overdramatically.

I can't disguise my envy. "Oh, shut up. You were not having sex that entire time. Were you?" I notice how high my voice gets on the question.

Ash bursts into a laugh. "Of course not."

I don't know why that makes me feel relief, maybe because if it hadn't been that way, it'd be like I was getting even less sex than I already am.

"We had to eat," Ash adds with a wink, but I'm not laughing 'cause now I'm thinking maybe that's closer to the truth than I figured.

"I know the feeling," Lance adds. "Ty and I had fun at Universal, but we were eager to get back to the hotel so we could have a different kind of fun."

"To think it used to be two straight guys and our bi bro Ash, and now I'm the odd man out."

"That's not true," Ash insists, sidling up close and hooking his arm around mine. "You were always the odd man out. But it is funny how many Alpha Theta Mus identified as straight freshman year, and now they're falling out of the closet left and right. Maybe keeping a whiteboard to track how many of the guys in the house come out wouldn't be so bad."

That's an idea I had when it felt like all my buddies at Alpha Theta Mu wound up with guys.

We share a laugh. Obviously, we'd never do that, but it's funny imagining scratching off the names of our bros as they discover this new side of themselves.

"But enough about the Alpha Theta Mu queers," Lance says, then to me, "How are things with you? I saw you chatting up Angie after TaskFrat on Friday. Any news there?"

"News? There's not gonna be any news. There's nothing there."

Ash angles his head, glaring at me.

"No, like, she's hot and fun and cool, but that's where it ends."

Do I wish she would go out with me? Absolutely.

Am I deluding myself, thinking that would ever happen? Absolutely not.

"Even worse, now she's ogling Ryan every time he comes around. Him and his beefy, Hulk-man body. If that's what she's into, I can't compete."

"That's true," Ash says, and Lance and I both glare at him. "I meant, if that's what she was into, but you don't know that. And speaking of the frathole, we've enjoyed an entire afternoon and you haven't brought him up, so I take it things aren't *as bad?*" The way he inflects that last part, it's clear he's hopeful things have improved.

"It's better," I confess, though I wish I didn't have to.

"Oh, really?" Lance says, sounding shocked, but like fake shocked, which makes me suspicious.

"Why?" I ask. "You didn't tell him I was keeping tabs on all that shit he was doing, did you?"

Ash purses his lips, like he's keeping a secret for Lance.

"Hey!" I snap.

"I did not tell Ryan anything," is as much as Lance reveals, which tells me all I need to know—he must've blabbed to Ty. Of course he did.

"So this is why he's better? Well, I guess I don't have to worry because I'm sure he'll be back to violating rules by Friday. Probably all sexed up from the girls he had lined up in Orlando."

"Um...you know we just went to Universal Studios,"

Lance says. "We weren't, like, having orgies at the hotel. Not all of us got Ash and Colin's vacation."

"I'm surprised he managed to go a whole week without."

Lance and Ash exchange looks.

"What? You guys think I'm being overdramatic? After all the stunts he's pulled?"

"I didn't say that," Lance says. "But you said he's acting better, and you're still bothered, so…"

"Yeah," Ash says. "Maybe…keep an open mind and give him a chance."

I huff. "He's had more than enough chances."

We head out to dinner, and when we're back at the house, I go to my room, where I discover Ryan sitting at my desk. I don't know that I've ever seen him there before, especially not in joggers and a tee. Is the asshole trying to hog the desk?

"I don't have any homework tonight," I tell him, and he glances over from his laptop and shrugs.

"Well, I do."

"Oh, just to keep me up late?" I ask, searching for the ulterior motive.

He shakes his head. "Nope. Just to get it done before class tomorrow." He turns back to his screen and keys away.

I search around my room uneasily. Things have been too calm recently. And tonight things are *eerily* calm, in a way that only concerns me that much more.

I approach my bed cautiously, pulling back the sheets to see if he has some horrible prank waiting for me—like he's slipped Payton's python under the sheets. It hasn't happened to me, but it's an easy enough prank to pull off, and I fucking hate snakes.

"If you want," he says, "I can finish in, like, five and do the rest tomorrow morning."

"What are you doing?" I ask.

He spins the swivel chair toward me. "I told you: my homework."

Finally something clicks into place. I know what's up!

"Do you have someone in here?" I check under the bed, then the closet.

His forehead creases as his brows knit together. "Do you think I would hide them in the closet?"

"You didn't put the door hanger out, so you'd be violating one of the rules Sigma Alpha agreed to. Maybe you forgot since you never honored them anyway."

"And I just jumped into these clothes when I realized you were coming up here?"

"I don't know. Maybe one of the guys texted you. Whatever. It doesn't matter. I see there's no one else in here. And no snake…that I've seen."

"Why would there be a snake?"

"As if you don't know."

He looks at me like I've lost it. Maybe I have.

"I'm trying to work out why you've been acting weird lately," I explain.

"You're searching the closet for girls and I'm the one acting weird?" he says as though he's the shining example of a roommate.

"Okay, this is entering full-on gaslighting territory."

He grins. "How is that gaslighting?"

"Gaslighting means trying to make a person question their reality, which you are doing by acting like it's this far-fetched idea that you'd do these things that you are entirely capable of doing, especially with how pissed you've been at me."

Ryan's gaze wanders as he considers this. "Is that what gaslighting is? Huh, who knew?"

"Is that a confession?"

"Nah, man. I've had a change of heart recently. And I actually kind of need your help."

"My help?"

I know this is somehow gonna end in a prank where he fools my ass, and tonight is not the night, mother-fucker.

But I go along with it to see where this leads. "Okay, what is it? Give it to me. But if you think anything you say is gonna get me to ask Lance to take you off probation, you've got another thing coming."

He chuckles. "It's not that. You know those tango

classes you're taking?"

Why the fuck is he bringing those up?

"That I just started taking?" I ask.

"I was thinking you could show me some moves."

I study his expression, trying to work out how serious he is, checking to see if he's moments away from busting out laughing or mocking me for them. There must be a reason he's saying this…other than wanting me to show him some moves.

"You want me to show you how to tango?"

"It's spring—formals season. Keegan knows how to ballroom dance, and it'd be nice to show him up for a change. Why are you looking at me like that?"

"I'm still trying to figure out what the angle is."

He pushes to his feet and approaches. Kind of strange seeing him in my room without his cock out or without it bulging in his pants.

"Look, I know I was a dick about you getting me put on probation, but I was thinking it over, and maybe I could be a better roommate."

"Whatever you're doing isn't gonna work, Ryan. I know Ty must've said something to you, but you can't pull a one-eighty and think we're gonna be buddies and I'm gonna show you how to tango so that I'll go easy on you. I know all this charm and sexiness works on the girls you're used to."

"You think I'm sexy?" he asks, quirking a brow.

I sigh, fucking exasperated. "I think that's how people perceive you. I also have eyes, so I know that you objectively meet the criteria for what people consider to be a hot guy."

"Can I ask what those objective criteria are?"

"Six foot two…"

"Three."

"Blue eyes, blond hair—"

"Like, dirty blond."

"Body that looks like…" I'm struggling with this one.

"A god, maybe?"

I cringe. "I was thinking a swollen Ken doll."

"I'll take that," he says, standing a little taller.

"None of this is meant as a compliment. And we're done talking about this. I don't know why you're asking to learn tango, but we're not magically gonna be friends now that you got in trouble and are finally thinking about getting kicked out of the frat. Now if you'll excuse me, I'm gonna take a shower while you're in this friendly spirit and not terrorizing me by staying in the bathroom for five hours."

I start for the bathroom when he says, "I could make it worth your while."

I stop in the doorway, turning back to him.

He folds his arms, sporting a particularly cocky expression that really sets off this fire in my chest. Because I know he wants me to push to know what he's offering, but another part of me doesn't want to engage.

"I don't want to hear it," I say, though I'm curious as hell.

I head into the bathroom and close the door.

"Okay, if you're not into Angie anymore, then ignore me."

Angie?

Fuck, this asshole really knows how to get to me.

I should ignore him.

I shouldn't press because that's exactly what he wants, but I can't help myself. I crack the door open. "What about Angie?"

9

Ryan

PEOPLE LIKE MARTY think I'm some dumb jock, but clearly not that dumb.

Took a couple of days, but since my bet with the guys, I came up with a plan that could earn Marty's trust and maybe get him off my ass long enough to survive this probation and prove to my fratbros I didn't get to be linebacker for Peach State without having some discipline and self-restraint.

I can only see a sliver of Marty as he stands in the bathroom, hidden behind the door, obviously enticed by the plan I've concocted. That he's even opened the door again assures me I struck a nerve.

I know your weakness, Marty McGovern.

"You want me to tell you through that crack, or you want to come back out here and talk?"

"I can hear you from here," he insists, so I approach him.

"I've noticed you don't exactly have smooth moves

with Angie, right? But you've seen the way I am, not only with her, but other girls. I could maybe help you out in that department. Be your coach, basically."

His eyes narrow as he studies me, as though still trying to work out if this is all a con. I mean, guess it is, but not in the way he's thinking.

He cracks the door open a little more.

"You'd help me flirt with Angie?"

"Hell, if you'd asked me before all this, I would've."

That's the truth. If we hadn't been down each other's throats, then I wouldn't have had an issue giving him some pointers.

"And all you want in exchange is for me to show you some tango moves?"

"Yeah, sure. Seems like a fair trade to me."

He angles his head as he glares at me. "You think I don't know what you're doing? You're trying to get on my good side so when you fuck up again, which you will, I won't get you expelled from the house, so I should warn you this isn't gonna work."

"Then what do you have to lose?"

"Besides my pride?"

I throw my hands up. "Okay, guess you didn't like Angie as much as I thought."

As I spin around, he says, "Wait, wait, wait. I didn't say no."

I can't help but smirk, appreciating that I have some

damn good negotiating skills. Those guys will have to pay up.

I turn back to him, and he bites his bottom lip, clearly thinking it over. "I feel like I'm gonna regret this. I don't want to, like, trick Angie into liking me back."

"Is that what your flirting is? Tricking someone into liking you?"

Misguided as his comment may be, it's sweet that he wouldn't be interested in tricking someone into dating him. He's got good parts to him that, whether he shows them to me or not, a girl would be interested in.

"Honestly, I'm not even sure I know what flirting is," he admits. "Isn't that obvious?"

Fair point.

"It's about being comfortable with yourself and confident," I explain, "and if she's into that, then she'll be into you. I don't know her type, and I can't guarantee she'll like you back, but at least, even if it doesn't work for her, maybe you can use it when you run into another girl you like."

"Confident and comfortable? Great. Two things I'm shit at." It's like he's already talking himself out of it. "And if we agree to do this," he goes on, "does this mean you're gonna stop flirting with her around me?"

This again.

"I've never flirted with her," I insist. "Maybe I talked to her more than I would have normally for, like, a day to get under your skin, but trust me, if I were flirting, I would've already sealed the deal."

He studies my face as though trying to work out if I'm being sincere, but he's seen me operate, and I'm sure somewhere in that messy head of his, he knows it's true. His gaze wavers before he says, "This is a horrible idea."

Fuck. Well, I tried. Of course it couldn't be that easy.

"When are we starting?"

My lips twist into a smile. Touchdown.

"Then it's a deal?"

He extends his hand, and we shake on it. I'm impressed that this is going according to plan.

"So," I say, "how about, in the name of good faith, you go ahead and show me something?"

It's not that I'm excited to learn how to tango, but the sooner I can get Marty to let his guard down and chill, the easier it's gonna be for us to get along…and maybe get him past writing down every infraction he could potentially use against me.

"We're starting this tonight?" he asks.

"We don't have to get into anything complicated. Show me some basics. Did you have something else you were planning to do instead?"

"No, I mean, I guess we can. Uh…" He pulls out his phone and fidgets with it. I can tell by how quick he is to do this that he really wants to get with Angie. When the music starts up, I recognize it from when I've caught him practicing. He places it on the desk before saying, "Okay, let me figure out how to do this without making it awkward as hell. Sit on the bed."

I plant my ass down on the edge.

"So this is a basic move…" He raises his arms, positioning them like there's another person there, before showing me some basic steps as he counts out loud. Looks kind of ridiculous as he does it by himself. "That's the thing we come back to every time, and then we can get more creative after that," he explains. "Here, get up, and let's try together. I'll start off leading, and maybe we can switch out once you figure it out. I don't know that it's the best way to do it, but it's the only way I know how."

I laugh, pushing to my feet. "Show me what to do."

"So this is, like, the basic move that we do in a circle, which will be kind of weird given the lack of space here, so we'll have to get creative, but I'll do the counting, and you'll follow my lead."

"You're gonna be leading me?"

"Like I said, this is the only way I know how to do it."

"Okay," I concede.

He positions one of his hands on my lower back and takes the other in his hand. The only time we've ever been this close is when we're getting onto each other. I notice how warm his hand is and the light scent of his cologne—cedar and citrus. It's a nice fragrance that hits my nose just right.

"Now your other hand goes on my shoulder," he says.

As I follow the instruction, he gulps, not making eye contact as he begins counting. I try to follow the movement, and he steps on my toe.

"You have to actually follow," he says.

"Whoa, whoa, I'm the student. You can be patient with me."

"You're right, sorry. I'll go slower. The way I learned it, don't try to pay attention to my feet, but feel when I'm shifting my weight, and that's how you'll know which leg to step back with."

"Okay…"

We start again, and Marty counts out loud. We fumble a bit to start, but gradually, as I start to realize what he's doing, he gets a little less self-conscious, and we manage to make a complete circle.

As we continue, I can't help but notice the way he's counting, his gaze shifting around as he clearly stresses about his movements. It's kind of adorable.

The thought catches me by surprise and throws me off-balance, and he steps on my foot again. As I halt, he practically slams up against me, face into my chest. After he recovers, he glances up at me.

"You good, man?" I ask.

As I study his face, I notice the pink in his cheeks. But my gaze settles on his mouth—those smooth, thin lips.

"Those are pretty lips." I figured I was thinking that in my head, but it comes out of my mouth, and his eyebrows shift quickly, his forehead creasing.

"What did you just say?"

"I was only making an observation. I mean, you have some qualities girls would be attracted to, and that's one of them."

Yeah…that's a good excuse. Not really sure why I was thinking it, let alone saying it.

"Oh…" he says, nodding. "Maybe we should call it a night on the tango lesson. That's a good start, and we can practice some more until you get the hang of it."

"Sounds good." As he pulls his hand away, my thumb lingers against his flesh, caressing. He's got nice, smooth skin too.

"So now you gonna give me a tip or a pointer or something?" he presses.

"Patience, young Jedi."

His head tilts slightly. "You like *Star Wars?*"

"You kidding? I used to watch them all the time as a kid."

"Like…*The Phantom Menace?*" he asks, like that wouldn't have counted.

"No, like *A New Hope, Empire Strikes Back, Return of the Jedi*."

"Hmmm…interesting."

"What? Did you think a dumb jock couldn't be a fan of *Star Wars*?"

"You never bring it up."

"There's a lot of things we haven't brought up since we've gotten to know each other."

And it seems a stretch to even suggest we know each other.

"That's a fair point," he says, "but I just showed you some moves. What happened to the whole I show you something, you show me something? Is this the part where you say you duped me and piss me the hell off?"

"Relax. There's a party on Friday, and there'll be lots of girls around. I'll show you then. In the meantime, maybe a couple of nights this week, you show me more of this."

"Wait, a party? You're gonna throw me into it like that? I'm not making you compete in a tango championship to start with."

"I got you." I rest my hand on his shoulder. "Where do you think Keegan got his moves from? Not to brag, but I know what I'm doing."

"Yeah, I guess," he says, as though still waiting to find out this has all been a prank.

"Come on, you gotta shower off, and I've gotta get to

bed. We have a long, painful journey ahead of us if we're gonna make you fuckable."

"Shut the fuck up. At least I know you're not gonna be any less of a pain in the ass."

"*A* pain in the ass? Excuse you. I'm *the* pain in the ass."

This earns a smile from Marty, and I'm kind of proud I managed that much from a guy who's usually barking away at me. It makes me think that despite our differences, he might not be as unbearable as he sometimes acts.

10

Marty

"**M**ART! OVER HERE!" Ryan shouts from across the yard.

I'm on edge, and not only because the TaskFrat Challenge earlier involved wrestling with a bunch of guys in a pool full of Jell-O.

I'm suspicious as hell about my agreement with Ryan.

This must be a trick to get me back for having his ass placed on probation, which was one of the reasons I shut his idea down at first, but as he pushed, I realized this could work in my favor. If it is a trick, then I won't have my documentation for his nuisance behavior, but bullying, if that's what he's planning, for that he deserves to have his ass kicked out. Still, I hoped Ryan was sincere about his offer, and not only because I spent two nights this week showing him what I'd learned in class (three if you count the first night when we made the agreement).

I've seen the way this frathole is with girls. Of course,

I'm sure his appeal is in no small part due to being a hot jock, but I'd be curious to see if he really has some tricks up his sleeve that could help me at least be bold enough to let a girl know I'm interested in her.

I approach Ryan, who's hanging with Dax, which makes me feel less threatened since Dax and I get along. Really, Dax gets along with everyone. He's the kind of guy who's never met a stranger…which is an odd thing to say about a guy who apparently hooks up with plenty of strangers.

Dax runs his hands through his wet bangs, which must've happened when he tackled me in the pool. "Sorry again about earlier," he says.

"Eh, all's fair in love and TaskFrat, right?"

"Guess so," he says as we fist-bump.

"I see you showered off too."

"Yeah. Found Jell-O in some surprising places."

I laugh. "I'm not even sure I got it out of all the surprising places."

"You think you'd be that nice to me if I tackled you during TaskFrat?" Ryan asks me.

"Shut it," I say.

Dax laughs. "Okay, you two duke it out. I've got a Zeta Tau I've had my eye on all night."

"Of course you have," I say in a knowing tone.

"I'm surprised you haven't torn through all the frats yet," Ryan says.

"Is that a challenge?" Dax asks, which gets us laughing. "It's not the kind of thing you want to rush," he adds. "Take your time, enjoy every fucking drop."

A part of me thinks *drop* might not be what he meant to say, but I've known him long enough to know better.

"Go get 'em, champ," Ryan tells him, and Dax heads off.

I search around, making sure no one's in earshot. "Okay, this is the part where you make me regret agreeing to this?"

Ryan grins. "Nah. You're gonna be great. And even if you suck, I'm a great teacher, so…"

He says that in that arrogant-ass way he has, the sort that has me rolling my eyes.

"Now…" He signals to someone, and before I know it, there's a Phi Lambda blonde at his side, as indicated by the Greek-letter charms on her necklace. Her hair falls just past her shoulders, her blue eyes bright in the outdoor lighting.

She sports a bright smile as she says, "Hey, Marty, I'm Gisele."

"Um…hi? Ryan, what is happening?"

"This is why we're doing it at a party. You need practice chatting up girls, so I figured, what better way to do it than to have a real live girl to work with."

My face heats up. "Can you excuse us for a moment?" I grab Ryan's shoulder and usher him away from my new Phi Lambda friend. "I knew you'd do something like this," I say through my teeth.

Ryan's expression twists up. "What's wrong?"

"You didn't say anything about telling other people about our agreement."

"Gisele promised to be discreet, and doesn't she look trustworthy?" He waves to her, and she waves back with those bright eyes on Ryan.

"Okay, it's pretty apparent why she's offering to help, and it has nothing to do with me."

"She's in the drama department. I said it might be good practice for her with character work."

I feel a migraine coming on. "I never should have said yes to this. I had this gut feeling you'd find a way to turn this into the perfect opportunity to humiliate me, and congratulations if that was your goal."

"Whoa, whoa. You can ask Keeg and Jaxon, I did the same with them. How did you think this was gonna go down?"

"I was expecting pointers. Like tips. I showed you moves *in private*. I didn't bring in a hot girl to judge."

"You need practice talking to a girl, and given how red your face is, Gisele is gonna be perfect for you because she makes you nervous. And the more you sit with that, the less uncomfortable you'll be during the real thing because you'll be used to having that feeling and knowing what to do when it comes up."

Wait a fucking second… "Exposure therapy?"

"Huh?"

"You're talking about exposure therapy, essentially."

"I'm lost."

"You get me to do the thing that makes me uncomfortable until I'm familiar enough with the discomfort that it doesn't intimidate me."

He shrugs. "I guess."

It's stunning that an idiot like Ryan has inadvertently stumbled upon his own version of exposure therapy, which when he pitches it like that, I must admit might work.

But I'm probably gonna hate every second of it, which is kind of the point.

"I'm listening," I say, "but just know, I've still got some Jell-O up my ass from earlier. I'm on edge, and I'm more than a little annoyed that you didn't give me a heads-up."

"If I'd told you, would you have said yes?"

"Absolutely not."

"Exactly. So why don't we get back to Gisele and get to work."

I hesitate, still unconvinced. "You're saying you did this with Keegan and Jaxon?"

At his nod, I search around, spotting Angie chatting with Ash and Lance. I think about how many days I've spent chatting with her, fumbling my words, pining away, knowing I'd never have the confidence to flirt with her. It gives me the boost I need to surrender to Ryan's plan.

"Okay. Let's just get through it."

"That's what I like to hear." He slaps my back, urging me toward Gisele.

"Okay, don't touch me like you do your football bros," I say, and he backs off.

"It's nice to meet you," Gisele says before turning to Ryan. "Ooh, is that not how we should start? You should probably start, Marty." She giggles, as though she's the one who should be embarrassed about what's happening.

"Uh…"

"Here's the scenario," Ryan interjects. "Gisele and I are having a conversation, and you approach and insert yourself into it. Easy enough?"

"Why not?" I step away and approach.

"So then Carmichael was coming down the field for a Hail Mary when—" He acts like he's just spotted me and says, "Ah, hey, Mart. This is… Sorry, what was it again?"

"Gisele," she replies, and it's fucking surreal how much they're selling this bit. I imagine she does very well in the drama department.

"Hi." I reach my hand out, and we shake. "Nice to meet you."

She stares at me, clearly waiting for me to initiate some sort of conversation, but it's not easy to do all this stuff on the spot.

"So…you enjoying the party?" I ask since that seems like a good opening.

"I am. It's fun."

"That's good. That's real good." And as ridiculous as I assumed this would be, it's apparent I'm as awkward as I would be if I were flirting with any other girl. Tension twists in my gut, my face is hot, my palms sweating, even though it's a cool night. I cut Ryan a look, and I see the disappointment in his expression. I sigh. "Never mind. This is too humiliating. I really can't."

"Hey, hey, hey," Ryan says. "When Miami was down 24–27 against Duke, did they give up? No, they played the hell out with laterals like you can't even imagine, scoring a touchdown and winding up beating Duke 30–27."

"It sounds like some luck might have been involved there."

"You need to YouTube that play because you'll see it was smarts, not just luck. Now you need to be Miami and believe there's a way to win this. Here, I'll make it easier."

"Because I'm sure you've noticed in the time you've known me that I'm an optimist by nature."

He chuckles, his gaze wandering. "I'll be the optimist

for both of us. I've got an idea. I'll be like the director of the scene, and I'll tell you what to do, and you just listen, okay?"

"This seems even worse."

"It'll be fine," Gisele assures me.

Despite the ball of tension I've become, who am I to be the ass and bail when she's so willing to help me?

"Sure, why not?"

"What do you think is attractive about her?" Ryan asks. "Say something you think is hot about her—don't say breasts because that's inappropriate as fuck."

"I agree. Don't say that," Gisele says, shaking her head.

"To be clear, in no universe would I have said that."

As hot as my face has been throughout this, I can feel myself getting used to it, so in some way, I know Ryan's plan is working. But if this is all just to humiliate me, I wish Ryan would get it over with. Since this is still happening, I go along with the plan, studying Gisele.

"She has a nice smile," I say. "I like the blue in her eyes."

"They're not simply blue, though, are they?" Ryan says. "What kind of blue? What do they remind you of?"

"I'm not really sure."

"Well, tell her she has pretty eyes, and since it's kind of dark, ask what shade they are."

I follow his lead, and she replies, "Baby blue-ish, but

there's a bit of sapphire if you look real close."

"Now move a little closer to get a better look. That was an invitation to move in."

I follow his instruction, and she sizes me up. She's really in it to win it—maybe he's paying her or maybe because she knows she has a better chance of getting laid by going along with this.

"That's good," Ryan says. "Now you've established interest. In a real-world setting, if she backs away, then you're a creep, so back off. And now wait for her to move closer to you," which Gisele does.

Ryan guides us through some basic shit, the sort of conversation we might have if we'd just bumped into each other, then says, "Okay, now we need to ramp things up a little. Keep sort of looking her up and down—your eyes should let her know you think she's gorgeous—and pay attention to how she responds."

I feel like a goddamn idiot as I try to somehow look like I think she's gorgeous, which I don't know how to do because I've thought she was gorgeous this whole fucking time.

"Gisele, you're doing great here, exactly like that," he says. "Nice and receptive. Observe how she's moving closer."

"It sounds like you're directing porn," I say through my teeth.

"Quit breaking the fourth wall."

"The huh?"

"That's when you address the audience," Gisele explains. "Unless it's done really well, it pulls the audience out of the story."

"Aren't you breaking the fourth wall?" I ask Ryan.

"I'm the director. I can break the wall all I want."

"He's right," Gisele says. "He can."

"Well, now you're breaking it too," I tease, earning the first genuine laugh from her.

Which makes me pause, wondering, is she into me? Or is this part of the act?

"You have a cute sense of humor," she says. "You should do more of that too. That's hot."

Now she's calling me hot? What is happening?

"Now," Ryan says, "you're gonna say, 'your eyes aren't the only thing I noticed' and then look at her lips."

"What?"

"Just do it."

"Your eyes aren't the only thing I noticed," I repeat, checking out her lips.

"Oh yeah?" Gisele asks. "What else were you noticing?"

"Tell her, 'You know what I'm talking about.'"

"I know what you're talking about."

"No," Ryan says. "That doesn't make any sense. Quote me exactly."

"Oh...*you* know what I'm talking about."

"Now do the lean-in, and you're gonna whisper if you can kiss her, in, like, a really sexy way."

A jolt of panic surges through me. "Wait, what? How far are we going with this?"

"You're gonna kiss her, of course." He says that like it's plain as day.

I turn to Gisele, hoping she'll be appalled at the idea.

"I'm fine with it," she assures me. "Ryan already mentioned we'd be doing this."

"He sure as hell didn't mention it to me," I snap.

My face is so hot, now for a very different reason than when we started. My gut is knotted up. I need to get away, but I take a measured breath. "You know what, Gisele, I appreciate your taking time out of your night to help me out, but I can't—"

I hurry away, and I hear Ryan tell her, "Give me a minute."

He catches up with me, and there's that hand on my back again. "Don't touch me," I insist, jerking away from him.

He raises his hands, wide-eyed. "Okay, dude. What's the issue? Before I brought her in, I showed her your pics and she thought you were cute, which is why I recruited her to help."

This is new information. "She thinks I'm cute? What? I wanna die." As my chest tightens like I'm about to have a panic attack, I press my hand against it and hurry off, Ryan keeping right behind me.

"Dude," he says en route to my room.

"Just leave me the fuck alone, will you?" I spit out.

I keep on to my room, and as I get to it, I head in, slamming the door behind me. Right now, I'm really hating that it was my idea that he roomed with me, since I wish I could lock him out. I'm waiting for him to barge in, but he knocks.

"Mart...come on. Talk to me. Please."

This must be one of the few times he's actually respected me enough to give me space and not come barging in.

I take a few breaths, feeling the tightness in my chest loosening, but not much.

"Please, Mart," he says again, his voice muffled from the other side.

At this point, I'm so worked up, I feel like it'd actually-ly feel better if we were fighting, so I open the door, and he stands on the other side, his head tucked low, like a kid who's gotten into trouble.

"Can I come in?" he asks.

"Sure."

I start toward my bed, but now that he's in here, all the pent-up frustration and rage from downstairs breaks through the surface.

"Why did you do that to me? Why would you put me in a situation with a girl I actually stood a chance with and torture me in front of her?"

"Okay, clearly the kiss was a bridge too far and touched a nerve. What's going on?"

This is what's been building since he first made the suggestion. This secret I keep that feels so goddamn shameful, it hurts. So I tell him. "I suck at kissing. Are you happy?"

His expression sobers. "Huh?"

He says that like he can't fathom the idea—and of course he can't! He's fucking Ryan Lorde. He's got game. He's had so much practice, he couldn't suck at kissing if he tried.

"I'm not a good kisser," I repeat, mortified I've revealed this much, but glad it's out and now he can leave me the fuck alone. I spin back to the bed. "Will you leave now?"

Now that my anger has settled, I realize what a stupid-ass thing it was to share with him—this vulnerability I wouldn't even confide in Ash or Lance. I don't want him to see me like this.

"Please go," I whisper.

Ryan doesn't budge. I'm about to demand he leave when he asks, "How do you know that?"

"I've had girlfriends tell me."

"Like, many girlfriends?"

It was one girl, but he doesn't need to know that.

"Why didn't you tell me that sooner?" he asks.

I glare at him. "This is your response when I tell you this deeply personal thing? It's not exactly something I'm proud of."

"This is important information, though. If you'd told me, we would've started in a completely different place. This is like emergency-intervention shit."

Emergency intervention? He sure has a way of making it sound even worse. "Will you stop making fun of me?"

Ryan approaches. "Dude, I'm not making fun of you." He starts like he's about to put his hand on my shoulder, but stops himself, surely because of all the times I've told him to keep his hands off me tonight.

"You think maybe that's why you have a hard time flirting with girls?" he asks.

He has a point.

"Maybe. Because I know even if I got to that moment, it would suck, and that would scare them off, and then…it just seems so fucking humiliating. Why are you still here? Leave me alone. Go tell your friends what a prude I am and have a laugh. I know you guys make fun of me."

Ryan nods, turns and heads to the door, closes it. He pulls his phone out of his pocket, keying away.

My nerves quickly transform into hot fury. I can't believe he's texting his friends about this in front of me. "Okay, I meant leave and tell them, not send a group text."

He side-eyes me. "I'm texting Gisele so she knows she doesn't have to wait for us."

"Oh…"

After he sends the text, he approaches me again.

I'm totally thrown. After what I just shared, why is he still here? Why won't he leave me the hell alone?

11

Ryan

I'VE LEARNED A lot about Mart in the last few minutes.

Not just that he's a bad kisser, but that he thinks even less of me than I realized. We aren't on great terms, but I never would have guessed he'd assume my reaction to hearing him share something so personal would be to run off and start sharing that with my friends.

A part of me thinks I should do what he wants: leave.

But this is my fault. If I hadn't pushed him with Gisele, he wouldn't be so worked up.

As he stands there, his expression locked in a scowl, I approach. The way he glares at me, if I didn't know him like I do, I'd think he was gonna haul off and hit me.

"What. Do. You. Want?" he says through his teeth.

"Let's sit on the bench for a minute."

"You mean my bed?"

"It's an expression. Come on." I approach the edge, take a seat, patting the spot beside me.

"Whatever," he concedes, plopping down beside me.

"I'm sorry." My apology seems to catch him off guard because his scowl shifts to confusion. "I clearly didn't read this right. I should have asked more questions before making assumptions. As I said, if I'd known this was an emergency situation, I would have started in a totally different place."

He glares at me. "Can you stop calling it an emergency situation?"

Me and my dumb mouth.

"I didn't mean—"

"Oh, no, you definitely meant it. *Sooorrrry*..." He couldn't be more sarcastic if he tried. "Not all of us have had hundreds of girls to practice on."

"Hundreds seems..." I consider it briefly...well, not as brief as I would've expected...because wow, I guess my numbers are up there. "I mean, that has to be wrong. Right?"

His eyes narrow.

"Okay, so this kind of talk isn't helping. Let's scratch all the shit we did downstairs. I'm getting where this insecurity is coming from now, so I can help you." Because, really, this has given me an important insight into why Marty's so insecure.

"Help me? No, no. We're done with this. I'm out. I'm not showing you how to fucking tango. You're not showing me how to flirt. We're not doing this teaming-up thing. We're going back to the way things were."

I've had guys get like this on the team before. Wigging out. Being irrational because they're so caught up in the emotional after missing the catch or fumbling. I need to keep my cool and be here for him the way I would for one of my guys.

"Hey, hey, look at me. Mart, come on…look at me. Marty."

He's as stubborn as always, but he finally breaks, and I can see the hurt in the subtle downturn of his lips, the softness in his eyes. When he's not being a complete dick, it's possible for me to sympathize with him.

"This is clearly hitting a nerve," I say. "I'm sure that wasn't great to hear from girls, and it's obviously left an impression, but if you want me to be honest with you—"

"I'd rather you not."

I need to be more careful with my goddamn words because I don't really care whether or not he wants me to be honest. "Even if you don't want me to be honest, here it is: I think this is what's getting in your way. If you felt confident about kissing, maybe you'd feel like you could hit on Angie or another girl because you'd know you have the skills to back it up with."

He breaks eye contact. "I can't say you're entirely wrong."

"I feel like I'm not even a little bit wrong."

He shoots me another dirty look. He's full of those tonight. But we might've hit onto his core issue around flirting, which is a win in my book.

"If it's only kissing, that's something we can work on," I tell him.

"If you think you're getting Gisele back so we can kiss, you are dead wrong."

"I wouldn't do that to you, man. Or Gisele, for that matter, because wouldn't that suck to team her up with someone who can't even kiss?" I'm hoping the joke will lighten the mood.

It doesn't.

I start to reach for him to rest my hand on his shoulder, but thinking about how he reacted before, I stop myself. As he notices, I say, "See? I can learn."

He snickers, which makes me feel some relief, like I've broken through whatever barrier he was keeping between us.

"I'm not gonna bring another girl into this because with where you're at, that's too much."

"Okay…" he drags out. "So you have some other plan for how to deal with me being a shit kisser?"

I take a breath, accepting this isn't gonna be an easy job, but someone's gotta do it. "You're gonna kiss me."

Seems like the obvious solution, but his eyes widen, and he jumps up from the bed, as though the suggestion meant I was about to lunge at him and force a smooch on his lips.

"The hell is this weird shit?" he asks.

"What? How is that weird?"

"How is that *not* weird?"

"We're in frats. You had to have kissed guys before."

"No, I haven't. *You* have?"

He can't be serious.

"You never played spin the bottle and it wound up on a guy? Or had a TaskFrat challenge where you had to kiss?"

"I don't play spin the bottle for obvious reasons."

Mmmm. That tracks. If I sucked at kissing, guess I'd avoid situations where I had to do just that.

"I should have figured that one out on my own."

Maybe he's right. I could just be an idiot. I sure am acting like one tonight.

"Well," I go on, "having kissed guys before, I can tell you it's not a big deal. And it'll help me see where you're at. Kissing can be taught. It's a skill like anything else. And I don't know if you think you need references, but I'm pretty damn good at it."

Marty's shoulders relax before he searches around the room, as though the walls are gonna start making fun of him for even considering the idea. He runs his hand through his hair. "If this is a trick…" he says, the threat in his tone.

"No trick."

I guess it's a little bit of a trick since I'm helping him so I won't wind up on probation, but the kissing itself is not a trick.

"You know this is a weird-ass idea, right?" he says.

"Seems practical to me. What, you got some kind of queerphobia that makes you worried about kissing a dude?"

"Ash and Lance are my best buds, so you know that's not it."

"Oh, is this *I have a queer friend, so I'm not queerphobic?*" I tease.

"That's not how I meant it. I'm just—"

"I'm giving you hell. Get your ass over here and plant one on me. And I'll give you instructions. We can work on it."

He scratches at his arm, clearly thinking it over, which is better than where things started. "Maybe we should call it a night."

He doesn't want to do this, and I get it, but I need to get through to him if there's even a chance of helping him get over this. "One time when I was a kid, I was really struggling with my throw, so Dad got me down to the park every day. And I didn't want to because I thought it was embarrassing and that it wouldn't do any good because I was crap at it, but we kept drilling away, and you know what happened?"

"It worked?"

"Exactly."

"I don't like what this implies about how much we'll have to do this."

"Sit on this bed," I instruct, my tone letting him know I won't back down until he caves.

He eyes me uneasily before settling beside me again, which is a relief because a minute ago I thought he was gonna rush out of his room.

But despite how pushy I'm being, I also don't want to push him too far before he's ready. "Mart, you can do this. I won't judge you or tell anyone about what we do…or how bad of a kisser you are." At his look, I add, "Sorry again. Hey, words aren't really my thing. Let's do this. Come on. Give it to me."

"This isn't gonna work," he mutters.

"If you're that shitty, I'll let you know," I joke.

"I can't believe this is happening."

"Meanwhile, some girls would kill to be in this bed with me right now, having me as their kissing instructor."

"Kill?"

"Stop stalling."

He takes a breath and leans toward me. I'm surprised he's going along with it. Maybe this is really happening…

But he stays stiff in place.

"You need me to close my eyes?" I ask, batting my eyes playfully.

"I need you to shut your dumb mouth."

"That might be what your issue with kissing is."

"Can you cut it with the jokes?"

"I'm trying to lighten the mood."

"Trust me, Lightness is downstairs, enjoying himself at the party."

He leans a little closer, staring down at my mouth like it's a bug. I can tell by the way he's all tensed up that he's stressing himself out even more. I try to think of a way to make this easier on him, so I lean toward him. I'm waiting for him to back off, but he doesn't budge.

"Here," I say. "Let me help you. Are you ready?"

He sighs. "Just do—"

Before the word *it* even has a chance to fully escape his mouth, I press my lips against his, pleasantly surprised by how soft they are. I start small, lips barely parted, easing him into the experience, noticing how warm his flesh is against mine. The way his breath brushes up against my skin as he breathes.

He moves closer, opening his mouth more, pressing harder.

Naughty Marty.

The move sends a surge of adrenaline through me, and before I know it, my dick's getting kind of hard. That's wild, but now I'm curious when the shit-kissing part is gonna start, so I grab the back of his head, keeping him close as our tongues meet. There's something very intuitive about his movements, how his tongue teases mine, which shocks the hell out of me, considering I've seen this guy trying to dance.

Where the hell is this coming from?

And what was that bullshit about being terrible at this?

My dick is quick to respond, firming right up before his tongue slides back out, leaving me hanging, and I find myself craving more.

His breath hitches as he searches around, looking as confused as I feel.

"That bad?" he asks, his cheeks pinkening, and I realize I'm staring.

I was expecting it to feel like the other kisses I've had with guys.

Clinical.

Maybe a little fun.

I wasn't expecting that rush…or what felt like more expertise than he'd led me to believe.

But that can't be right.

It was just nice to make out with someone, maybe?

"Um…" I finally manage, struggling to understand what happened. "I didn't get what these girls are talking about. Can we try one more time? Like really throw yourself into it. Do whatever you'd do naturally."

It's the right way to sort this out, but also, I feel guilty because I know I'm more curious than I should be, not about him, but about what it was doing to me.

Marty doesn't hesitate like he did before. His lips are

locked against mine in no time, tongue back in my mouth. Fuck, he's really going for it this time, and it's fire searing across wet flesh.

I can't even think straight. I just follow where it leads. As he cups my cheek, I guide him onto his back. I'm enjoying every moment, forgetting what the hell I was even doing, when he starts to pull away, but I lean forward, keeping him in place.

My cock stretches in my briefs.

Damn, this has really got me going.

But now that I'm stiff as a board, I realize I'm being greedy as hell.

This isn't about me.

I think it's gonna kill me to break the kiss, but I force myself, muttering, "Sorry, I think I got a little carried away there."

"Yeah…uh…"

My gaze is drawn to his crotch, where he sports a—

"Mart, what the hell is that?"

"Oh fuck," he says, sitting up quickly. "Nothing."

"That's a lot of inches of nothing."

"Shut it!" he says, pushing to his feet and turning away from me. "I don't know why it did that."

I have a few ideas, but also more questions. "Where do you keep that concealed weapon? I've seen you in a fucking G-string."

"I'm a grower, not a shower."

"Apparently." I'm awestruck by the bulge.

"And TaskFrat challenges don't exactly get me wound up like that," he adds. "Jesus, I knew this was a crap idea."

I'm making him self-conscious, so I try to set him at ease. "Sorry, Mart. It just surprised me, but I'm hard too."

"What?" He sounds offended.

He spins back around, and I can't take my eyes off the bulge in his pants.

"Why are *you* hard?" he asks, studying mine.

"Probably for the same reason you are."

He shakes his head. I imagine he's struggling to make sense of this too. I'm racking my brain, trying to think if I've ever experienced anything similar to this with a guy before. There were times when the kissing was fun, but nothing like this.

"Well?" he spits out, looking at me as though expecting me to say something.

"Um…I'm trying to figure it out too."

"What?" he says. "No, the notes. The whole reason we are in this mess."

"Notes? Oh yeah, notes." His size made me totally forget about what we were even doing in here. I'm not thinking straight right now…no surprise there, I guess. So I certainly can't come up with a critique. All I know is I've shared enough kisses to know a good kiss when I feel one, and that was an incredible kiss.

Which only adds to the questions this whole kissing thing has brought up.

"I'm sorry," I say, "how many girls told you that you couldn't kiss?"

"It was only one girlfriend, but obviously when she said that, it stuck with me."

I'm relieved to hear it because otherwise whatever the hell just happened might've just been completely in my head. But I'm not done interrogating him. "What exactly didn't she like?"

"That I like to kiss with my mouth open like that, and with tongue. She preferred closed-mouth kisses."

"Ah!" It dawns on me. "I think what you're looking at is people who have different preferred kissing styles because I can assure you, having kissed a lot of people, that was fine. More than fine. It was *exceptional.*"

He studies my expression. "Why did you say it like that?"

"Because I'm being honest. What was it like for *you*?"

He blushes, tucking his head low as he indicates his raging hard-on. I mean, that better be raging because what else is he gonna do with that thing if it gets any bigger?

"Okay," Marty says. "I told you this was a weird idea, and it was, so can we stop now?"

"Wait. No, no. I think there's definitely more to talk

about here. That felt good to you, right?"

"Yeah, but you told me you're a good kisser, so it's not a huge surprise."

"But did it feel like…*good* good?" I press.

His eyebrows twist up. "That's the least descriptive way you could have phrased it."

"You liked it, though?"

"Is this why you wanted to set me up? So you could make fun of me?"

"I'm asking a sincere question. And how can you even say that? I'm hard too."

He seems to relax as I remind him of that important fact.

"It felt good, and that causes an erection," Marty explains.

"Yeah, 'cause I need the middle school sex ed class now. No, it felt good for you, kissing *me*."

"We've been over this part."

"You bi?"

"What, no?" Although, he doesn't sound as confident as I'd expect from someone who knows they're straight. "I have never… I'm into Angie. That's why I was even doing all this. So I could get with a girl."

"And…?"

"I don't know why you had to make this so fucking complicated."

"Hey, you were fine with giving this a try."

"Because I thought you were gonna help me, not scramble my fucking brain."

"Okay, come here," I say, pushing to my feet and approaching him.

"Don't touch me."

"I'm not going to touch you. Just sit on the bed, and let's talk this out."

He glares at me as I approach, and I'm admiring that even as my dick is going soft, his is still standing firm. And that's making my mouth water for some reason.

I guide him back to the bed, and we settle beside each other again, quieting as we think this through.

"It could have been a fluke," he finally says.

"Twice for me, at least. Both kisses I was getting hard during."

"Same here."

Oh, really?

"Were you thinking of a girl while we were kissing?" I ask.

"Honestly, I wasn't doing much thinking. You?"

"Wasn't doing much thinking either."

He studies his crotch like he's realizing that here we are, even after all this awkwardness, and he's still got that baseball bat between his legs.

And I'm not sure why the hell that intrigues me so much.

"Maybe we try it again," I suggest.

"Huh?" His brows tug closer together.

"To see what happens."

"We did that already."

"Yeah, you're right. I think I would want to try it again…"

"Why?" He eyes me suspiciously.

"Clearly, you're not where I'm at, but I'm wondering if this means something about me, and it would help me figure that out, but maybe it's only me, so never mind."

As many questions as he's got in his head, I have my own too.

"Not sure I've ever heard you ramble before." He nudges my shoulder with his.

"Shut it," I throw back at him.

"Okay, so no notes on the kiss, then?" He turns to me, quirking a brow.

"Not sure I've ever seen you cocky before." I must admit, it's kind of hot.

"Well, that's good to know that I've been freaking out the past few years of my college life about something that isn't even a thing for me."

"Could be worse. We could have had to keep on practicing until you got it right."

It's the sort of thing I might've teased him about before our kiss, and I detect something in his expression as he studies my lips again.

"Yeah, that would have sucked," he mutters so low,

I'm surprised I can even make out the words.

"I mean…" Before I can finish my thought, he moves quickly, and our jaws clash before his lips are back on mine, Marty pouncing me like an animal, and soon I'm on my back, sliding my hand around his waist as that tongue slips back between my lips.

I'm not sure what the hell he's doing, and I don't really care so long as he keeps on kissing me.

12

Marty

WHAT THE FUCK is going on?

Ryan is one of the biggest assholes I've ever met.

With the most kissable lips, apparently.

Not that I have too much experience with that, but when our lips are locked, all the clutter, all the sound and fury that usually preoccupies my brain finally quiets, allowing me to be absorbed by the pleasure.

Even with all the questions that have come up since we got back to my room.

Am I a shit kisser?

Am I attracted to guys?

Am I queer like my best buds?

Maybe I attacked Ryan with another kiss because this could be the only way to answer these questions. But this could all be because I haven't had a real kiss in so long, what I did with Ryan finally gave me some much-needed relief.

It was wild.

It was exciting.

And when he's not talking, it's easy enough to forget what a dick he can be.

As I pin his wrists to the bed, making out with him, I savor the swirling sensation in my chest, the pricking in my fingertips and lips, the soothing warmth in my cheeks.

Who knew the guy who can get me the most worked up could also act as a sedative?

I don't know how long we've been making out, but I finally manage to pull away, catching another breath without his tongue down my throat.

Ryan lies on his back beneath me, his shirt hiked up slightly to show the grooves in his abs, which for some reason is catching my attention right now.

"Everything cool?" he asks, which considering everything that's happened tonight, seems like a wild-ass question.

"I think my lips are starting to get chapped," I admit.

"Should I put on some ChapStick before I kiss you again?"

I laugh…fucking laugh over something Ryan Lorde said. Wow. This is new territory.

"You really are something," I say. "You're acting chill as ever after what we've been doing?"

"Should I be freaking out?"

"One of us should be."

"Isn't that kind of *your* thing?"

In that case, I'm not doing a bad job. "Shut your fucking hole."

"You know how to make that happen." His gaze settles on my lips again.

He's not wrong about the worrying bit being my territory, so I do my job, letting the questions this provokes dominate my thoughts.

"You think we're attracted to guys?" I ask, and his brow creases.

"What's the answer you need that gets those lips back on mine?"

I roll my eyes. "I'm starting to see why the girls find you so damn charming."

"Bet you are," he says before offering a soft peck.

My dick is really straining in my boxers, so I have to adjust it for what must be the tenth time since we started making out.

"Let me just…" I unfasten my belt and notice Ryan looking at my crotch. "Don't look!" I insist.

"Oh, sorry." His gaze shoots right for the ceiling in a way that's more considerate than anything I would have expected from him.

"Somebody's being nice now that he wants to kiss me again."

"Hey, I'm always a gentleman."

"You haven't felt that *gentle* the past few minutes."

"Neither of us has really been all that gentle. And I think it's cute that you believe it's been a few minutes," he says as I unfasten my fly and fix my dick so the head has some breathing room.

"It hasn't been that long," I say, and he retrieves his phone from his pocket, revealing it's almost two in the morning, so it's been like thirty. "Ugh. I need to get some sleep. I'm volunteering with Activate Kindness tomorrow. And I still don't know what the hell this is all about."

"I think you have a little idea of what it's about."

"I just need to think it through, and doing this with you isn't helping me get any thinking done."

"You think too much."

He's not wrong.

"Have you decided to go back to being a fucking asshole?" I ask.

He sits up, getting right in my face, so close I'm waiting for him to plant another one on me, when he says, "Dude, whatever it is, it's not a big deal. Would it be so terrible if you were into guys and girls?"

"Not really, I guess."

"And I might be too, but we don't have to put a label on it in one night."

He's right for a change, but that's not really my thing, and without his lips pressed against mine, I'm already starting to spiral, reflecting on my other experiences with guys, searching for clues that might have indicated interest that I haven't perceived that way.

"In case you haven't met me, I don't love uncertainty," I say.

"Then I'll have to help you get some clarity around this later. Besides, I'm starting to question my initial conclusion. You could use some work on your form." The playfulness in his expression suggests he doesn't think that's even a little bit true. Here's the Ryan I'm more familiar with.

"Oh, really?" I say. "At what point did you determine that?"

"Probably when you were pinning my wrists and nibbling away at my lips like your life depended on it."

"Is that why you were moaning into my mouth?"

"I was trying to make you feel better."

Liar.

"I'll bet," I say, inching toward him, getting my lips close enough to earn a look that assures me he doesn't have any issue with however I was working my mouth. "If I'm so bad, then you need a break from these sloppy kisses."

His jaw stiffens. Even though we're teasing, I can tell he's being serious when he says, "I don't think that's a good idea." He offers another peck but lingers before slipping his tongue out and sliding it along my bottom lip.

"Really?"

"Yeah, well, I told you earlier it's all about practice."

I chuckle into his mouth before he kisses me again. I kiss him right back, appreciating that once again it helps diffuse all the questions that would otherwise feel overwhelming.

What the fuck are we doing? I fucking hate this guy, but tonight he's actually been cool with me. Very generous with helping me work this out. And his skin against mine…Jesus, nothing beats it.

Ryan finally pries himself away, grunting in a way that makes my cock twitch. That's definitely not a straight reaction. But this guy could probably have chemistry with a house plant. He's sex on legs.

He groans. "I do think we need to get to bed. Feel like I've done a proper assessment and this will help me with your Angie situation. But don't forget you still owe me tango lessons."

Angie? Tango? That's how we wound up in this confusing mess to begin with.

"Yeah, you're right," I say.

"Night, Mart," he says, licking up my lips before rolling off the bed.

He plops down on his air mattress, and I collapse back in bed, resting my hand on my chest as I stare at the ceiling.

How the hell am I gonna get any sleep after all that?

Although, I figure the answer is: I probably won't.

"MARTY, WHERE DID you head off to last night?" Lance asks as I step into the kitchen. In only pajama bottoms, he strokes Frat Cat with one hand and eats cereal with the other.

I agreed to show Ryan some tango moves if he would help me with girls, and somehow that resulted in us locking lips and leaving me questioning everything I've ever known about myself.

Not actually saying that. Obviously. So I keep those words locked in my throat, replying, "I headed up to bed early."

He shrugs, then glances my way, his eyes bulging. "If you went to bed early, why do you look like you didn't sleep all night?"

While it took Ryan maybe ten minutes to doze off, releasing that familiar deep breathing he does when he's out, I spent the night rolling around in the sheets, my brain scrambled and my cock refusing to give me a moment's peace.

Maybe because I was busy thinking about Ryan's touch, his tongue teasing mine, his hot breath against my face. And while Ryan was sleeping like a baby, I found myself resenting him again, only this time because he left me in this confused state.

Am I into guys? I must be. But if that's true, why didn't I find that out until last night?

"I went up to bed but stayed up thinking."

"Ah. Sounds about right."

Nice to know I'm known for being so packed full of anxiety that this doesn't raise any red flags for my buddy.

Last night, I considered whether I should say anything to him. He's my best friend. He knows what it's like to be attracted to guys and girls. Maybe he could help me understand what's going on, but I'm such a bad liar, if he starts probing, he'll work out it was Ryan I was doing stuff with. No matter how much I don't like the guy, I wouldn't put him in that position.

Not that he seemed particularly rattled, but it was easy to leave the world behind and be stupid in bed together, letting those primal urges control us when we didn't have to think about what it'd be like this morning. Or how it would impact our lives beyond a few kisses.

"I'm gonna make an omelet," I say, imagining if I got busy with something, it would help me relax. "You want one?"

"That'd be good. Thank you! Was gonna need something else besides this cereal anyway. Gonna get my workout in at the weight room in a bit."

"Mmm," I hear from the living area before Ty saunters in. He's got this look in his eyes, like he doesn't even see me—can only see Lance as he approaches him, his hands sliding around his body as he effortlessly pulls him close and kisses the back of his neck.

A wave of heat moves through me. In the past, I would've assumed it was embarrassment from them being so intimate in front of me, but what if it's because I find this hot? My therapist and I once talked about how I sometimes lack nuance in understanding my emotions—extreme, at times, black-and-white thinking. What if some of my confusion is because this uncomfortable emotion wasn't embarrassment after all?

"Ty, would you like an omelet?" I ask.

"Sure, man. I appreciate it."

"I'll make one for Ash and Colin too."

"I'm sure they'll appreciate that," Lance says. "I know for a fact those guys were up all night."

"How do you know that for a fact?" I ask.

"Before they went to bed, Ash said he was determined to keep his man up all night, and I believed him."

"Oh…"

I get cracking on omelets, considering if I should make Ryan one, but no, that'd be weird.

I'm being weird.

I've split one for Ty and Lance by the time the back door opens and Dax heads in, wearing a Zeta Tau jacket.

"You fucking traitor," Ty teases, and Dax unzips it, revealing he's shirtless underneath.

"Okay, how did this happen?" I ask.

"Isn't it obvious? Ended up with a guy at Zeta Tau."

"Yeah, but why do you have his jacket? I assume you messed around at his place. He couldn't give you a shirt?"

"We were at the park, actually, and I'm not sure where I left my shirt. I asked to borrow his, but he wanted me to take something more substantial to make sure we'd get together again."

"Pretty smart," Lance says.

"Hey, I don't go after idiots."

"Did I hear my name?" The voice has goose bumps pricking across my flesh.

It's the familiar annoyance I feel whenever I know he's nearby, but it's different this time. There's something else mixed in. Probably the thing making my dick a little twitchy.

My face is red even before Ryan's in the kitchen, bare-chested, only in boxers, minus the tent he was sporting most of the time he was up with me. Ty, Lance, and Dax laugh at his quip, but I can't appreciate the humor.

I sneak a look his way, and unsurprisingly, the guy looks cool as ice. He breezes in, offering shakes and fist bumps with the other guys as though nothing happened last night. Maybe because it was nothing for him. For a guy who goes through girls faster than Tic Tacs, I guess I shouldn't be surprised. To him, I was probably another in a long list of the people he's mouth-fucked with his tongue.

"Fuck, those abs!" Ryan says to Dax. "You looking good, man."

"Ya think?" Dax asks, flexing them for the frathole.

Seriously? It's been less than twelve hours since he made out with a guy, and now he's already hitting on Dax in front of me? I clench my fist, tightening my grip on the spatula.

"What you changing up in the gym?" Ryan asks.

"I saw Jaxon getting some nice definition from those hanging leg raises, so I added them to my routine."

"Very nice," Ryan says as Dax invites him to feel.

And for the first time I have the thought: What if Ryan was lying to me about not having messed around with guys before? No, that's too douchey, even for him. Still, this is grating on my nerves, and just as bad, I know it shouldn't be. We made out for a night. Would it really be a shock if after Ryan found out he was bi, he'd run through the house faster than Dax?

I'm focusing on the omelet when Ryan appears beside me, leaning against the drawer by the stove. "Morning, Mart."

He's got this broad grin across his face, knowing in his eyes. I'm waiting for him to say something dumb and out us to the guys, which only keeps me on edge.

"That one for me?" he whispers. "You know I'm kind

of hungry after last night."

I grit my teeth, checking over my shoulder, but the guys are busy catching up with Dax about the night before to notice what he said.

"This one is for Ash and Colin. I wasn't planning on making you one."

Ryan leans closer. "That's fine. Would prefer a nice big hunk of sausage anyway."

He looks me dead in the eyes, and I gulp as I think about the way he was eyeing my cock last night. Admiring it.

His gaze sinks toward it, and despite how tense I am, I can feel myself getting a little hard. My eyes settle on his lips, some part of me wanting to get back to what we did before.

Where is this coming from? I've never been the type to get horny like this over someone.

"Should start with a protein shake, though," he says.

"Don't you have to eat the sausage first to get that?"

I can't believe I said that, but I couldn't help myself, and Ryan grins. "That's true."

"Ryan, will you leave Marty the hell alone?" Ty says, sounding annoyed on my behalf.

"We're getting along fine."

If only Ty knew just how fine.

"I have a hard time believing that." Ty drags Ryan away, which is probably for the best, but now that he's not beside me, I'm trying to work out if this heat is from the range or from the way he was talking to me.

"Okay," Ryan says. "I gotta get some hours in at work. Then hitting the gym before I have dinner with my parents."

I hate that I'm in the middle of making omelets since I really want to pull Ryan aside and work out when we're gonna meet up again. But that's not something I can do in front of the guys.

I watch as Ryan heads out of the kitchen, noticing that decent rump he's got. Wondering what it'd feel like to get a good grip on those cheeks.

My face flushes with heat again, though this time I know it's not from the stove.

13

Ryan

AFTER WORK, I hit the gym, and during a break between deadlifts, I pull up Insta and see that Marty's not only followed me, but sent a DM.

Maybe don't make such a production in front of the guys about what we did.

They could have overheard something.

I can imagine the exact expression of annoyance he's making.

Me: Relax. I'm not as stupid as you seem to think. I didn't say anything that would have clued anyone in.

Me: Think you just wanted an excuse to hit me up on socials.

I'm about to put my phone back in my pocket, but a reply comes right through.

Marty: Trust me, this morning reminded me why this might've been a terrible idea.

Me: Dude, how did you reply so fast?

Me: Just sitting around waiting on a notification from me?

Marty: I don't even know why I feel like this is some

kind of insult.

Me: Not an insult. Kind of adorable.

Me: But a terrible idea? Nah.

Marty: For a guy who said kissing guys wasn't a big deal, you suddenly seem eager to explore your options.

I'm totally thrown.

Me: ?

Marty: Didn't seem shy about hitting on Dax right in front of me.

Now that one's really got me laughing.

Me: Dax?

He's a hot guy, sure. But I've never thought about him like that. Although, I never thought about Marty like that either until he showed me how he could work that mouth.

Marty: Oh, you loving on his abs for some other reason?

A warm sensation radiates in my chest. So that's what his attitude is really about. And for whatever reason, it's got blood pumping through my veins like when we were messing around last night.

Me: Kind of loving that we made out once and you're already jealous of other guys.

Me: Hot.

Ellipses appear, showing he's typing, then disappear, returning just as I hear, "Look who's slacking off now."

I tuck my phone away as Keegan approaches with Jaxon. We came to the gym together, since Keegan and Jaxon are regulars here too. Jaxon's put on a lot of muscle thanks to Keeg's mentoring.

"Chatting up a girl, I imagine," Keegan says.

"Something like that." I don't want to lie to my buddies, but also, none of their business what's going on with Marty and me...not that either of us really understands that anyway.

We get to chatting, and while they're doing bench presses, I figure it's a good chance for us to spot each other. I'm curious what Marty replied, so while Jaxon spots Keegan, I check my phone.

Marty: I may be a lot of things, but jealous isn't one of them.

Marty: Know what, it doesn't matter. If you're around tonight, I could show you some more tango moves.

Me: Needy for it all of a sudden, huh? I must be that good.

I imagine how that'll get under his skin, but I'd rather be doing that in person.

He doesn't reply right away—I assume he's busy at Activate Kindness now—so I hit the locker room and change before heading out to meet up with my parents.

When I get there, about an hour from Peachtree Springs, I park in front of the picturesque two-story house. The place where I was raised.

Where Dad and I used to spend time out back throwing the ball around.

Where we would open Christmas presents in the

living room, by the bay window.

Where I used to have to time things just right, like a spy, to sneak girls up into my room in high school.

Spending so much time at school and work these days, it's nice to come back every once in a while. My home—my family—always grounds me, no matter what else may be going on in my life. Plus, it's been a minute since I've seen Mom and Dad at the same time. Feels like she's been really busy with friends recently.

Dad greets me at the door. "How's my champ, huh?"

Well, he's messing around with guys now.

A guy, at least, but not something I have to share with my parents right away. Would prefer to get a handle on this first, get an idea of what's happening between Mart and me.

Dad pats me on the back, ushering me inside. "Must be killing you waiting for the draft. And we need to make some time so I can see where you're at with training."

"Yeah, sure."

That's a topic I was hoping to bring up over dinner. At least plant the seed, let him know I'm reconsidering going pro so he's not blindsided later. But first, I'd rather just enjoy the afternoon with them than...I don't know...crush Dad's NFL dreams.

We step into the kitchen, where Mom's standing in a skirt and blouse, her hair and makeup done, which isn't the norm. She's more of a ponytail-and-jeans kind of mom.

"Were you out?" I ask her as I approach for a hug.

"With some friends for brunch."

"Friends *and* brunch? Wow. You are all over the place these days."

She searches around uneasily, which catches me off guard, as though I said something that made it awkward, but I can't imagine what that could have been.

"Sit down," she says. "It's been too long since we've talked. We have so much to catch up on."

I settle at the table, expecting Dad to mosey on over to the oven to finish with dinner and Mom to sit and talk with me like we normally do, but they both sit, their expressions tense, and I quickly recognize what this is.

"What is going on?"

Dad winces. "Why do you look worried?"

"Not sure. This reminds me of how you sat me down after you found that condom in my room."

Mom and Dad exchange a look before Mom says, "We were very happy you were using condoms, but we did need to have a talk with you. We didn't traumatize you, did we?"

"I mean, it's not the only serious conversation we had. There was the time I snuck out."

"You're saying it like that was only once," Mom observes.

"And the time the cops came over because they caught me and some friends in a park after it was closed. And that one time when I was making out with Mandy Forbes at that house that was under construction."

You know, as much as Marty can get to me, he wasn't that off about the kind of person I am. But I haven't even been home, so I'm stumped about what I could've done.

"And…" I'm about to go on.

"You're not in trouble," Dad insists quickly, like a lawyer trying to keep me from incriminating myself more than I already did. "But we wanted to talk to you about something."

"We don't have to get to it right away, though," Mom adds. "Why don't you tell us what you've been up to?"

I search around the kitchen, sniffing… "What's for dinner, exactly?"

"Oh, we were planning to go out," Mom says. "We didn't have time to get something together, but also, this is important enough that we figured we'd want to discuss it before eating, hence meeting here first."

That's unusual…

"If it's so important, why didn't you tell me over the phone?"

"It's the kind of thing you deserved to hear in person, Ry," Mom says. "And it's something we probably should have told you sooner."

Now I'm really on edge. I wait for one of them to explain, but they're quiet, as though each is waiting for the other to tell me this news.

"Someone has to say it now. Is it Grandma?" She had a stroke last summer, but from everything they've told me, she's been fine recently. It's the only thing that comes to mind, though.

"No, no," Dad rushes to reassure me. "Grandma's fine. This is not about anyone's health."

"Okay…" I drag out.

Between the odd way they're acting tonight and the way Mom's been acting recently, I have a pinch in my gut, some instinct that I'm hoping once they share what's on their minds, I'll reveal what I feared they were about to tell me, and they'll laugh it off as a wild thing to conclude.

Unfortunately, Mom says, "Your father and I have been doing a lot of thinking the past few years, since you've been in college…"

The blood in my face drains as her words confirm what was already stirring in my mind, a fear I have a word for, though I keep trying to pretend the word doesn't exist.

"It doesn't have anything to do with you," she says. "We both love you."

"So much."

"Someone just say it," I force through my teeth.

Mom takes a measured breath, the sort I recognize from other times when she's had to deliver bad news. "Your father and I are getting a divorce."

There it is. The word I was trying desperately to avoid, and now that she's said it, I feel even more oblivious than usual. And not only oblivious, but selfish. Was I so self-involved that I didn't consider this could have been on the horizon for the two people I care about most?

I'm waiting for a torrent of emotion—rage, guilt, shock—but I'm surprisingly numb. To make matters worse, they're silent, staring at me, as if to gauge my reaction. I open my mouth to say something, anything that will make this stop, but words catch in my throat. Not that I'd have any even if I could think of something.

After a stretch of time, I finally manage to get out, "What?"

"Divorce," Dad says, avoiding eye contact. "We're getting a divorce."

"Not, like, a separation?"

They turn to each other but won't look each other in the eyes either, and again, I know them well enough to have an idea of what they won't say. "So you've already been separated?"

"Not a legal separation," Dad says. "But we've agreed we would do that."

"How long has this been going on?"

"About a year."

Now they've got me running back through the past year's events—Christmas, a vacation to see our extended family. "Even when we went to Maui?" I ask, since that's just a regular trip we have over the holiday, and everything seemed totally normal, but again, it reminds me that I haven't been paying attention as they nod to confirm.

"And you didn't want to tell me *anything*?"

"We wanted to be sure first," Mom says.

"Did something happen? Or…" My stomach churns at the thought that either might have betrayed the other.

"Nothing happened," Dad insists before I can sit with that for too long. "But your mom was expressing frustrations for some time—"

"Aster, don't put this on me."

Dad hangs his head as he chews his bottom lip.

"We agreed to this together," Mom adds.

Dad nods, his face red, but he's quiet, unusually quiet for him.

"Dad doesn't want this, does he?" I ask, choking up.

He still won't look at me, and I can see the tears forming in his eyes as he says, "Things don't always work out the way you plan. You know that, champ. But I adore your mother, and she knows that."

Mom shoots him a subtle look, and her stoic expression and the way she tilts her neck has me thinking his confession has irritated her arthritis.

"Is there something you could do?" I ask. "Like see a therapist?"

"We've been to couples counseling before we made this decision," Dad reveals.

Another thing I've been oblivious to.

Fuck.

That numbness is quickly being replaced by all these feelings I'm not ready to handle.

Anger.

Frustration.

Guilt.

And a sense of helplessness because it's clear they're only telling me after the decisions have already been made.

"Are you okay?" Mom asks.

I push to my feet. "I don't think so." The tightness in my chest is intense, like a pinched nerve in my heart, if that were possible. I head right for the door, wanting to get the fuck away.

"Ryan!" Dad calls after me.

"Sweetie." Mom's voice isn't far behind as they tail me.

"Sit down so we can answer any questions you have. We said we'd go to dinner."

I turn around, summoning all my strength to keep

control of the torrent of emotions moving through me. "Please, I need to get out of here for a bit. This was…a lot. And I love you both, but I need to think about it." I can't even look at them right now.

"Okay, just reach out if you need anything. We're happy to talk," Dad says.

They say more, but I'm too busy leaving to hear any of it, maybe because I can't process any more new information. I hurry to my car, not even safe once I close the door because Mom and Dad stand on the front porch, watching me. I put the car in Drive and head down to the next cul-de-sac in the neighborhood, parking before the tears overwhelm me.

14

Marty

"COME ON, WE got this," Lance says.

"Bi powers activate!" Ash follows, spinning the cursor on his controller.

"If that existed," Colin adds, "we would have cleared this game already."

Ash and Colin are stretched out across the bed. Since they can't keep apart from each other, they're like a four-armed monster, with Colin spooning Ash as they play.

After I finished up at Activate Kindness, I joined the crew for video games in Ash's room. Angie's here too. Normally, that would be enough to put me in a good mood, but today it's not setting me at ease. Neither is petting Frat Cat.

I check my phone for what must be the dozenth time since I last messaged Ryan.

There's only my DM: **What time do you think you'll be back here?**

That was three hours ago.

I remind myself he's with his parents, but that

doesn't take the edge off, especially given the way we were sparring via Insta earlier. I'd say I'm worried I might've pissed him off, but considering how we've been at each other's throats in the past and how he still wound up kissing me, that can't be it.

No, but there's another worry, much worse.

It was one thing to mess around last night. And then joke about it this morning. Ryan's good at showing everyone this chill, easygoing side, but he's got feelings, same as the rest of us, even if sometimes I forget that. He has worries and fears. What if, now that he's had time to process, he's regretting what we did? Maybe he realized there could be consequences for discovering this queer part of himself. He's a popular jock who'll likely go pro. Sure, the world's made a lot of progress, but it's still a big deal. I also don't know his parents. What if seeing them has brought up all sorts of issues—

"Everything okay?" Angie asks, yanking me from my ruminations.

She sits on the edge of the love seat Lance and I are playing from.

"Huh?"

"You seem anxious, even for you," she teases, and I force a smile.

She would notice as much in any of the other guys, but it's one of the things I enjoy about her. She's thoughtful.

Kind.

Caring.

Pretty much the opposite of a dick like Ryan, who can't even be bothered to reply to my text about tonight's tango lesson. Don't know why he can't do the bare minimum when he knows he's gonna have to deal with me sooner or later.

"Nothing. I think I need to head to bed. It's been a long day, and I have a test tomorrow."

Frat Cat meows, either demanding more scritches or saying *liar*. Maybe a little of both. I wait for a good stopping point in the game, then say my goodbyes to the crew and Frat Cat, knowing full well I won't magically be able to get to sleep.

When I reach my room, I hear music on the other side of the door. Not blaring, but loud enough to pinch at my nerves before I hurry in. The heavy metal assaults my ears, agitating me even more than seeing Ryan standing at the mirror in the bathroom, a towel around his waist, his hair messy since I guess he just took a shower.

Now I'm really pissed.

I head over to the desk and turn off the music, which doesn't elicit any response from him. Is this some fucked-up silent treatment?

"Thanks for replying to my last message, by the way," I say, not attempting to disguise my irritation.

"No problem." He applies lotion to his face, his words the only assurance that he heard me or is even willing to acknowledge my existence.

I rest my hip against the doorframe, folding my arms. It's like I'm posing in the mirror in the perfect frustrated stance. "I was being facetious because a reply would have been nice."

He still won't look at me. Maybe I was right about his visit with his parents.

"Sorry, man," is all he says.

This is not the Ryan Lorde I'm used to. Where's the sarcasm? Where's the assholery? Where the hell is my frathole?

"I'm tired," he adds, wiping his hands on his towel. "I don't think I'm up for any dance lessons tonight. Probably just gonna pass out."

He tosses the towel off, granting me a full view of the moon and his North Star before approaching me. I stay in his way, but when he still won't look at me, I finally give him space, and he breezes into the room and rolls onto his air mattress.

Despite my annoyance with his behavior, I have to believe I was right. Maybe what we did has caught up with him, and he can't play it cool while he's struggling.

"Hey," I say, forcing myself to say the word in as calm a manner as I can manage. "Will you talk to me?"

He closes his eyes as though he's got a migraine.

"Something on your mind?"

"Ryan, you don't have to do this."

"Do what?" he asks, opening his eyes and wincing.

"Pretend nothing happened last night. Or be weird about this."

"I'm not being weird about anything."

I glare at him. "It's pretty clear something's happened between this morning and now. You didn't reply to my text. And now you're practically giving me the silent treatment." I take a breath. "This is a lot. And you like to pretend nothing fazes you. Like you don't give a shit about anything, but it's okay to not be okay with everything you're going through right now."

He sits up, his eyebrow quirked. "And what, exactly, am I going through right now?"

I want to meet him at his level, so I get down on my knees. "Whatever we're trying to figure out, we can help each other. Don't shut me out. We don't have to do anything else. That can be the end of it, and I'll be fine…" Even as I say the words, they're hollow because part of what's bothering me so much is not having those lips again; life feels so much worse now that I know how good it can be with his face mashed up against mine. "…but I'm dealing with the same stuff, Ryan. You're not alone."

He huffs. "You know, you can be a lot less of a prick than you act like most of the time."

"I wish I could say the same about you," I tease.

His lips curl into his dimples, so at least that cheered him up.

"So let me get this straight," he says. "You think I'm acting this way because I regret what we did last night and now I'm questioning my sexuality and wanting to pretend it never happened?"

"Oh, look. You're also not as dumb as you act most of the time."

Even though I'm joking, I'm tense too because that is my fear.

His gaze settles on my lips, and he comes at me quickly. It's the sort of move that, had it happened before last night, I might've thought he was gonna punch me, but his lips crash against mine, and it's like my whole body releases all the tension he created by avoiding me.

He hooks an arm around me and tugs me close to his body. I can feel the heat he's still giving off from his shower, his oatmeal-scented soap tingling in my nose as his tongue sweeps across mine. He doesn't hold back, he's not hesitant, and that tongue sure as hell doesn't seem confused about what it's doing. Meanwhile, I'm back to being confused as fuck.

He guides me onto my back, our lips parting briefly as he positions his knees on either side of my waist. He rocks his hips, his crotch pushing against the fresh boner he's got worked up. My breath hitches, and he finally pulls away, giving me a chance to collect my thoughts.

He's wearing this cocky smile, the sort that would normally irritate the hell out of me. "You know," he says, "now that I've had this mouth, you look a lot cuter when you're annoyed with me."

Heat flares in my chest, and my cock assures me I'm not bothered by what he said, but aroused as fuck. Hell, it's hard to even remember why I was frustrated with him to begin with, but as it comes back to me, I have to say, "So you're definitely not weird about what we did."

"I'm weird all right." He leans down and licks up my lips. It should seem strange, but it's fire.

"You're not acting like yourself, though."

His playful expression softens, his gaze wandering. "Got some bad news today. News I can't even process, it's fucking with my head so much."

I don't know that I've ever seen him look like this before. Ryan's range goes from laughing, give-no-shits to teasing to all-out ready to kick someone's ass, which I've only seen a few times at parties when guys have made the dumbass decision to try and step up to him.

"Did something happen at your parents'?" I press since that's the only thing that's changed since the last time we chatted.

He nods. "I didn't stay long. They dumped news on me, and I had to get out, get my head on straight. Well, maybe not straight." I can tell he's trying to be his usual playful self, but it falls flat. His lips twist into a frown. "Wasn't what I was expecting today."

"I can tell you're trying to be evasive, and I know we're not the best of friends or anything, but if you did want to talk about anything, believe it or not, I can be a good listener."

He presses his tongue against the inside of his cheek, studying my expression.

"I'm good for things other than my mouth," I add to lighten the mood.

He cracks a smile.

Success.

"I honestly don't know that that's true," he jibes.

"Frathole."

Even with a smile playing across his lips, I can still see the pain lingering in his blue eyes.

"So as soon as I got home, my parents sat me down and told me they were getting a…"

He hesitates, but I already know even before the word *divorce* slips past his lips.

Fuck. That explains his sullen mood.

"Now who's the frathole for coming in after that and giving me hell?" Despite his attempt at another joke, his eyes water. "I probably shouldn't have even told you that much. It's been stuck in my brain since they told me. I went to the park for a while after the talk, and my phone died because I forgot to charge it last night, which is why I never responded to you."

"Oh…"

"It's been a day, and I'm just in a funk."

He stares off. I imagine it's the look I get when there's too much going on and I don't even know where to focus my thoughts.

"I'm very sorry," I say.

"For being a dick?"

"No. Well, yes, that too, but that's a shitty thing to have found out."

"That's part of it, but also, I really didn't see it coming. And I know I'm oblivious as fuck, and especially with how busy I was during the season, trying to keep on top of frat responsibilities and then the fire stuff… They told me it's been going on for a year, and I thought we had this perfect family. Like the kinds that TV shows are about. But suddenly, in an instant, it's like I haven't even known what my parents have been dealing with. So I guess you're right. I am the frathole."

I notice the water in his eyes stirring like he's about to drop a tear, and he turns away. I rest my hand against his arm. "Hey, hey. It sounds like something they were keeping from you. It wasn't your job to read their minds."

"I think it's over…like really over," he blurts out. "There's a part of me that feels like if I'd caught it sooner, maybe… I know it's stupid, but like I could have done something. Like *Parent Trap* shit."

"The movie? You think you could've set up some situation to make them fall in love again?"

He cringes. "It's worse when you say it out loud."

"I mean, not necessarily. You happen to have a British Ryan around somewhere?"

"Well, his name wouldn't be Ryan, and I wouldn't know about him yet." He sneaks me a playful look, more like the Ryan I'm used to.

"That really sucks, though. I'm sorry. And sorry for assuming your mood was about all this stuff."

"What stuff is that?" he says, his brows popping up as he feigns ignorance.

"You know what stuff."

"*Stuff* is a vague word." He's really playing it up, overdramatically shifting his expression about. "You could mean *anything*."

"Definitely referring to the fact that you were probing my mouth last night with your tongue."

"Oh, the we-might-not-be-as-straight-as-we-thought thing?" he asks, his cocky grin returning.

"Yeah, sure."

He shrugs. "I guess I shouldn't be surprised I can turn a guy. Just got the talent."

I have to keep from rolling my eyes, since I'm sure that would give him exactly what he wants. "Technically, that means I turned you too, so do I have the talent?"

"Who says I'm turned? I'm totally straight." That charming smile suggests he knows damn well that's not true. "I told you I was just trying to help you out with getting girls. And I assessed your kiss. Saw there were no major issues there."

"No *major* issues? So there are minor ones you wanted to discuss?"

He tilts his head, his lips twisting downward. "Eh…I think it's something we should work on together." He leans closer, the tip of his nose brushing up against mine, his minty breath filling my mouth.

For some reason, that smart-ass attitude that normally grates has me worked up. "Well, when is our next session gonna be since you're about to go to sleep?"

He licks up my lips before kissing me again, his tongue sweeping across mine, and I understand now why I was so pissed with him. Because when he didn't reply, I was afraid I wasn't gonna get this again.

"I think I can take a little time for another study session," he whispers into my mouth. "You need all the practice you can get."

Our lips smack with wet kisses.

His hand travels to my crotch, pressing along my cock until it's peeking out of my pants.

"There it is," he says.

As he applies more pressure, I roll my head back,

breaking our kiss. His breath slams against my cheek as he continues stroking me.

"Are you sure you haven't been with a guy before?" I ask because I don't get how he knows exactly how to get me worked up.

"Not yet," he says. "But we could change that. Do you want to change that?"

He offers another generous stroke, and my body vibrates, clearly eager to explore more. There's a cluster of confusion spinning in the back of my mind—all the valid reasons why we shouldn't do this.

This isn't like me at all.

I'm not impulsive or sex-crazed. But especially with how on edge he had me over not responding to my texts, and now to have him working my cock, it's more than I can bear.

On top of that, I like that he's in a better mood now, and maybe this could offer him a distraction from the shit news he found out today.

"What do you want to try?" I ask.

"Wouldn't mind getting this fat thing out and playing with it some."

The fuck?

15

Ryan

I WAS IN such a funk after my parents told me about the divorce. Spent hours feeling more down than I've felt in my entire life. But now that I have Marty's lips against mine, feeling that hard girth under his pants, hell, it's the only thing that brings me relief.

"Uh…" Marty says, which makes me pull away from him.

"Uh…? Well, that's not something anyone's ever said when I've offered to get them off."

"But with everything that happened, you want to do stuff?"

"Not sure if you've noticed, but getting off with girls is one of the ways I de-stress, and I could use a release right about now." I press up against his crotch again, feeling how tight his cock is. "And it looks like you could use one too."

"I don't want you to do anything you might regret because you're vulnerable."

"You worried about taking advantage of me?" I tease.

He angles his head, shooting me a look. "You know what I'm saying."

"I do, and it's cute. But unless you don't want me to play with your dick, then I say it might actually help me get to sleep. Come on, Mart. Let me play with it." He seems to be considering it, so I press, "Pretty please."

He practically snorts. "I mean, I would be curious to see what happens."

"I think you know what happens."

"Whatever. You know what I'm saying."

I grin. "I do."

Is it weird that our combative dynamic makes this all even more fun?

He starts to reach for his fly, but I bat his hands away. "Hell no. I got this. You gotta let me do this for you."

He raises his hands, surrendering, I know not only in this moment, but to messing around. I roll onto my hip beside him, then loosen the buttons on his jeans. His cock is already an inch stretched out from the waistband of his boxers.

"That's nice and thick," I tell him. "I've always been proud of mine, but you got a real monster down here."

I watch his expression as he glances around uneasily, his cheeks pinkening.

I take him in my grasp, gulping. "I have to admit,

I'm kind of intimidated by this."

"By how big I am?"

"Not that. I've just…had plenty of sex, know exactly what I'm doing with women, but no experience with any other dicks than my own. But I'm confident I can figure it out."

As I stroke his cock, his body vibrates, and I stare at his expression as his eyes roll back. Fuck, what that does to me.

"Yeah, doesn't seem like you're gonna have an issue with that," he mutters.

A burst of heat swirls in my chest.

"Guess I can work on this while you work on this." I kiss him while jerking him, my cock firm as fuck while I play with him. Can't believe I'm locking lips and jerking with Marty McGovern, who was bound and determined to get me kicked out of Alpha Theta Mu's house.

His dick stiffens even more in my hold, our lips tightening together as I speed up my movements.

"Marty McGovern's getting real stiff for me," I whisper into his mouth. "Dirty bastard."

That plumps him up even more before I steal another kiss. I don't feel like an expert at this, but I certainly know how to please my cock, and what I'm doing seems to be working just fine as my hand glides up and down his shaft, which swells until it feels like I'm jerking off marble. Between how hard he is and the way he arches his back, I'm sure I'm getting him close, so I speed up my movements, determined to take him all the way.

He pulls away from our kiss and says, "Ryan, I'm gonna…"

"Give it to me," I tell him.

He hikes his shirt up and shoots across his abs with a load that's as impressive as his size. I keep pumping him to make sure to get every drop out, feeling like I just made a touchdown. He continues twisting his head either way, his expression locked up, again looking more adorable than I ever thought the guy could look. His body finally stills as he catches his breath.

"You liked that," I say.

His gaze travels to my crotch. "You clearly did too."

"Mind if I get off too?" When he shakes his head, I grab my shaft. "Don't think it'll take me too long either. You…mind…if I come on you?"

"Huh?"

"You're already messy. I'll just add it to that." It's not only the mess, though. "Come on, Mart. Let me paint you with my cum." That excites me for reasons I can't wrap my head around. Well, aside from the fact that it's hot as hell.

He stares at me blankly, in a way that makes me worry he'll say no, but then shrugs. "Sure."

I kiss him again, rolling toward him as I continue pumping. The thought of mixing my cum with his on his belly, and the sensation of kissing him…it's all too much for me. There's an urgency in me, pushing me toward the edge.

"Mart, here it comes. Here I fucking come…"

I roll closer to him, my cum shooting across his torso. I enjoy the release as I paint over his fair skin. When I'm finished, I run the head of my cock through my cum, spreading it across his abs.

We gaze at each other, and he asks, "Feel better?"

"Much. But I definitely think you're queer, man."

He rolls his head back, laughing.

It's a side I get to see him let out around his friends, rarely with only me, and I enjoy seeing that I can bring that out of him too.

"I think you might be right," he says.

"Glad I could help you figure that out. Maybe tomorrow we work on sorting out how to get you with Ang?"

"Angie."

"Yeah, whatever her name is."

"Sure."

A knot constricts in my chest, this tension I can't explain, so I disregard it. "Well, so far we know you're a great kisser…and I do mean *great*, and considering what an ass you've been to me, you know I wouldn't fuck around about that. You also got a nice, thick dick, so…like most of the things in your life, I think it's only in your head. Why are you looking at me like that?"

His expression is twisted up, his brow arched. "One minute you're coming on me and the next you're talking about giving me pointers to get together with Angie? Really?"

I shrug. "I mean, you're not with anyone now, so what's wrong with a little friends-with-benefits situation? Unless you think because we mouth-fucked once, you got feels, in which case I feel bad for you."

He laughs before cringing. "Mouth-fucking? Really? And we just did more than that, but either way, you're definitely safe there."

We share a laugh, and I must admit, this was a nice end to a crap day.

With Marty McGovern covered in cum.

"I'M SORRY FOR the way I handled that," I tell Mom as we chat the following day.

I've come down from my mood, in no small part due to the way Marty helped take the edge off. He's fun, despite normally being the Ruiner of All Things Fun. Evidently, he's a lot easier to get along with when he's soaked in cum. Or when my mouth is keeping him from talking.

"You didn't do anything wrong," Mom says. "We

knew it wasn't going to be easy, and you handled it the best way you could in the moment. I love you. Your father loves you. And we both agreed that maybe you needed a minute. We have plenty of time to discuss it more."

There's that tension again because I don't want to discuss any of this. But I get what she means. It's not a one-and-done deal. This is part of our lives now.

"It was hard hearing how certain it was. But I do want you both to be happy."

"I know that, Ryan. And your father knows it too."

"Speaking of, I better give him a call. Gotta make amends with everyone today."

"Okay, I love you."

"I love you too, Mom."

After we hang up, I call Dad, who answers before the second ring, as though he's been waiting for me to return his call all morning.

"Champ?"

That twists like a knife. Not exclusively because I can hear the affection in his tone, but because it reminds me of the news I haven't shared with him yet—the news I was planning to bring up before they told me about their divorce. The news that certainly isn't gonna make any of this any easier for him, given he clearly doesn't want this divorce either.

"I just talked to Mom."

"I'm glad. We were worried about you. I'm not sure we handled it the right way. And, really, I was holding out hope..." He stops himself. "I shouldn't say that. I'm not putting any of this on your mom."

It chokes me up to hear him say that because just as when I was in the kitchen with them, I can feel this is more Mom's decision and he still loves her.

"It's been a shit year so far," he says, "but won't be once my son's drafted, right?"

Another blow.

Part of me thinks now would be a good time to tell him, while another is certain this would be the shittiest time with everything he's going through.

"Honestly, Ry, it's the only thing I really have to look forward to right now."

A bleak confession, and the words catch in my throat. "Yeah, uh-huh, Dad. You know, I need to get ready for my next class, so..."

"I'll let you go, champ. Thanks for being such a good sport. I promise I won't let any of what's going on between your mother and me stand between you and your big break."

"Mmmm-hmmm." Now I can't even get words out, I'm so uneasy.

Fortunately, it's not much longer before I get off, but now the lingering disappointment of the news they shared yesterday is mixed with the guilt about not sharing the truth about my feelings about the draft. But if I shared that, it'd break his heart on top of everything else that's going on. And I can't bear the thought of doing that to him. Not yet.

After we exchange I-love-yous, I find myself pulling up Mart's number. And I know why too. Talking to my parents worked up plenty of stress, and he was a great source of relief yesterday, so I DM him on Insta: **You planning to head back to the house soon?**

I notice bubbles pop up on my screen. **You sent this on Insta? You have my number.**

Me: Does it matter? You get notifications either way. ;)

Me: Or you were just waiting on me to text so you could get some more of this action.

Marty: You know I can block you, right?

I'm wearing a ridiculous grin. Wild that Marty is the one who's able to take me from feeling like crap to feeling good. Who would've thought?

Me: Doubt it. Pretty sure you want another taste of this mouth.

Marty: You're the one who DMed me, so I think I know who wants another taste.

Me: Nah. I could just feel how much you needed it.

Me: Besides, we both know you need more practice.

Marty: I thought you said it was good.

Me: Yeah, and I just have to practice until I can get that confidence up and you'll know it for when you're smooching on Angie.

Marty: Smooching??????

I chuckle.

Me: So make-out session in our room later?

Marty: MY room.

Marty: And why do I feel like it's not gonna only be making out?

Me: Probably because you're so horny. You haven't had a good lay in a long time, so we gotta get all that bad sperm out of you.

Marty: *eyeroll emoji*

Me: Oh, okay. Never mind. I'll just hit up Dax. He's probably free.

I shouldn't bring him into this, but remembering how Marty was fussing about me chatting up Dax, I can't help myself.

Marty: You trying to emotionally blackmail me into messing with you again?

Me: Depends. Is it working?

Marty: *eyeroll emoji*

Marty: If you haven't fucked your way through all the available queer guys at the frat before I'm back, sure.

A jolt of excitement pulses through me at the thought of getting to reenact that first experience.

Me: And don't forget, you have to show me some more tango moves.

Marty: We'll see if we can keep your hands off my dick long enough for that to happen.

Me: We should definitely do that after because I don't know that it's gonna work if I'm not fully drained first.

16

Marty

I T'S BEEN A great week.

Part of being roommates with Ryan means I haven't had any alone time to jerk off, but since we started fucking around, Ryan and I have gotten off every day—twice yesterday.

Now that he's shown a side of himself that's more than an oblivious, broey jock, he doesn't get on my nerves as much. Probably in no small part due to what I've learned his mouth can do to me—something that's hard to take my mind off as we work through a little tango coaching from one of the least qualified instructors in the dance world.

Both of us are dressed for tonight's TaskFrat challenge, in gladiator outfits we put together with the guys earlier in the week. I wear a chest plate, but unsurprisingly, Ryan's shirtless, with just a harness like he's He-Man, which is about as distracting as his mouth.

That might be why I fuck up the ocho.

"That was me," he says.

"No, that one was definitely me."

He tilts his head. "You sure? I was supposed to step back when you stepped forward."

"Oh yeah. That's right. I guess it was you. My mind's all over the place right now."

"Maybe we take a break for some of those smooches."

I laugh—a full, uninhibited laugh at something Ryan said to me. Wow. Things have changed over the past week.

"Don't laugh at me too much, or you won't get any smooches."

"You can only get away with saying smooches so many times."

"Just trying to gauge where the line is."

"That's what you do, like, all the time, isn't it?"

He surely knows I'm referring to his mischievous behavior because he arches his eyebrows. "I've been good this week."

He's not wrong.

"Since we started messing around, you have been," I observe. "Maybe you just need to make sure to get off a couple of times a day, and then you're not so bad."

"*Not so bad* supposed to be a compliment?"

"I didn't think a guy like you needed any of those."

"Guess you don't know me as well as you think because I love a compliment. And I think I know how to get one from you."

He leans in, moving slowly, and as much as I want another kiss, I sneak a look at the clock on my nightstand. "We've got ten minutes before we have to be out of here." Ryan groans before I add, "We need to get through this routine once more before TaskFrat. Then we'll call it for the night."

He leans back, his gaze wandering before he turns a mischievous glance my way. "Or we could sneak in a quick jerk-off session?"

"Is that all you ever think about?" I ask, though his inquiry makes my dick a little twitchy. "If we only ever fuck around, then you won't learn any tango moves and I won't get any practice."

He sighs. "No fun, but sure." He offers a quick peck before we get back up, finding our rhythm and completing the half-turn, two ochos, before we stop again.

"There we go," I say. "We actually made it through a tiny circle around my room."

"I think I deserve a smooch for that."

I laugh and offer a quick kiss, which apparently isn't enough for him, since he grabs the back of my head, keeping me close, and my lips surrender to him. We release each other's hands, and his settles on my waist, navigating around the chest plate to my back. His tongue sweeps across mine in that expert way he has—in that way that makes me forget about everything, even what the hell we were doing.

He squats down, hooking his arms around my thighs, lifting me before setting me on the bed. That's a first, and it's hot as hell. A jolt of excitement sweeps through me before there's a knock at the door.

"You guys about ready?" Ty asks.

"We'll be out in a minute!" Ryan calls before kissing me again.

"We need to get going, like, now."

Ryan grunts into my mouth, then asks, "You feel like we've had enough practice for when you see Gisele tonight?"

The plan is to meet her at afters for another session. And though I'm not excited about it, he's right that I need the practice if I'm ever gonna stand a chance with a girl like Angie.

"We might be starting to get a little too much practice," I tease.

"No such thing. But if you're real good with Gisele later, maybe I can offer you this as a reward."

"Oh, now your kiss is so good, you're offering it as a reward?"

He nods, full of all the cockiness that makes him Ryan Lorde.

"Perfect," I say. "In the meantime, I guess I should add our names to that whiteboard."

"Whiteboard?"

"Nothing," I say. "It's an Alpha Theta Mu inside joke." Which seems real fucking apt right about now.

He laughs. "Dork."

We get our things together and head out to TaskFrat.

Sigma Alpha stomps our asses, and then we meet at Alpha Theta Mu for afters. I chat up my friends for a bit before receiving a text from Ryan that it's time for my lesson.

On my way to find him and Gisele in the living area of Alpha Theta Mu, I can still feel the twist in my gut, like I had the first time, though it's not as bad. Probably because this time, I know what to expect, and also because Ryan's definitely improved my confidence about my kissing skills.

As I near, Ryan's expression stretches into a grin—like when he sees one of his buddies. Never before for me. And I wouldn't say we're friends just yet, but it does make me wonder, considering what we've been up to, if maybe we're on the way there. Still, if he thinks I'm letting him get away with breaking rules because we're make-out buddies, he's got another thing coming.

I settle beside Ryan, and Gisele angles her head in a way that's particularly flattering, offering a warm smile. Is this an acting bit for her? She did say she liked me, and she is hot, so maybe this wasn't the worst idea Ryan could have come up with.

"How've you been?" she asks.

"Good. Sorry about last time. I was surprised, and then…" I shrug.

"You don't owe me an explanation. And I'm here now. Happy to help." She rests her hand on my arm, which catches me off guard. Though it's nice.

Ryan's expression turns from playful to serious in an instant as he reaches over, swatting the air near her arm. "Okay, none of this. He needs to learn to initiate."

She removes her hand. "Sorry, I didn't mean to interfere with your process."

"It's not a big deal," he says, but judging by his tone, he's not entirely sincere. "Okay, so just like last time. Mart, you approach and start engaging. And I'll coach you through a conversation." He motions for me to go.

"Oh, you wanted me to actually pretend the whole bit?"

"It'll help you get into the scene," Gisele assures me.

I wish I'd been less in my head the last time we did this. She's really friendly, and I like how she gives a damn and tries to set me at ease.

I step away a few feet and reapproach, working my way through the greeting part.

"Nice work, Mart," Ryan says in a way I'm sure he's heard from coaches throughout his life.

He encourages us to bring up different topics, and

Gisele tells me about her major, a little about her family, and that she's apparently into gardening like Dad, which is a great conversational bit for us to roll with.

"Okay, now move a little closer," Ryan directs.

As I step toward her, she sizes me up. If this is acting, fuck, give her the Academy Award.

"Not this close yet," Ryan intervenes once again. "Give her some breathing room."

"How close do you mean, then?"

"Like an inch less?"

I'm a good bit from her, so that seems silly, but he's the teacher, so I follow his instruction.

"I don't think that was too close," Gisele interjects, earning a glare from Ryan, who seems a lot testier tonight than last time we attempted this. Although, I remind myself that at the time he didn't know his parents were planning to divorce, so he's got a lot going on.

"Who's the director here?" he asks.

Gisele laughs. "I was trying to offer some creative input."

"Noted," Ryan says, "but he needs to get this right if he's gonna stand a chance in the wild."

"Okay, okay," she says, clearly trying to placate him. She turns to me and widens her eyes. They seem to say, *He seems like a lot,* and I can't help smiling, since that's usually the way people look to others when they're dealing with me.

We continue working through the scene until I get a little closer.

"Now you're gonna go in for the kiss," Ryan instructs.

There's that tension, but the confidence I've developed from working out my mouth with him makes it easier as I lean in. She moves close, studying my expression, our lips inches apart, before resting a hand on my chest. At least I think it's hers, until it starts pushing me back.

"Okay, okay, we get the point," Ryan insists, forcing me away.

"What?" Gisele asks. "Doesn't he need to practice kissing?"

"No, I think we're good there. Right, Mart?"

"Last time you said he needed to kiss me," she says. "Oh, I'm sorry, are you not comfortable with that?" She directs this to me, her eyes wide with concern.

"I'm actually over that issue."

"So it's not an issue anymore," Ryan states.

"It wouldn't hurt to make sure," Gisele says, and the way she's debating this with him, it sounds like she actually wants to kiss me, which is a first for me in a while.

And judging by the tension in Ryan's jaw and shoulders, if I didn't know him as the big manwhore he is, I'd say he was jealous.

He flinches, scratching at his neck like he does when he's agitated. "Yeah, you're right. I guess a little kiss would be totally fine."

"Hey, man, looking good," comes from nearby, and Dax approaches Ryan, offering a fist bump and stopping to admire his physique in his costume.

I was feeling fine until now, but suddenly that tension is back as Dax and Ryan smile at each other.

"Great job at the challenge tonight," Dax says. "You really kicked ass with the arm wrestling. Not that I'm surprised with these guns."

Dax rests his hand on Ryan's arm, and my tension ratchets up a few notches. Dax would fuck around with Ryan in a minute, and Ryan's so promiscuous, I have no doubt that given this new thing we're discovering, they'll hook up at some point. I don't know why it bothers me so much. Maybe I'm jealous about how easy it is for him, like I was when I kept catching him with girls.

Still, discovering he's interested in guys because of my mouth doesn't mean he owes me anything, but maybe because I'm not like him, some part of me feels like he does.

"You okay?" Gisele asks, pulling my attention from the guys.

"Did you think I was doing badly?" I ask, assuming she's talking about the exercise.

She chuckles. "No, you just seem…off right now."

She must've picked up on my discomfort with the way Dax is chatting up Ryan. Not that I have a right to be uncomfortable about that. It's not like we're dating. Fuck, he's helping me figure out how to flirt with girls so I can maybe have a chance with Angie, so this whole thing is ridiculous.

"I'm fine, Gisele. As you've probably noticed, this is really fucking awkward, and I don't need any help in the awkward department."

"You're too hard on yourself. You're very attractive, and I think you have an adorable personality."

"Is Ryan paying you to say this? Or is it helping you with your acting?" I'm only slightly joking because a part of me feels like that's what this must be.

She shakes her head and steps toward me. "If you'd approached me at a party, I'd be very interested in a guy like you. And I know plenty of girls who would feel the same."

Now my face is warm.

She sneaks a glance toward Ryan and Dax. "You know, maybe you should kiss me now. It'll be easier without Ryan hovering over us. I think it's making you too self-conscious."

"You don't have to do that."

She laughs. "Marty, you are ridiculous if you don't get that I'm into you. I want to kiss you."

Not sure why that's so hard for me to believe, especially when she can't seem to take her eyes off me.

She creeps closer, resting her hand on my side, near the chest plate. It's a nice sensation, and once again, I'm getting twitchy, reminding me I'm most likely bi.

As I lean toward her, I'm waiting for her to pull away or laugh in my face, but she closes her eyes in anticipation. Excitement rushes through me as I move in—before a hand against my chest is shoving me back.

"Hey, hey," Ryan says, intervening once again.

Fuck, that was so close too.

"What the hell?" Gisele asks.

"I leave you alone for five seconds, and you're running the scene without me?"

Dax watches us, his twisted-up expression suggesting his confusion about whatever the hell he thinks he's witnessing. I mean, I really can't imagine what's going on in his head.

Ryan turns his attention back to Dax. "Sorry, we're helping Gisele with a scene for class," he lies, surely to get him off the scent, which I appreciate since it'd be embarrassing as fuck if he knew the truth.

Dax shrugs. "Cool, man. Catch up with you later. See you, Marts."

He heads on his way, leaving us in this weird-ass situation, and I find myself less stressed with him gone, but also annoyed at Ryan for interrupting my moment with Gisele.

"I'm really confused right now," Gisele tells Ryan. "I thought you wanted him to get practice."

"Yes, that's what we're doing, but we don't need to rush anything."

"You wanted him to make out with me the last time we got together."

Ryan flinches and stammers before explaining, "I realized I was moving things too quickly. You're gonna make him uncomfortable."

"I'm fine with it now," I assure him, and he shoots me dagger-eyes. I don't get what the issue is.

He shakes his head. "Look, we're doing like you would in a play. I cut the kiss from the scene."

"But both actors want it back in the scene," she insists.

His eyes narrow as he glances between us. "Fine," he says through his teeth. "You're both right. I'm wrong. Let's go for the kiss."

"With pleasure," Gisele says, turning her attention back to me.

I move closer, leaning in and pressing my lips against hers. I'm curious to try this out with the confidence Ryan's given me, and as I do, I notice Gisele is much more receptive to my kisses than my ex.

But...it's not the same as it is with Ryan. Doesn't have the same spark, though it's still pleasant enough.

As I pull away, Gisele smiles, and I look to my mentor for feedback. He's got his fists clenched, and his shoulders are as tense as the time he got a pinched nerve in his neck. "How was that?" I ask him.

"It was very good," Gisele replies.

"Yup," Ryan says, sounding annoyed. "No issues. You did it."

"Should we practice again?" Gisele asks.

"Nope," he answers on my behalf. "You know, I think that was more than enough for tonight, but thank you."

She shrugs. "Okay. I need to get up early tomorrow anyway. I'll see you guys for the next session."

She sets her hand on my arm, gently caressing before Ryan takes hold of my other arm and starts to pull me away. "We should definitely recap, go back through everything," he rushes out. "Later, Gisele."

17

Ryan

I'M SURPRISED I can even see straight as I escort Marty back to his room. I don't know what the hell has got me so worked up. It's not like I wanted to kiss Gisele.

I told myself it was because I didn't want Marty to be uncomfortable. That had to be the reason I was so defensive about it. That had to be why, when I saw him leaning in for it, heat fired up in my chest, which flared up even more at the thought of them going at it. Then when they kissed, it was like a knife. Not sure why it's affecting me like this when Marty was doing what I told him to do last weekend.

I finally get him back into his room and close the door.

"What did I do?" he asks, wide-eyed.

Aside from depriving me of that mouth so you could give it to Gisele?

What?

That's such a fucked-up thought. This was the whole

point of making out with him to begin with.

He wears a concerned expression as he says, "I couldn't have been *that* bad."

"Huh?"

As if I wasn't confused enough. After having had my tongue down this guy's throat, I can't imagine why that would even cross his mind.

"Isn't that why you got me out of there? Because I messed up with Gisele?"

"That wasn't it." I run my fingers through my hair, closing my eyes and trying to think this through like I would after fucking up a play.

"So I did good?"

The knife in my chest is twisting.

"What the hell is going on?" I spit out, grabbing at my chest.

"Ry, you okay?" Marty approaches. "Do you need to sit down? You look like you're having an anxiety attack."

Despite how thoughtful he's being, I shoot him an angry look. "How was it?"

"What?"

"The kiss. You enjoyed kissing Gisele, didn't you?"

"It was…fine."

The pain intensifies, and I realize what I'm dealing with here. It reminds me of when I get jealous over another guy taking a touchdown I thought would be mine.

"I think I might be jealous," I admit.

Marty's sympathetic expression shifts quickly—now he looks pissed, which throws me even more.

"Oh, so you can fuck two girls at once in my bed, but I kiss one and you have to have her too?"

The hell is he on about?

"I should have known better than to agree to this," he says. "I have one nice experience with a girl, and that's too much for you while you were flirting away with Dax…and I'm sure you guys will be fucking in no time, but no, please, it would be terrible if anyone else in this frat got to have some fun with someone you haven't already fucked."

I'm starting to realize why he's so worked up, but before I can respond, he starts for the door.

"I swear, you're even more of a frathole than I thought." He turns the knob, but I'm already at the door beside him, pressing my hand against it to keep it closed.

"Let me go," he insists.

"Aren't I supposed to be the idiot here?"

His brow creases, and before he has a chance to come up with any other ridiculous theories, I rush him, taking that mouth again.

Those lips give me much-needed relief, that knife being pulled from me, allowing me to enjoy this moment. I shove him back against the door. Despite how annoyed he seemed, he doesn't resist me, relaxes as I push my tongue up against his, toying with it in a way that helps bring me down from the heat I'd worked up. He moans into my mouth, and as I taste the peach in the cider he was drinking, I once again feel like myself. I finally pull away.

"I'm so fucking confused," he mumbles.

"I was jealous of you kissing Gisele because I wanted *you* kissing *me*. Make more sense?" But even as I say it, I realize it doesn't make much sense even to me.

"Is that why you were trying to stop us from kissing?"

"I guess so."

"What do you mean you *guess so*?"

"I've never had this feeling before. Like, my friends can hook up with whoever they want. Or girls can go hook up with whoever after me, and I've never thought twice about it. I don't get why this is different."

Marty chuckles, which activates that pain in my chest again.

"What's funny about that?"

"You must admit, it's a little funny. You're saying you were jealous of me, a guy you don't even like, kissing a girl?"

"I didn't say I understood it, but it's what happened. Don't act like I'm the only one either. You were awfully worked up when you mentioned me chatting with Dax."

That smug smirk across his lips disappears real fast.

"I was worked up because you were being a hypo-crite…or at least, that's what I thought. Now I'm not even sure what to think."

"That makes two of us. And by the way, I maybe haven't liked you since you got me into trouble, but lately…you're not the worst to be around. Still, why would I be jealous over you? No offense."

"None taken."

I consider where this could be coming from.

"This is uncharted territory," he says, "so it's reason-able to assume we might not understand everything that's going on. Let's talk it through."

"Yeah, that's a good idea."

Marty steps past me and starts pacing.

"That definitely doesn't help me relax any."

"I think best when I'm moving. If you don't like it, look away."

I take a breath and turn to face the wall, though it doesn't take the edge off when I know he's doing it right behind me, so I turn back to him.

He stops pacing. "What if you were jealous of Gisele?"

"Okay, we established that."

"No, I mean, you mess around with girls all the time. You know exactly how to please women…whether I like to think about it or not. But what if you're jealous because, now that you know you like guys, you don't know how to please them the way she would."

"I haven't had any issues getting you off," I tease. But it's a good point. "When I think about football or messing with girls, I know exactly what I'm doing. I'm a pro, I've put in the hours and seen results, but this is all so new, something I'm unfamiliar with…maybe the thought that I wouldn't be good at this bothers me, puts me on edge."

Marty cringes. "I'm right, aren't I? You're getting worked up because you don't know if you would be as good in bed with me as Gisele?"

"Not you, specifically, but men in general."

He rolls his eyes. "You know that's what I meant."

I take a deep breath, relieved to have some clue about this.

"So…we're good?" Marty asks.

"Yeah. Sorry for freaking out. I just didn't know what was going on, and—"

"It's okay. It was a weird night for me too."

"No, I shouldn't have interrupted you and Gisele. It was a dick move. I was cockblocking, and that's not the kind of guy I am." I approach him and rest my hand on his shoulder. It's what I would've done with any of the guys if we'd had an issue, but this feels different, especially after what I've done with him. "I guess it's part of us sorting through this new stuff we're feeling, and I'm being weird. I'll probably be a great lay for a guy."

He quirks a brow. "There he is again. My cocky, asshole roomie."

I laugh. "Hey, it's not like I'm cocky for no reason. You like everything I've done with you."

"And as you keep talking, you make me regret it even more."

"Shut that pretty mouth of yours." My gaze lingers, and his lips part, like an instinct, his mouth inviting me to take it once again. But as I move in, he turns away, catching me by surprise.

"Something wrong?"

"Um…so if you realized you're feeling insecure…"

"I didn't use that word."

"Uncomfortable."

"I didn't use that word either."

He huffs. "What word would you use?"

"I'm feeling *underprepared.*"

He snickers. "Well, if you're feeling underprepared for being with guys, what do you think you're gonna do about that?"

I shrug. "Dax seems interested. Maybe he would practice with me."

The muscles in his shoulder tighten against my hand. Weird.

"But that's like going to an NFL player when you've never held a football before, right? Don't you think you should have a little experience first?"

"Like…find someone else to mess around with?" I ask, and as he angles his head, I realize what he's getting at. "Oh, like you and me?"

"Why not? I don't know what I'm doing either."

I laugh. Sneaky Mart.

"Why is that funny?" he asks.

"I know what you're trying to do."

"And that is?"

"It's adorable, actually."

He scowls. "What is so adorable that you think I'm doing?"

"It's pretty obvious you're projecting because you're worried about hooking up with someone experienced and not knowing what you're doing, so you're trying to convince me to do more stuff with you."

"Whatever," he says, pulling away and starting toward the bed.

"Where is this attitude coming from? I told you it was adorable."

Odd that a lot of things he's done have been adorable to me lately.

He spins back to me. "It's patronizing. And you know what, maybe you're not wrong. I'm not a fucking manwhore like you who can go do whatever with anyone. And I don't know that I'll do much better with men than I do with girls, so while you're out there figuring it all out, what? Are you gonna give me lessons on how to flirt with guys too?"

An idea springs to mind. "That actually makes sense."

"Fuck off."

His face is red, his jaw tense in that all-too-familiar way before he turns and starts for the bathroom.

"Whoa, whoa. Hear me out. You gave me an idea."

When he turns back to me, he's still got a shade of red in his cheeks. I definitely stirred something in him, and for a change, unintentionally.

"What is it?" he says through his teeth.

"The lessons part. What if, like we've been doing with flirting and girls, we helped each other out with other stuff…"

"Like?"

"*Fucking*, duh."

His eyes bulge. "Wait, what?"

"We both already know we're into guys. We can research this stuff together and then experiment like we have with kissing and jerking off."

"You're talking about like blowjobs and…" He stops himself.

"*Anal* is the word you're looking for."

"I know what it's called."

"I've had it with girls, but they don't have prostates, so it'll be different. Figure out like, positions guys get into and stuff. Come on. You gotta hand it to me. That's not a bad idea. We can take a few days to research."

"Research?"

"Watch videos. Read some shit, watch some Toks about it... Then decide when we want to give it a go. Then when we feel like we've got it figured out, we can go mess around with guys or girls, and we don't have to be totally embarrassed about not knowing what we're doing. Not that *I'd* be embarrassed, but for you." As his eyes narrow, I quickly say, "Kidding. Jesus, we've been getting along fine. Figured you can take some jokes. It would be a win-win for both of us."

His gaze shifts, and I can't tell what he's thinking until he says, "Sometimes you don't come up with totally shit ideas, I guess."

As his smirk returns, I notice that burning sensation in my chest is practically gone, and I've got this lighter feeling in my belly. Playful even.

"When was the last time you were tested?" I ask before volunteering, "I tested negative in my panel right after the last time, with uh...Em and...Dani, I think?"

He groans. "You could at least pretend to remember their names."

"I remember it was fun."

He cringes. "More things I don't need to hear, but I was tested after my last time with my girlfriend, also negative."

All that anxiety has quickly turned to eagerness.

"Well, sounds like we're all set for a *real* good time."

I move in and take a kiss, pushing him back beside the doorframe of the bathroom, my hand under his chest plate. I kiss down his chin to his throat, and he rolls his head back, moaning, "Fuck."

"See how much better things can be when we work together?" I tease him before running my hand down to his crotch, where I can tell that monster dick is already expanding. I pull back the elastic waistband of his gladiator skirt and shove my hand down, feeling his girth. "Is that for me?"

"Don't be a dick when I just started not being mad at you again."

He's back to being fun and playful Mart, the one I prefer.

"We gonna shake on our new agreement?" he asks.

I stretch his waistband some more, glancing down to get a good view of him as I jerk him.

A wicked idea springs to mind.

"I got something better than a shake…"

If we're going for this, then I might as well really go for it.

I squat down, dragging his pteruges with me until I'm on my knees, that thick cock pointing toward me, slightly angled up, letting me know exactly how hard Marty is.

"You're not seriously about to do this, are you?"

"I mean, gotta start somewhere...unless you don't want me to."

"You think I'm gonna say no to a blowjob?" His lips twist into a smile.

This is a wild thing to try, but I want to show him how serious I am about our arrangement. And I notice what the idea's doing to my own dick.

"Well, you just let me know what feels good." I study his cock, his balls. Licking my lips, I move closer and run my tongue from the middle of his shaft to the head.

"Fuck," he moans as I probe some more.

There's this uneasiness in me, and I know it's because I don't know what the hell I'm doing with a cock, but I'm determined to figure it out. I think about the way girls have gone down on me in the past, and I raise my hand, gripping his balls, applying a little pressure, which makes his cock angle even more.

"That firms you up," I observe.

I offer another lick, but I realize I'm stalling. It's time to go for it, so I take some of the head into my mouth, feeling as his cock pushes at the insides of my cheeks, opening my jaw up. Marty's hand rests on my head, stroking. Fuck, if I knew it would feel this good to have my lips around a man's dick, I would've tried it a lot sooner. Seems to be a theme with Mart.

I descend farther onto him, taking him deep, but there's still a good chunk I can't get in, and when I try, it's getting too close to my gag reflex. I run my tongue along the bottom of his shaft as I pull off, giving an extra tease under the head before letting it drop, that wet dick shining in the room light. I look up to Marty, whose eyes are closed. He was clearly letting himself enjoy the head.

When I push to my feet, he opens his eyes, panic in his expression, as though he thinks I'm gonna leave him hanging. "Wh—wh—"

"Come to the bed," I instruct, and Mart doesn't ask questions, just follows as I hop on and lie back so that my head's off the side. "One time a girl was struggling to take me, and we did this, so I think it might help with that Hulk cock. Come on, slide it in." I open my mouth, eagerly anticipating getting that thing back in me.

Marty feeds it to me inch by inch, getting farther back than I was able to when I was on my knees. It's so fucking satisfying—I'm impressed with myself, and I'm sure Marty must be too. He rocks his hips as my mouth serves his cock's needs.

"Oh hell, Ryan. Your mouth feels amazing."

He keeps on before I get a salty taste of precum. Fuck, that makes me so hungry for more.

I reach back and grip his ass, encouraging him to speed up.

"Holy shit...holy hell..."

Where there was tension and heat in my chest earlier, there's now a swirl of excitement, radiating outward, the pride of knowing that, for a guy who's never done this, I'm clearly not doing such a bad job. Keeping one hand on his ass cheek, I slide the other under my waistband and grip my firm cock, stroking as I continue taking all that he has to give me.

"I don't know how much longer I can go like this," he warns. "I'll pull out when I'm close." He must be waiting for a response because he says, "Squeeze my ass twice if that works."

I have to keep from chuckling, but I also appreciate his consideration, and I give two squeezes to confirm.

When he picks up his pace, I do the same with my cock. He expands even more in my mouth. I'm sure it can't be much, but with how much space he's taking up already, it feels like a lot. There's another burst of precum, the flavor exploding in my mouth.

"I'm about to—fuck," Marty warns before sliding his cock out. He grabs at his dick, and I don't know what's come over me, maybe from tasting his precum, maybe because I'm so into it, but I say, "Stick it back in."

"No, I'm about to—"

"Give it to me. I want it."

It's not a request, it's an order. I'm fucking feral to know what it'll feel like.

And Marty hasn't even gotten it into my mouth before he explodes, the warmth rushing across my cheek before he sticks himself back into my mouth, his load assuring me he's far from finished.

I never imagined it'd feel so good to have cum coating my tongue, but it's apparently all I needed to take me to the end, and a quick jolt pulses through me before my release shoots across my abs, leaving me in a fit of quivers and spasms as I swallow him down.

Between his release in my mouth and my own, I'm lost in pleasure, gasping as I recover from the thrill of everything that just happened. As I catch my breath, Marty says, "Hey, you're about to get some cum in your eyes. Keep them closed, and I'll grab you a towel."

I hear his footsteps, and I can't help but laugh.

Even though we don't always get along, Marty has this considerate side to him. Not exclusively because I helped him get off. I see it all the time around the other frats.

He returns and wipes up my face. "Okay, you can open them now."

As I do, I run my tongue along the inside of my cheek. Fuck, I'm hungry for him.

He gazes down at me, looking stunned.

"Impressed?" I ask.

"Shocked, for sure."

"Wish I'd known how good you tasted. I would have made you shoot in my mouth sooner. Told you I'd be good at this."

He rolls his eyes, but his lips curl into a smile. "Well,

like you said, this was our shake on our new agreement."
That excitement in my chest intensifies.
Because I know it's fucking on.

18

Marty

AFTER CLASS ON Wednesday, I meet with Ash and Lance in the library. I don't always study with them, but this week I could use a little time to concentrate, especially when I've had sex on the brain since Ryan and I made our agreement.

What did I get myself into?

The last thing I was expecting last Friday was to have Ryan's lips around my cock, but I must admit, all that jealousy he felt about not being good at it was for nothing because I couldn't even get my cock back in his mouth before I was shooting.

Shouldn't surprise me. Ryan's a sex god, and clearly I'm no more immune to it than any of the numerous girls he's hooked up with.

I've never been the kind of guy to be obsessed with sex, but since we started kissing, it's been like when I was thirteen and first discovered how amazing my dick could make me feel.

I'm catching up on some reading when I notice a DM notification on my phone.

Ryan: Check out this one too.

"We can take a few days to research."

Since he blew me, we haven't done anything more than jerking off, kissing, and him sucking me off. But I've been scouring the net to find out more about anal and what that will entail. Reading about other guys' experiences. Meanwhile, Ryan's been sending me clips and screenshots from gay porns he's been watching. He says they call it "watching film" in football.

My thumb hovers over my phone screen as I peek at Ash and Lance. Ash is focused on his phone, probably chatting with Colin. Lance seems absorbed in his reading.

I make sure the volume is turned down on my phone, since one of the links in a DM from him was loud and graphic when I opened it around some of the guys back at the house. Not making that mistake again.

I open the message, discovering a screenshot of a guy—what I guess is considered a twink—facing the ceiling, holding the headboard of a bed, suspended in the air, while a much larger, hulky guy fucks him. Under the photo, Ryan's DM reads: **This position looks fun. *devil emoji***

My cheeks heat up the way they do whenever he sends me something like this, my cock twitching. If I hadn't already realized I was into guys, I've definitely realized it since he's been blowing up my phone with these kinds of messages, making me think of the wild sort of guy Ryan is.

Although, I'm also a realist…

Me: Did you mean to send this to a gymnast you were planning to fuck?

Ryan: You can't do that?

Ryan: Maybe I need to look for a guy who's a little more adventurous.

Me: I'd need to work on my upper body strength to even try.

Ryan: Depends on which position you're playing.

Me: Pretty sure for either.

Ryan: Nah. The bottom's more about the core. *winky face*

Me: Any recommendations? Crunches? Ab rolls?

Ryan: Planks, for sure.

Me: You know I'm joking, right?

Ryan: And you know one of us has always had a sense of humor, even before we started making out…right?

I chuckle, but then quiet, looking to Ash and Lance to see if either noticed. Neither looks up, and another DM comes through.

Ryan: I'm feeling good to go on my end. You?

My thoughts scramble, my anxiety shifting gears.

Me: Good to go? Actually do this…like soon?

Ryan: Why not? I've been watching a lot of videos and reading subreddits. And I told you, I've had anal sex with a girl before. I get the gist.

I've hit up my share of subreddits about anal. And

despite the tension in me, there's eagerness too. What we've done so far has been exciting and intense. I can't help thinking this will be too.

I chew at my bottom lip.

Me: So when would we do this?

Ryan: Tonight? You have plans?

Fuck, how is he so damn casual about everything? Especially this.

Me: I'm tempted to make some up.

Ryan: Obviously we don't have to if you don't want to.

Me: No, no. I didn't say that.

I couldn't have messaged back faster, and I wish I'd thought about that before replying because I sound desperate.

Ryan: Because you wanna fuck me?

Me: Shut it. I'm trying to figure if my core will be up for it.

Ryan: Who says you'll be the one bottoming?

My face warms.

I can't tell if he's serious, but it's something we haven't really gotten into since our agreement—something that, as we researched, it became clear we'd need to discuss, and I guess I should bring it up now rather than dealing with the awkwardness tonight.

Me: So...since you brought it up, I figure whoever is bottoming will need to take care of things to make sure everything's good.

Ryan: You mean douche?

I'm gonna give myself an aneurysm from this eye roll.

Me: Yeah…that's what I meant, Mr. Subtle.

Ryan: You gonna get nice and clean for me?

Me: Do I need to?

I see that he's typing, but then he stops, and this happens a few times before I push:

Me: I can see you typing. You're making me anxious.

Ryan: Oh, sorry. I was trying to work out who was bottoming. I think I'd want to try that too.

Reminds me of all the things we haven't discussed. Are we jumping into this too quickly?

Me: Maybe the fair thing is for us to switch?

Ryan: So we need to decide who will bottom first…

Ryan: I mean, I can do it, if you want me to.

Me: Honestly, I've been so anxious about it, I'd rather get it over with.

Ryan: How romantic for me…

I can't believe he's even joking about anything we're doing being *romantic*.

Me: I thought a guy like you would be allergic to the word *romantic*.

Ryan: Well, now I know what that itch is, so I guess I don't need another STI test. ;)

Ryan: You know that's a joke, right?

What does he think of me that he believes I'd take that seriously?

Me: I figured as much.

Ryan: Never know with you. *winky face*

"Who are you messaging?" Lance asks.

I drop my phone, and it slams against the tabletop, earning not only Lance's and Ash's attention, but other students' around us.

Ash winces. "Um…"

"You seemed awfully invested in that conversation," Lance observes. "Was it Angie?" He grins like he knows me so well. If only he knew, Angie hasn't been on my mind nearly as much since Ryan and I have been experimenting.

Oh, just talking to Ryan about bottoming for him to-night.

I don't say that, but I can imagine their expressions if I did.

"It's only Ryan," I reveal. I'm not lying to my friends, but they also don't need to know everything that's been going on with me lately. Especially not what Ryan and I are talking about doing tonight.

"You've been texting a lot with him," Ash says.

"How would you even know? You've had your face buried in your phone since I got here." No doubt sexting with his boyfriend.

"I'm pretty observant. And I've noticed you guys have been getting awfully close recently."

"What makes you say that?" I didn't mean for it to come out so defensively, but it earns looks from both my guys.

"Last Friday night, you were hanging together, and

you seemed cool."

"Oh…yeah."

"Things seem better since probation," Lance adds.

Better? That's an understatement. "He hasn't done anything so bad." Nope. Everything he's done has actually been pretty great.

"That's good," Lance says. "Guess we just needed to get up his ass."

Or maybe he just needed to get up in mine…

"You guys want to get together for some games to-night?" Lance asks.

"I was gonna head to bed early." I don't know why I'm saying it so weirdly—it's not a strange thing—but it's like I'm worried my buddy who knows me best will read all over my face, *Because I'm planning on letting Ryan fuck me tonight.*

But Lance shrugs. "Cool."

I pick my phone back up and see a message from Ryan: **I'll be back from work around 8…**

I PREP BEFORE Ryan returns to the house, and after he gets home, he hits up the bathroom for a shower to wipe the sweat and shop smell off.

This gives me plenty of time to entertain my anxiety-ridden thoughts. I'm doing some last-minute browsing of the videos we swapped throughout the week, putting one on repeat as it shows a cock entering the guy's ass. That's what will be happening to me. Fuck. This is starting to feel very real.

When the water shuts off, I close the video and set my phone on my nightstand, but now I don't have anything to do with my hands, so I look like a virgin sacrifice waiting for Ryan to come and deflower me.

Awkward.

I pick my phone back up and pull up my news app, but then I realize that's not going to put me in the mood, so I tuck my phone in the nightstand, retrieve the box of condoms and the lube, and set them beside me. Although, it's not like we need a whole damn box. I pull out part of the strip of condoms, and as I tear one at the perforation, I accidentally cut into the package, exposing the condom.

Smooth.

The door to the bathroom bursts open, the surprise jolting me, sending the box of condoms tumbling off the side of the bed. "Fuck," I mutter as it rolls all the way to his air mattress.

Ryan stands in the doorway, his hair wet, messy, only a towel around his waist. I'm sure his towel always hangs this low, but I must admit, it's a nice view of the ridges defining his waist, lines seeming to draw the eye down to what I know is under the towel.

He folds his arms, studying me. "Are you doing something adorable?" He winks, smirking like he's feeling charming as fuck.

"Could you get that for me?" I ask, indicating the fallen box.

"All over it." He retrieves the condoms and sets them on the nightstand, towering over me. "Come on, scoot." I make room for him, and he crawls into bed, lying back on the pillow beside me, groaning. "How you feeling?"

"Honestly, fairly anxious."

"Really?"

"I fumbled my way through prepping earlier, and then I've been thinking if it's gonna hurt or if I'm gonna have a panic attack in the middle of it."

His brows knit. "Maybe we pushed this too quickly."

"What? No, no, no. I did not spend the day stressing and getting ready so that you can bail. Unless *you* want to bail."

"I have zero issues with whatever happens." He rolls closer. "How about we take the pressure off? If you get uncomfortable, just let me know, and we can decide we're not doing this or maybe choose another day to experiment?"

I'm kind of annoyed. "Don't worry, you'll *know* if I'm uncomfortable."

"I don't doubt it."

"Why are you so chill about this?"

He shrugs. "It's only fucking. It's not a big deal."

"It's a big deal to me—a guy who hasn't been with a girl in about a year now and who has zero experience being with a guy."

"And we've covered the fact that I've never been with a guy either, so we're on the same page."

He rests his hand on my leg, stroking with his thumb, which surprisingly has a calming effect. Reminds me of when my Xanax kicks in during really bad anxiety attacks. Like somehow he knew I needed that.

I take a breath.

"Hey," he says. "I know I'm acting humble…"

"I don't think you've ever done that. Like ever."

"Okay, maybe I should have said I know I don't brag as much as I could, but I'm very good with girls because I take my time. I probe and explore to make sure it feels good, and I intend to do the same with you."

As my dick shifts, Ryan's gaze goes right to the crotch of my boxers, like he's some kind of hunter who finally noticed his prey moving in the bushes.

"Well, that perked you right up."

Of course it did.

"I don't doubt you'll be good at it, Ry. But it's one thing to read about it on a subreddit and another to actually do it. Not knowing what to expect." I take another measured breath. "Okay, let's do it. I think I'm ready for you to fuck me now."

His eyes widen like he's startled by how direct I was. Although considering how direct he tends to be, it's easy to get to the point. I move quickly toward him, knowing I'll get relief once we're kissing, the way I usually do.

As soon as his lips are pressed up against mine, I get a hit—that rush sweeping through me, like a messenger sent to let all my tense nerves know everything will be okay. As though all they had been waiting for was his kiss.

Ryan rolls on top of me, propping himself up with one hand while sliding the other under my shirt, his warm fingers trailing across my skin. "One thing...I know..." he says between kisses. "Is...we gotta get you outta these."

He starts to remove my shirt, and as I try to help, I become a fumbling mess, somehow getting stuck with one side too high for me to keep pulling it up.

"Fuck," I mutter. "That was supposed to be smoother and sexier."

My arms are locked upright, and Ryan helps me navigate out of it before tossing it off the bed. At some point he threw off his towel, and his cock is erect, ready to go.

I gulp.

"Look how ready I am for you," he jokes, moving in for another kiss.

I eagerly accept it before pulling away and gazing

down at his length. Since we started messing around, I've been curious about something, but now I finally have the courage.

"You curious?" he asks, rolling onto his back. I study him—the tight muscles, the grooves and dips between them, showcasing the hard work he puts into his body. His thick cock shifts subtly right below the grooves in his abs. I get on my knees, crawling down to face it.

I take a moment, staring at it as it pulses before I grasp it in my hand, repositioning it to face me so I can see the slit. Sliding him between my lips, I allow it into my mouth. He has a subtle salty taste, but it's nice, inviting. As I move up and down, I'm surprised by how soft it is against the sides of my mouth. It's interesting that, though I'm a bundle of nerves about this, when I have his cock in my mouth, I don't ask questions, just enjoy myself.

"Fuck, apparently, you don't have issues with that either," Ryan says, making my chest swell with pride.

A new taste fills my mouth; he must be leaking. Despite how good he tastes, I pull off because as much as I wanted to try that, there's something else I'm eager to try more.

Ryan sits up, practically attacking my mouth again, and we're all tongue and heat as he gets me on my back. Soon he's kissing down my throat, down my body to my navel, taking a gentle bite out of my abs. When he reaches my trunks, he pulls the waistband down. In that expert way he has, he slides them down my legs and tosses them off. Now we're both lying in my bed naked, that much closer to making good on our agreement.

"Mmmm," he says as he tastes my cock before wrapping his arms around my thighs and angling them, exposing me to him. He kisses down my balls, making his way to my ass before I feel him against my hole. He offers a kiss first and then lets his tongue glide around the rim, displaying as much expertise there as he does when kissing my mouth. "Fuck, that's a pretty hole," he whispers, his hot breath slamming against my flesh.

My skin prickles with sensation as excitement courses through me. As much apprehension as I had leading up to this moment, I find myself so willing, curious about what the hell he's gonna do to me.

He makes out with my ass, tongue pushing in deeper as he buries his face against me. "Mmm," he finally says, leaning back. "How's that?"

"That's…lovely," I assure him.

He snickers. "Lovely? Okay, well, hopefully I can do better than that. You think you're ready for a finger?"

My muscles tense up again, but I know this is what has to happen next.

19

Ryan

I CAN TELL he's not as tense as when I first stepped out of the bathroom, but he wouldn't be Marty if there wasn't some of that, and his anxiousness is starting to grow on me. Kind of makes him even sexier, which is wild since it must be one of the qualities that annoyed me about him most.

It's not only his anxiety that I like, though. I enjoy being the one to set him at ease, like I did with my tongue and I intend to do with my finger. I've approached this like I would a game—prepped and mentally worked myself into the right headspace. Now it's time to put all the videos I watched and subreddits I explored into action.

"You ready?" I ask. "I'm gonna start with a finger, and we'll go from there."

He bites his bottom lip, then closes his eyes. I can tell by the way his chest rises and falls, slow, controlled movements, that he's really focusing on his breaths, trying to keep calm.

"I'm ready," he whispers.

The invitation sends a surge of excitement pulsing through me. Maybe because the idea of giving him more pleasure than he's ever felt in his life thrills me. At least, that's what I intend to give him.

I grab the lube and ready my finger before playing along the rim of his hole, which contracts for me. "Love seeing how eager you are," I say, massaging gently, probing with the tip before pressing and watching as it steadily slips into him. He's so tight, but I love the thought of being the one to open him up, both in his body and mind. "I love knowing you took extra care to get it ready for me," I admit as I push farther in.

His muscles loosen up as he rolls his head against his pillow, moaning.

"You're doing so good," I assure him, and really, I'm impressed by just how good.

I make a little more progress before I feel what I've been waiting for—that soft, rubbery spot, what I've read about and what I've been curious as hell what it would be like when I discovered it on him.

As soon as I touch it, Marty spits out, "Whoa. Oh..." His body trembles, his muscles twitching around my fingers, though not resisting or working against me.

"That okay?" I ask, to be sure.

"Oh, fuck yeah." He blinks a few times, his mouth

hanging open as he adjusts to the sensation of having my light touch against his prostate.

I wait for him to settle, and his upper body jerks forward slightly a few times as even this much clearly keeps him stimulated.

"You like that a lot, don't you?"

"Wow…wow…"

My dick couldn't be much harder. "Have I left Marty McGovern speechless?"

"Holy hell. How is that—how did I not know about this sooner?"

I feel the same way. This feels as good as knowing when I've hit a girl's G-spot, knowing what it's doing for them.

I wait until his initial shock subsides and he's lying back, his muscles loose once again, my finger still gently against his prostate. Then I offer the subtlest of rubs. Marty reaches out to either side, grabbing at the duvet, his abs tightening as he arches his back. A bead of precum spills from the head of his cock, descending onto his belly.

"Fuck, that's hot," I tell him as I continue teasing his prostate. "You like how quickly I found it? You like me playing with it?"

"Fuck yes, Ry."

Hearing him call me Ry while I've got my finger buried inside him is deeply satisfying.

As his body relaxes, adjusting to me, he says, "You can try another finger."

I don't love the idea of getting off this spot—not when I know the power it gives me over him—but if one finger against it is making him do this much, maybe two will show me another side of his pleasure that'll excite me that much more. I pull out enough so I can work my middle finger in with my forefinger, steadily creeping back until I'm against his prostate again.

"Don't hate me nearly as much when I'm in charge of your pleasure, do you?" I ask.

"I hate you just fine," he teases with a smile until I hit that spot again. There's that slight shift of his upper body again as he gasps and it turns into a moan, which hits my ear just right.

"Mmmm," I say. "You're making me feel like I'm already a pro."

"Jesus Christ, like that. Whatever you're doing. Keep doing that."

It's as though he can't help but beg for more. He's left behind all the worries and stress and is absorbed in what I'm doing to his body.

I run my fingers in light circles around his prostate, occasionally lifting off enough to ease the pressure, but clearly it's doing what it needs to. As I work it out, his ass loosens up even more for my fingers, as though his body is welcoming whatever is giving him so much pleasure.

"Loving me being in control?" I say. "Tending to your needs?" I love it too, especially as another bead of precum leaks from his cock.

"Ryan, I think I'm ready…"

"You sure? I don't want to move too fast."

He angles his head so he can make eye contact, nodding. "Let's do it. Please."

I don't want to pull out of him when I know what I'm doing to his body, but after exploring this much, the idea of having my cock in him, working him up like this, is more than I can resist.

"One last rub," I warn before generously offering it, watching him twist up, ease into my touch once more, before I'm steadily pulling out of him.

I rise on my knees, crawl over him, and retrieve the condom on the bed, which is already torn open.

"Is this one good?" I ask.

"Yeah, the wrapper tore when I was tearing it off the strip."

"You're not trying to get a baby out of me, are you?"

"Trust me, I have no interest in having any of your asshole babies," he jokes.

I can tell from that smile how much more relaxed he is, not only for tonight, but than I usually see him.

"You know, for a guy who's always tense as hell, you sure know how to enjoy yourself."

He's grinning as he says, "It'd take a lot of effort for me not to enjoy that."

"Makes me eager to see how much you'll enjoy my cock."

I ready myself with the condom, and Marty grabs the lube, passing it to me.

"So how do you want to take me?" I ask. "I've read it can be better—"

"If I ride you," he finishes for me. "Yeah, I read that too, but I just know if I'm on my knees and trying to be the one getting it in, that's gonna stress me the hell out. You want to try missionary and see what happens? Seemed to work fine with your fingers."

That stirs something in me—this deep, primal desire. I don't know why it feels so good, the thought of dominating him like this, claiming his ass with him under me.

"I'm sure I'll be good however I do it. Feel like you're lucky to take me."

I can tell he's fighting a glare, but he can't fight back the curl in his lips. And I'm glad because I said it to keep things light. This isn't the time Marty needs to be stressing about anything.

I kneel between his legs, readying myself, and he repositions his legs, as though trying to find the perfect placement for them.

Once I've lubed up, I toss the bottle aside and grip

his thighs, adjusting him so that his hole is on full display. It puckers for me, and a rush of saliva fills my mouth.

"You're making me thirsty for this ass," I warn as I line myself up with him.

"Just go slow," he spits out, maybe because he could hear the pure, raw desire in my voice.

And all I want to do is assure him I would never take advantage of this moment he's offering me.

"I'm gonna go very slow. Until you beg me to go fast." I push the head against him, testing to see how much give there is, if I've opened him up enough for this.

He takes deep breaths as the head starts to push in, but his muscles tighten, creating a wall to prevent me from entering any more.

He cringes. "Ooh, no, no."

I pull back out, panic whirring in my chest. "You okay?"

"I don't think it's a good idea. I'm too tight. It's not gonna work."

"Oh—"

It's like the guy's the Flash as he hurries out of the bed, and I'm right on his tail. He searches around for his clothes, then sees them on the bed.

He starts past me again, but I rest my hand on his arm. "Hey, hey. It's fine, Mart. We don't have to do anything. There's nothing wrong with bailing if that didn't feel right. Are you okay?" Given how quickly he got up and the way he's biting his lip, I'm worried.

He finally makes eye contact, studying my expression. "Yeah, I'm fine."

But the way he quickly looks away concerns me. "Did I hurt you?"

"No. That wasn't it. It just felt tight, and I got nervous…and then I was in my head about it."

"Come here, man."

It doesn't surprise me—not only because he's Marty and gets into his head, but that happens sometimes, and there's nothing wrong with it.

"If you don't want that, we toss that out. Off the table. Cool?"

He nods.

"Come on. Let's lie down for a minute. Relax."

I remove the condom, toss it into the trash while Marty crawls back into bed. I settle beside him, rolling toward him and resting my hand on his abs. He's still shaking.

"I'm so embarrassed," he says.

"What's there to be embarrassed about?"

"I spent all that time talking to you about this and getting you worked up. Then freaked the hell out. What's not to be embarrassed about? I'm always fucking like this. Like all the videos we saw, and it's clear that this is something people do, and I'm in my head about it, the way I am with everything."

"You wouldn't really be Marty if you weren't that way."

He glares at me.

"Sorry, I didn't mean that in a bad way. I think it's cute when you get all worked up about stuff."

"You think it's cute?" he asks skeptically.

"I don't know that I always knew that's what I was feeling, but looking back, feels like that's what it was because it kind of gave me a thrill. I thought I just enjoyed teasing you, but now I'm not sure that's all it was."

"What is that supposed to mean?"

"You're easier to talk to than I ever would have guessed. Like when you talked to me about my parents and their divorce shit. I'm glad I talked to you about it that night."

"I haven't asked because I didn't want to press, but how is that going?"

Ugh. This went real fast from a really hot night to a not-so-hot conversation. "I can't say it's really *going* at all. I haven't gotten together with my parents. I've talked to them on the phone, but...I don't know." I hesitate, but given what we're doing now, I don't really see a reason in keeping secrets from Mart. "It's not only that, really. Before they told me the news, I was planning to tell them I don't want to play after college."

"What? Really?" He looks about as shocked as when he realized we enjoyed kissing each other.

"Is that so weird?"

"You've got to be a sure thing for pro, right? I don't know shit about football, but the way the guys talked about you after that NFL thing…"

"The Combine? Yeah. I did pretty good."

"I heard it was better than that. Like, were you as good as you are at blowing a guy?"

"Even better."

"Oh, wow," he teases, and I can tell he's trying to cheer me up. "Seriously, though. What's the issue?"

I quiet, thinking through all the shit I've kept to myself since the Combine. "It feels like I did it already. And the schedule's wild. I don't want to spend the next several years of my life training and playing."

"What would you do instead?"

"I enjoy working at the shop. I wouldn't mind doing that for a bit, see where that takes me. But…it's a lot of change, really fast. Now that they're getting a divorce, I've been having second thoughts. Wondering if it would be better to not have everything in my life change next year, you know?"

His gaze is distant as he says, "Better than you might think," and I can tell by his somber expression there's more to it. A lot more.

Now he's got me curious. "Anything you want to talk about?"

His mouth opens like he's about to say something, but then he purses his lips, as if determined to keep it in. I don't intend to push, but finally he says, "When my brother was twelve, we were supposed to go visit our cousins. I wound up sick that weekend, so I stayed home. While he was on the trip, our cousins got the bright idea to get out the ATVs and take them through the woods. My brother was on the back of one when it flipped, and…" He chokes up before continuing, "He was in the hospital for a while, and when he got out, he couldn't walk, and it was a very difficult time for him…for our family."

I knew his brother was in a wheelchair, since he's visited the Alpha Theta Mu house a few times, but I didn't know any of these details. And I really feel for the guy.

"I'm so sorry, Mart," I say, sliding my hand up from his abs to his side and gripping gently.

He rests his hand on top of mine, doesn't even seem to notice he's doing it as he tears up. "It was dark for a while. He was depressed, which I think anybody would be. And we had to help him a lot in the beginning. Gradually, things got better, and now he's totally fine and doesn't even want me to help him with shit. He's so much stronger than I would've been if it'd happened to me. I'm so proud of him, but…" He stops himself, and I can tell there's something else lingering on his mind.

"What?" I press.

"I can't ever stop thinking that had I been there, I would've stopped them."

My jaw drops. He blames himself for what happened to his brother. Suddenly his obsession with safety and rules makes a lot more sense.

"Oh, Mart." I flip my hand over, gripping his gently. "You know that's not how it works."

"He shouldn't have been on that ATV. I would have stopped it. I could have stopped all this. Saved him all this pain. Fuck." He bats at his eyes with the back of his free hand. "Sorry, that was not what I was expecting to get into. I wanted to say that I know what it's like to have your whole life—everything you knew about it and everything you thought it would be—change in an instant."

"I'm glad you told me. You know, despite what you think of me, I'm actually a good listener too."

"I'm learning…slowly but surely." He snickers. "I'm sorry you're having a hard time right now."

I shrug. "I'll figure it out. That's what college is all about, right? Now roll."

"What?"

"Roll. I'm gonna cuddle you. You look like you could use a good cuddle, and I could use one too."

I'm glad he doesn't put up a fight, just rolls away from me, and I move close, my pelvis against his firm ass. I drape my arm around him, tugging him close. He relaxes into my hold, taking a deep breath, offering me instant relief, and I nestle my face against his neck, thinking about all he just shared. It gives me a new perspective on the guy I thought was trying to be the biggest pain in the ass.

Maybe his best friends know this side of him, but most of the frats don't see this part. He doesn't let them see it. To them, he's the party pooper of Alpha Theta Mu, and now I feel I understand why he's like this. At least, something that contributes to it, for sure.

"Guess I'm starting to get why you're always looking out for the guys," I whisper.

"Maybe. I was always prone to anxiety, but what happened with Aiden definitely didn't help in that department."

"Marty, the more I get to know you, the more I think you're actually not such a dick after all."

"Funny, because the more we talk, the less I think you're a big frathole." He sneaks a glance over his shoulder, smirking.

There's a stir of sensation in my chest. "Eh, I can be kind of a frathole sometimes."

"And I can be a dick."

"Well, you're a pretty cute dick tonight," I confess.

"You should tell all the other guys in the house how cute I am since I don't think any of them even think of me as a sex object."

"I think I know who you want me to tell, and it's not anyone in the house. Maybe Angie?"

He shoots another look over his shoulder. "Shut it."

But despite how that cheers me up, there's some tension in me still, knotting up in my chest like the night with Gisele.

"That's interesting," I observe.

"What?"

"Just mentioning Angie bothered me."

"Why?"

"I don't know. Kind of wondering if maybe we were wrong about what I was jealous about."

His head jerks back. "What are you saying?"

"Here I'm the dumb jock, but we're in bed together, naked, I was about to fuck you, and I find it adorable when you get anxious…"

His brow creases, but he smiles. "I'm sorry, is Ryan Lorde admitting to having a crush on me?"

I glare at him, though he's right.

"Hey, glaring is my thing!" Marty insists, and now we're both chuckling. As he settles, he says, "But I'm still not understanding what you're saying."

I stop myself because there's something I have to get out of the way first. Something nagging at my conscience that has to be said before anything else. "The reason I first said that shit about you showing me how to tango and me helping with girls was a bet I made with Ty and Keegan. I figured if I could get on your good side, you wouldn't be riding my ass about probation."

"This is the least surprising thing you could have told me," he says, which is a relief. "Unless you're gonna say part of the bet was to seduce me and that your dick against my ass right now is part of it."

I laugh. "Definitely not. No, if anything, I'm starting to realize I actually like you." My cheeks warm. "Jesus Christ, are you making me blush too?"

"I'm really throwing you off your game, aren't I?"

"I don't play games, Marty."

He turns away from me, tucking his ass even closer to my pelvis, firming me up.

"Be careful what you do back there," Marty says.

"Or what?"

He rocks his pelvis, and I nibble at the side of his neck, whispering, "I guess we could use a little jerk-off."

Just saying the word, it's like my brain registered it as a done deal because I'm stiff as he continues working his ass up against me.

"What if I don't want to just jerk off?" He shifts, and I loosen my grip, allowing him to roll toward me until we're face-to-face.

"What do you want?" I ask, considering how our

attempt went earlier, yet looking into those eager eyes, I already know the answer.

He raises his hand, running his knuckles between my pecs. "Maybe we could try one more time? See what happens?"

The uneasiness our conversation brought up shifts quickly as I feel this soaring sensation in my belly. A surge of desire radiates through me as he kisses me, his hand resting against my cheek, and I reach down, feeling his cock, which is a stone.

I give it a generous stroke. "You want me to fuck you, Marty?"

"Oh, fuck yeah…"

And I want to fuck him so bad.

20

Marty

I'M NOT SURE what it is…

How good it felt when he was probing my prostate with his touch.

How he revealed a part of himself I know he doesn't share with most of the guys.

The cuddling.

His confession that he likes me.

Or the way his cock rubs up against me and how he's gripping my shaft.

All I know is I want him to show me the sort of pleasure he's given to so many girls.

He rolls toward me so I'm under him as his lips crush down against mine. His lips travel down my chin, to my throat, which he nibbles at. My body erupts with sensation, the tips of flames tickling across my flesh. When he finally leans back, he's already holding another condom.

When the fuck did he grab that? I guess the

nightstand isn't far, and he's got those giant-ass arms. But that required some serious multitasking, which only reminds me that if anyone can show me how good it can feel to be fucked by a guy, it's Ryan Lorde.

He tears the packet open with his teeth before readying himself and finding the lube in the sheets.

I study his shaft. Am I gonna mess this up a second time?

He leans down, kissing me again, his tongue wild in my mouth before he whispers between kisses, "If you…feel…any discomfort…tell me, and we stop."

I'm sure he knows I will, but he wants me to know that this is on my terms and help me relax.

"I will," I assure him before he wets his cock and my ass with some lube.

He's even slower than he was the first time, pressing the head of his cock against me. He looks to me.

"I'm ready," I tell him with a nod, and he pushes in again.

Nervous as I am, I don't feel that surge of discomfort and tension like I did the first time.

"Fuck, it's tight," he says, a sliver of a smile playing across his lips.

Looking at that mug makes me think that—even knowing all this time he's a hot guy—I haven't allowed myself to really appreciate it because of how much I hated his asshole behavior, but fuck, he's beautiful.

His cock steadily creeps farther in, my muscles remaining relaxed, and I'm anticipating that sensation he brought up in me, how it felt to have his fingers against my prostate, even before there's that sensation again. Ripples of excitement travel through my body as my skin prickles with goose bumps. I close my eyes and roll my head back, moaning as my body welcomes him.

"There we go," he whispers as he slides another inch past my prostate. "Wow," he mumbles so that it's barely audible.

I open my eyes. "What?"

"Liking how my cock looks inside you."

"That works since I definitely like how it feels."

There's relief, not just from having pressure against my prostate, but knowing that the hard part seems to have passed.

"I'm gonna stay here, let your body adjust," he says as he caresses the inside of my thigh, and the care he's taking with me lifts what remains of the tension in my chest. He moves close, until his face is only a few inches from mine. "In the meantime, I think you deserve a kiss for how good you took me."

Once again, he's generous with his kisses. Fuck, it's even better when he's inside me at the same time. I nibble at his bottom lip, then give it a gentle tug with my teeth, surprised how quickly he's cured me of feeling self-conscious about that. I'm eager to feel him stimulating that sweet spot, so I tell him, "You can try a little."

He offers a subtle movement, back and forth, and waves of energy rush right through me, spreading out, my nerves celebrating. My body vibrates as my eyes roll back and I call out.

"Oh, I like when you roll your eyes like this," he teases before his lips are against my throat, tongue in a frenzy as he keeps up his work, allowing me to lose myself in this realm of pleasure I'd only heard about but now know no amount of description could have prepared me for.

"You want me to speed up?" he asks at the perfect time.

"A little bit."

He offers broader strokes, and given that there was a moment when I thought my body wouldn't even let him inside, I'm shocked by how much I've opened up. It's a thought I can only enjoy for a moment before his lips return to mine and I lose myself again.

With each short thrust, I gain confidence in what I can handle, and I urge him to give me more.

And more.

Until soon he's thrusting in and out with ease and my body's pulsing with life, sparks igniting in nerves in surprising places, tingling at my toes.

"Fuck, it feels so good," I confess before one of those waves sweeps right through me, leaving me gasping.

Ryan rises on his knees, locking his arms around my thighs as he continues his work, getting farther back. Another wave is quickly followed by a rush of warmth to my face, the intensity of it sending an urgent signal through my pelvis.

"Your ass feels so good. Marty, I love the way you're gripping me."

"Oh my God. You're really hitting it."

"You mind if I try something?"

I snicker. With what he's doing for me, I submit. "You can do whatever the fuck you want to me."

He stops his thrusts, which is good because if he kept going, I was likely to blow at any moment. He leans down, wrapping his arms under mine and pulling me up. "Put your arms around my neck."

The way I obey, it's like my body isn't even giving me a chance to think about it, as though it knows whatever comes next means more of this amazing feeling, so we need to do whatever will make that happen. Once my arms are around him, he grabs under my thighs and wraps them around his waist, then leans back, pulling me off the bed so that he's on his knees and I'm held up, his cock buried deep in my hole, which makes him even harder.

"Fuck, Ryan," I call out, enjoying how firm he is inside me, the pressure that's hitting my prostate.

"One of the perks of fucking around with a linebacker," he says before thrusting much faster, and I cling to him as he's got me soaring, climbing higher and higher.

As we moan together, precum leaks from my cock and settles on my abs. It's hard to concentrate on anything, but I want his lips again. As I move in for a kiss, he tilts his head back, wearing a playful expression.

"Uh-uh," he says. "I need to save it for the right moment."

As annoying as it is, it's exciting too. I don't normally like it when he teases me, but I like this kind of teasing. "Fuck, it's no wonder everyone wants to fuck you."

"Damn right."

He keeps fucking me as though trying to prove himself the fuckboy he's always been. No matter what there may have been between us in the past, there's no denying the chemistry we discovered with our kisses is even more present while he's fucking me. We work up a sweat, his hot breath mixing with our body heat, and I'm proud when I see him wipe the sweat that's beading on his brow.

"That all you got?" I ask playfully.

"Like hell."

Ryan's clearly got a point to prove—at the least athleticism—because I'm suddenly a rag doll he's tossing about. First crawling on his knees to the edge of the bed and stepping off so he can fuck me on my back, really showing me how fast and deep he can give it to me. I reach out to the side, taking him fully, absorbed in every delicious moment, awakening to the nuance of each movement that stimulates me, keeps pushing precum out of me.

It doesn't feel fair, though. He's working so hard, giving me so much pleasure, so I tell him, "Ryan, I want to ride you."

He scoops me back up, spins around, and sits on the bed, crawling back before lying across it. I'm certain he's only able to move so effortlessly because of his extensive training, and I'm here for it.

"See, never even have to leave that cock when you're with me," he says with a cocky grin.

"Definitely a perk." I laugh, but nearly as quickly, feel another wave of ecstasy shoot through me.

But I can't be greedy. It's my turn to see what I can do, so I rise and fall, working to serve his fat cock. He grips my hips, his thumbs massaging my flesh as his body jerks and thrusts.

We work into a natural rhythm, something we don't have much of a chance to experience when I'm trying to show him my limited tango moves. We speed up until my ass claps against his pelvis, my cock bobbing up and down, leaking onto his abs now.

Only I'm climbing too quickly. My thoughts scatter, my muscles locking as I keep up the pace I know is taking me to the end.

"Ryan, I'm getting too close. Fuck…are you close?"

"I can be," he says, his eyes lighting up with excitement.

"I'm sorry. I don't think I can hold it—"

He pauses his work, rising up, resting his hand against my cheek. Then he draws me close until his lips are millimeters from mine. It feels like I should be coming already, my body vibrating and jerking, sensations pulsing through me.

"See, you can hold it after all," he teases.

I tremble with sensation, my body feeling like it could burst open at any moment. My mind is swirling, fixating on each individual spark that radiates through me.

"Ry, I—" I can't think long enough to make my request.

"I think you're ready now," he says, finally giving me those lips and several thrusts.

Between the way he works my mouth and how he rocks his hips, it takes me to the end.

It's like a bullet shooting out of me, and his kiss stifles the sound of me calling out my pleasure until he pulls away to warn me, "I'm coming too. Fuck, Mart…fucking hell."

We're all twitches and messy kisses, our jaws clashing, our rhythm broken in a frenzy of wild movements as

I feel like I'm having the longest fucking orgasm of my life. Ryan grunts, and I can tell by the way his body jerks when he's emptied the last of his load. As he pulls back, I see mine spread across his abs, dripping down them like on a wall of rocks.

We pant, and he moves close, resting his sweat-soaked forehead against mine.

"Fuck, Mart. Who knew you were such an animal?"

"You must bring it out of me."

"I think I put it into you."

My face is on fire, and I'm taking quick, shallow breaths. I chuckle—wow—I can't believe after all that just happened I'm chuckling because there wasn't anything funny about that.

He slides out of me and disposes of the condom before returning to my bed.

"Wow," he says, his eyes widening as he drops down at my side.

I'm still catching my breath, realizing I don't know that I've ever been so totally satisfied in my entire life, yet also so hungry for more. I figured he would be a hell of a lover, but I clearly had no fucking idea how amazing.

"I hope you know I intend to do that again," he says.

I laugh.

"What's funny?"

"If you think we're done for tonight, you are out of your damn mind."

I'm relieved when he grins—he's practically glowing—proving he's not finished with me yet either.

And I know it's gonna be a hell of a night.

21

Ryan

WHEN I CALLED Marty an animal, I didn't know the half of it.

After that first fuck, we stayed up the whole night, taking breaks between sessions to recover before I was back in him. It felt like the Combine, like I had to demonstrate every trick in the book to show Marty what a good lay I am. I worked to become an expert on his body, learning the little tricks to arouse him, or delay his climax. I have no doubt I proved myself worthy of that ass.

Missionary, doggie, cowgirl, and reverse cowgirl—or is it cowboy now?—against the wall, on the floor, on my air mattress, on the damn desk. I fucked the guy all over his room, and even after we showered off, he sucked another load out of me.

We've hooked up every night since.

Really, it's what I'd rather be doing than meeting with Dad today.

Not that I don't want to see him, but between my parents' impending divorce and what I need to tell him, I'd much rather be buried in Mart's ass. Is that a crime?

I've delayed this long enough, though, and with the draft coming up at the end of the month, it's now or never.

"Good to see you, champ," Dad says as we pull away from a hug.

We take seats at the booth in the Italian restaurant we agreed to meet up at.

We catch up a little about his job and school before he gets a glint in his eyes. "I can't imagine being you right now. Must be stressful being this close, and I'm on the edge of my seat. Who are you thinking will snatch you up?"

Here it is. My chance to get this off my chest once and for all.

"I guess, on that note…" I drag out. "I have something I need to tell you."

Dad tilts his head, curiosity and excitement in his gaze. There's no way he sees this coming, and for a very good reason.

"There's something I've been struggling with recently."

The excitement in his expression dissolves. "Ah…you know, your mother and I are fine. Or…*fine* might be the wrong word, but we plan to have a nice, smooth process.

No fighting over dishes and—"

"That's not what I was talking about." And not at all what I want to get into.

"Oh?"

Say it. Get it over with.

"I don't know that I want to play football anymore." I shake my head. That doesn't cover it. "I *don't* want to go pro."

The color in his cheeks drains. He leans back and stares out the window alongside the booth. We sit in silence as he takes a moment to process my big reveal.

"I'm confused," he finally says, returning his attention to me. "You've wanted this since you were ten years old."

"Yeah, and I've been thinking maybe a ten-year-old shouldn't be the one determining how I spend my life."

His lips twist into a frown. He's dedicated so much time to helping me get to practice and games, helping me train to make it through high school, then kept dogging me to be sure I'd make it onto a college team. Always with pride in his voice when telling his friends about his linebacker son.

"Do you need to talk to someone?" he asks. "Sometimes guys get burned out. It's a lot of stress, and I know I've put a lot on you, but this is a once-in-a-lifetime opportunity, Ry. You walk away now, there's no redo."

I can see why this is confusing for him. In all the

time I've been working toward this goal, I've never expressed discontent. Never questioned whether I should be doing it.

Not to him, at least.

"I didn't wake up this morning and start thinking about this," I confess. "Truth is, it's been about a year, especially after draft eligibility and signing with Rachel. I knew after the Combine, and I was gonna tell you sooner—the day you and Mom talked to me about…" I trail off. I don't want to say the word. "As much as I love playing, I don't want that to be my life for the next ten years, if I'm lucky."

"What would you do instead?"

"I enjoy working at the shop. I wouldn't mind being a mechanic. I like the way I can focus. The guys are cool. Money can be good enough to have a decent life, and if I need a backup, then I have my degree."

He sighs. "I just think you were born for something bigger."

There's a bite to it. I doubt he meant it that way, but I have to state the obvious. "Do you really think my not playing would make me smaller?"

His brow creases, and he immediately shakes his head. "I didn't mean it like that."

I know he didn't, and I can understand why it isn't easy for him, so I assure him, "This wasn't an easy decision, but I know it's the right one. You have to trust that I know what's best for me."

He wears a solemn expression, tucking his head close to his chest. I viscerally feel his disappointment in my chest—a sinking feeling, as though my soul's about to slip under the table.

Again, he's quiet for a few moments. "Here I was hoping this would keep my mind off everything else that's going on." He runs his fingers through his bangs. "That's not putting that on you, but it's just been a rough year. And I can accept that—if this isn't something you want anymore, I'll understand, though it might damn near kill me." He chuckles, though I hear the pain in it too, reminding me why I've had to wait this long before telling him. "It's gonna take me some time to wrap my head around it all, but like you said, you wouldn't have done this if you hadn't thought about it already." He sighs. "Okay. Come on. Give your old man a hug."

We scoot out of the booth to hug it out, and it's a firm, full-on hug, the sort I can tell he needs more than I do. I feel for him, but I know I did the right thing. That isn't the life I want for myself, and as much as it might have helped him to go along on this journey with me, I know he would prefer for me to be happy.

We work out the details. I tell him I'll call Rachel and sort all that out, and then we get on to more mundane topics, fortunately avoiding the big D-word I don't want to discuss today.

After we finish up, I head back to Alpha Theta Mu, where I find Lance, Ty, Ash, Dax, Angie, and Marty hanging out in the living area. I notice right away that Marty's standing beside the sofa, where Angie is twisted toward him, laughing at something he said.

I didn't realize how relieved I was after talking to Dad until seeing her with Mart makes my shoulders tense up.

Why's she looking at him like that?

What am I talking about? It's Angie. They're friends. And even if they weren't, that's totally fine. More than fine. None of my goddamn business. It's what he *really* wants.

Although, that doesn't magically take away the sting in my chest as I approach.

"Hey, guys," I say, frustrated that I can't go right to Mart and tell him about my conversation with Dad.

He turns to me, curiosity in his expression since he knew where I was off to and what I was hoping to get off my chest. I get a faint hint of that citrus-cedar scent, unbinding some of the tension that still lingers in me.

"How was lunch?" he asks.

"It went really well." I grin, and I can tell by the way he smiles he knows what I mean.

"That's great. I'm glad."

"You heading somewhere?" I ask Marty. "Why aren't

you sitting down?"

"Oh," Angie says. "Apparently, he pulled a muscle."

Now I'm really smiling, since last night was pretty intense, and I love knowing I put that ass through it.

"Did you take up squats all of a sudden?" I tease, since I can't say what I really want about working out those glutes.

"Something like that," he says with a mischievous smirk that's giving me a hard-on.

"I hope it's not preventing you from getting around campus," I add.

"It's not preventing me from doing *anything*." He tilts his head in a pointed way, as though making it clear it's definitely not enough to keep us from having our favorite nighttime ritual.

Thank fuck.

"Why am I not getting a fist bump or a hug?" Ty asks.

Fuck, I'm acting weird, and I don't want the guys catching on and thinking we're up to anything. Not that I'd have an issue with it, but I sure as hell don't want to put Marty on the spot like that. I have no desire to out him before he's ready, and besides, it's kind of hot letting this be our dirty little secret.

"I wanted you guys to get along," Ty adds, "but I don't need Marty replacing me."

"Does somebody need some attention?" I ask, heading over to Ty, tackling him with a hug.

"You ass!" he jokes.

"Nobody's replacing my best bud," I assure him. "Anybody want to head out for some ice cream?"

"You just ate."

"Eh, I had a tough conversation with my dad and wasn't too hungry after, but now I'm starving."

"Tough conversation?" Ty asks.

"Yeah, and I'll tell you about it over a peanut butter fudge buster."

"I want ice cream too," Ash says.

Everyone else chimes in for the same, and we head out to the nearby ice-cream stand.

I'm relieved when the rest of the guys grab a table, giving me a moment with Marty while we wait for the server to finish making our bowls.

"How did he take it?" he asks.

"Eh…I can tell he's gonna need some time. It wasn't an easy thing for him to hear, that's for sure."

"It's impressive you went ahead and said it, though. That had to be tough with everything else going on."

"Yeah," I admit. "Now I have to break the news to my friends, trainer, my old teammates, and my agent."

He cringes, as though he's experiencing stress by proxy. "Well, you seem good, considering everything."

I check to make sure our friends are at the table before I lean closer. "I can seem not good too if that'll convince you to mess around with me."

"I didn't think Ryan Lorde would ever want a pity fuck."

"I've never needed one before, but I'd make an exception for that ass."

There's the twist in his lips, and if this is the way he reacts to compliments, I'm happy to dote on him with more. I'm tempted to drag him around to the bathrooms and take that mouth of his, and he must notice because he licks his lips. I growl, but there's something still gnawing at me.

"This might be a weird time to ask, but…you and Ang?"

His eyes flare. "What do you mean?"

"I know she's a friend, but are you still into her?" As soon as I say the words, I wish I could suck them back in my mouth. "Never mind. None of my business." I'm fucking Ryan Lorde. I'm not intimidated by some hot girl.

"You jealous?"

I tense my jaw, struggling to respond before getting out, "Maybe a little."

The way his cheeks go pink make it worth the embarrassment of having to admit that out loud, and he says, "Strangely enough, since we've started messing around, I haven't really been thinking of her like that."

It shouldn't matter, but then why is there this swirling sensation in my chest?

Probably because I'm getting a little greedy for Marty McGovern…

"But she's a good friend," he admits.

I lean closer, whispering, "Guess she can't dick you down like me."

"I mean, there are ways that—"

"Shh…let that be hot," I mutter, making him laugh as the clerk approaches the counter with our bowls.

We fetch them and grab utensils, and as we head toward the table our friends are at, he says, "So…I'm gonna head up to do some homework once we get back."

"Oh, really? That's wild. I was gonna chill and play some video games."

"Don't keep the volume too high."

"Really, the volume is totally up to you."

He enjoys a last laugh before we near the table, and I'm thrilled knowing damn well that there won't be any homework getting done or video games getting played when we get back to the frat.

22

Marty

I WASN'T EXPECTING my senior year to end with a bang. But it's ending with plenty.

Ryan and I can't keep our hands off each other. Or really, he can't seem to keep his dick out of me, and I wouldn't want him to.

When we aren't fucking, I'm showing him the new moves I'm learning in my tango class—something we're keeping up with even after he confessed that the whole thing was just to help him win his bet against Ty and Keegan. My instructor's actually given me credit for improving, which I know is from my practice with Ry. Kind of stunning, considering all the distractions that come up when we're attempting to get a session in.

In other news, Ryan revealed his draft news to everyone, and since then, I can tell he's more at ease, especially since his former agent has stopped calling with one of her go-to strategies to encourage him to stay the course: a.k.a., guilting him about all the work she invested into his career, assuring him that he's blowing his big break, or recommending some great "wellness centers" that can council him through whatever issue he's going through. He was patient with her, and with the draft coming up at the end of the month, she must've realized her time was up.

Outside of this and the occasional reminders Ryan has of his parents' impending divorce, it's been a hot, fun time, something I experience in all its glory this morning, as I wake with a stir, feeling Ryan's arms tight against my waist, his pelvis glued to my ass.

His air mattress hasn't gotten much attention since we started sharing the same bed. It started with him falling asleep while we cuddled, and now it's become our new ritual. I like how tight he holds me; feels so protective. My big linebacker making sure his piece of ass stays close in case he needs to use it later. That, mixed with his fresh scent, gets my already thick morning wood that much harder.

It's wild to think that I started the semester totally infatuated with Angie, and now I'm so busy thinking about what I want to do with Ryan, I just don't think of her like that anymore. Like a switch flipped off.

I've been still for maybe thirty minutes. Don't know what time it is, but I'm guessing we don't have too much time before we have to get up and get ready for our first class.

I must've intuited it or something because my alarm sounds, and I start to get up to turn it off, but Ryan's hold firms and he grunts.

"No," he insists, burying his face against the back of my neck and pushing his crotch against my ass. Heat rushes to my face.

"I don't like it any more than you do. And if we don't get it now, your *noise* is gonna start going off. And MegaDie or Judas Kills or whatever the hell weird-ass-named band you have is gonna start playing."

"You know that's not their names," he says before offering a peck against the back of my neck, soft…sweet, even. I'm learning there are a lot of sweet sides to the guy I couldn't have found any redeeming qualities to a few weeks ago.

"Siri, could you please turn off the alarm?" I say, and it shuts off.

"It's adorable that you say please and thank you to Siri."

"I'm adorable like that." Guess I'm feeling a little flirty this morning.

"You know what wasn't adorable? Watching a scary movie before bed."

"*Alien?*" I ask. "It's more sci-fi." I sneak a glance as he tilts his head. I concede, "Okay, maybe Lance's movie tastes have rubbed off on me a little." Lance loves him a horror film.

"Rubbed off? Now you're playing with fire." As he says that, he slides his hand down to my stiff cock. "Oh fuck. Not again."

Not sure what he means. "Not again?"

"Yeah, now I'm gonna have to drain you before we go to class." He groans. "Such a tough job, but someone has to do it." He offers a few pumps, and I can feel his dick stiffening against my ass.

"I think we're both gonna need to be drained if you keep that up."

"Don't be rude and leave me blue balling if I'm kind enough to get you off." He bites at my shoulder, and a rush of adrenaline flows through me. It's like he gave me a taste of a drug, and now I can't be without it.

"I wouldn't want to be rude," I say, "but we have, like, thirty minutes before we have to be out of here."

"Then I'd better make it quick."

On cue, his alarm sounds. It used to bug the crap out of me, but now that I don't hate Ryan, I actually think it's pretty cute.

"Hey, Siri, fuck off!" he snaps.

The alarm silences, and I laugh. "You could be a little nicer to *your* Siri."

"Let's not start the morning with a fight. We don't have time to get that in and makeup sex." He slides his cock between my ass cheeks as he continues stroking me.

"Maybe we can have the makeup sex after classes," I tease.

"But we can still jerk off now?"

"Of course."

He pauses before saying, "I can work with that," which gets me laughing.

Fuck, the guy knows how to make me laugh nearly as well as he knows how to piss me the hell off.

He sweeps his hand over the head of my cock, and I can feel his warm, wet palm.

"I already got you leaking," he whispers. "Mmmm. Perfect. This is gonna save us time so I don't have to grab a protein bar."

"Oh, is my dick only a convenience for you now?"

"Hey, don't act like that's all I think of you for. You know your ass is a convenience for me too."

Still the same old frathole—although this is the only kind of frathole I'm interested in.

He shifts about, and it's like we're on autopilot as he gives me space to roll onto my back and he starts crawling down my body. He takes some nibbles and kisses on his way to service me. I can already tell it's not gonna take him long to get me off.

When he reaches my dick, he looks up at me. His bangs are flat against his forehead, with a stray lock rebelling against the others the way it sometimes gets in the morning. There's a wicked expression on his face— the expression of a guy who knows he's learned every trick on how to get me off and is fully prepared to use them.

He leans down, running his tongue along the shaft, and I roll my head back, gasping as a surge like a subtle electric jolt rushes through me. It's the sort of rush that assures me I won't need coffee this morning.

He offers another lick when a loud knock comes from the door.

"Fuck," I mutter, but Ryan doesn't seem to give a fuck as he takes my cock into his mouth, like he's so greedy for it that he can't even hear the interruption. The way he works his mouth has me vibrating and shifting about before there's another knock.

"Uh…yeah?" I call out. My eyes widen as Ryan works his magic tongue, apparently not at all fazed.

"Quick question," Lance's voice comes from the other side of the door.

Ryan's already got his lips trailing down toward the base of my cock. As he stimulates my nerves, I grit my teeth to keep down the moan I'd normally let loose.

"Which is?" I ask. He doesn't reply, so I call out again. "Lance, what did you need?" I'm sure I sound like a dick right now, but it's Ryan's fault.

"Oh," Lance says. "I thought you were coming to the door."

"I'm…kinda in the middle of someth—oh…"

Ryan's tongue just ran the full length of my shaft, and I roll my head back, enjoying the sensations running through me.

"I can wait. It's not a big deal."

Ryan swaps his mouth for his hand, stroking as he gazes up. "I don't know. It's pretty big to me," he whispers.

"Shh," I hiss as he refuses to leave my cock alone, that urgency in me hastening. *Focus, Marty.* "Are you, like, waiting out there for me?"

"Yeah," Lance says. "On TikTok."

Ryan sneers at the door as though he has a grudge against it. "I used to like that guy."

He gives me another stroke, licking the head of my dick before offering a kiss. "Don't worry," he whispers. "I'll still be ready to service you when you're finished." And when he releases my cock, I feel like I could fucking kill my bestie.

I push to my feet and throw on my boxers. As Ryan gets off the bed, he grabs the back and tugs them down, like he wants to get a quick glimpse of my ass. It snaps back up as I lean down and grab my tank off the floor, throwing it on.

Ryan's settling on his air mattress, lying back.

We don't have to do this often, but when something like this has come up, we always make sure we're conspicuously where we would normally be in the room at the same time, since it would be odd if Ryan was naked in my bed or I was naked at my desk, which is one of our favorite places to fuck.

I'm about to open the door, when I check to make sure Ryan's settled, but he's sporting a hard-on, looking like a fully erect Greek statue on the air mattress.

"Ry," I snap.

He looks to me, that oblivious expression on his face, searching around as though he's trying to figure out what I want. I indicate the issue, and he chuckles before draping a sheet over his waist.

When I open the door, Lance looks clueless as hell.

"Yeah?" I ask.

He looks up. "Huh?"

"You needed something."

His gaze shoots right to my crotch. He looks away quickly. "Whoa, is that what you were taking care of?"

I see the tent in my boxers.

This is all Ryan's fault.

I cover it with my hands.

"How have you smuggled that giant sausage around here without anyone noticing?" he asks.

I never gave much attention to the fact that no one knew my size—really never thought there would be a reason for them to know, but it seems to keep coming up since Ryan started working me up.

"I knew he had a giant sausage," another voice comes from farther down the hall before Dax walks into view. "Morning, guys."

"How did you know he had a giant sausage?" Ryan

asks from the air mattress, and I can tell he's a little annoyed he's not the only one who knows this about me.

Dax shrugs. "I get a feeling about things like that. My ass gets a little twitch in it. Kind of a superpower, I guess."

I glare at him. "That's ridiculous."

"*That's* ridiculous," Dax jokes, pointing at my crotch.

"Okay, you guys need to stop talking about my dick."

"Yeah, talk is cheap," Ryan says.

"I gotta head to class, guys," Dax says, "but I want you all to remember, *this*"—he gestures to indicate all of us—"could have been fun, but you all playing." He winks, clearly teasing. Or is he? Has he picked up on something about Ryan and me?

"Later, man," Lance says as Dax heads down the hall.

"Now," I say, "is there a reason this morning, of all mornings, you needed me to come to the door and you couldn't text me?" I can't disguise my frustration.

"You planning to do that thing with Activate Kindness?" Lance asks.

"Huh?" I already volunteer when I can.

"Atlas and Troy were looking for some extra help on the builds they organized with the local housing project."

"This doesn't sound even a little familiar."

"They sent out the email this morning. It's for this weekend. You don't need to decide now, but just trying to see who's interested so we can work out cars. Ash, Colin, and Dax will be there. Obviously me and Ty, and I'm sure he'll get Keegan and Jaxon on board, and—"

"You had me at Activate Kindness," Ryan says.

Aside from being annoyed at having my morning BJ interrupted, I hate having surprise plans, but I'm not gonna say no to something that's for a good cause.

"Me too," I say. "But really, you couldn't have texted this?"

"Maybe I wanted to see my friend who's been squirreled away in this room for the past few weeks. I thought Ryan might've hidden your corpse in the walls."

He's being overdramatic since we bump into each other plenty. But since I've taken up Ryan's dick as a hobby, I must admit I've been scarcer than usual.

"I'm only giving you hell, man," Lance assures me. "It's the end of the semester. I know everyone's cramming for their projects and finals."

Yeah, well, I can definitely say this month has been a lot more exciting than projects and finals, but I get his point, and I know my friend well enough to tell he's a little sad.

"Yeah, I'll be there. It'll be fun, man."

"Cool, man. And let's try to make a little more time for each other."

Again, I can tell he genuinely wants to spend more time with his buddies while we still have the chance. And he's right. We need to take advantage of the time we have left.

"I will," I insist. "I'm sorry I've been busy lately."

"It's cool, bro." He offers a fist bump before heading off, and once I've closed the door, Ryan says, "That was pretty damn precious."

He pushes to his feet. His cock isn't as hard as when we were messing around, but still firm as fuck.

"I guess we have been a little selfish." As he says that, he approaches, pulls back the waist of my boxers, and grabs my cock, perking me right back up. "We need to make sure we're also spending time with our friends. This is our senior year anyway. And we don't have much time left."

"I think I'm in a little bit of denial about that," I admit.

"Same. It's hard to think that we'll be moving on from all this soon."

We gaze into each other's eyes. And I wonder if he's thinking what I'm thinking—that we've been taking advantage of whatever the hell this is because we know we only have so much time to continue experimenting with each other.

Ryan steps forward, cornering me at the door, his hand still around my cock. When my back's against the wall, he goes down on his knees, dropping my boxers and licking up my shaft, getting it nice and thick again.

My body trembles with anticipation for how this guy's learned to work his mouth.

But he raises my boxers back up, then pushes to his feet. "Guess we need to get ready for class."

"You seriously gonna leave me edging like that?"

He tilts his head back, like he's putting that impressive jawline on display for me. "I kind of like the idea of edging you a little. Make you that much hungrier for me when you get home later."

"Seriously?" I ask, unable to disguise my irritation, given how horny he's made me.

"Oh yeah." He heads to the bathroom, leaving me suspended in this state between arousal, confusion, and rage.

As he reaches the bathroom, he grabs a towel and starts toward me. "I'll head to the communal shower to give you time to head out. That's pretty considerate of me, right?"

"Still a fucking asshole," I say as he opens the door, clearly not caring about covering that fat hard-on.

"Nothing wrong with edging you a little." He takes hold of my cock and gives it another stroke, rubbing it in. "See you later, honey," he teases with a wink.

"Honey?"

"You heard me."

"Get the fuck out of here and take your shower."

"Okay, see you tonight?"

"If that's how I'm gonna get a BJ, I guess."

He leans closer. "See you then." He offers a quick peck on my lips…which I return without even thinking about it.

What the hell was that?

23

Ryan

I ENJOY MY time with Marty.

This isn't like when I was first staying with him. The fights.

The walking on eggshells.

The steadily intensifying resentment…between both of us, really.

I've successfully passed my probation period, and now Marty and I are playful, jokey even. Like when I first called him *honey* the other day. I went in for a peck, like someone who would say that to a boyfriend. I figured it'd be funny, but turns out, I liked it enough that now I keep doing it as a joke whenever one of us is about to head out, even demanding that he make sure to kiss me before he leaves, which we did this morning before heading over to the build Lance asked us about. A lot of the frats and sororities help out, especially when the housing project is running low on volunteers, so we recognize plenty of the people here, waiting in the front yard of what's mostly a frame of two-by-fours and plywood. In a few minutes, the project coordinator will assign our responsibilities for the day.

In the meantime, I hang with my crew—Ty, Keegan, and Jaxon—but I keep glancing over at Marty, who's with his buddies. Since Lance reminded us of how little time we have left of the semester, with finals looming in only two weeks, we have to take advantage of these final days with our buddies. Which means less fucking.

Not that either of us has gone without sex for very long. Hell, I'm pretty sure I'm drained from what we got up to last night.

Marty chats up Angie, and I must admit I have a bit of a jealous streak. Although, he doesn't look at her the way he used to—all doe-eyed, mouth hanging open. I try to keep from looking too much, but I can't help myself, and when he catches my gaze, a visceral relief moves through me. It really shouldn't feel as good as it does. Like, him winking at me shouldn't make me smile, but there I go. It's the sort of moment that reminds me Ang ain't got nothing on me.

"Keeg, what do you think of her?" Jaxon asks, displaying his phone to Keeg. He's always showing us some guy or girl he's checking out on the apps.

"I *think* you're surrounded by plenty of options," Keegan says, "and maybe that's where you should focus your attention."

"Okay, so that's a no? Swiping left."

"That is not what I said."

"Too late."

"You seem even more anxious than usual," I tell Jaxon. "Someone not been laid for a while?"

Jaxon chuckles uncomfortably. "I've had a lot to do at work and school. And this one keeps me up all night." He indicates Keeg.

"Oh, really?" I ask.

I never would have imagined the two of them fucking around, but if Mart and I are, I guess you can never tell…

Keegan quickly says, "Playing video games."

"Oh…" I'm kind of disappointed. Would have been cool as fuck if we had all been hooking up all night, but if all they're doing is playing video games, sucks for them.

"You're one to talk," Ty says, which catches my attention.

Why would he say that? Does he know something about Marty and me? Did I say something obvious? Am I the bastard who accidentally outed Mart because of my idiot mouth?

"Yeah, telling Jaxon he needs to get laid," Ty explains. "When was the last time *you* got laid?"

Last night, thank you very much. Of course, I can't tell him that without him being suspicious about who it was with, but I'm relieved he's not onto me and Mart.

"I'm just giving you a hard time, man," Ty says, patting my arm. "We all know what's going on."

A rush of panic rises up my spine. "You do?"

"You've got to be kidding," Keegan says. "You think you could keep this from your best friends?"

Sweat beads across my forehead.

It's not that I think my friends would give two shits about what we've been doing, but no one should know what's up unless Marty wants them to.

"Listen, you guys, you need to keep this—"

"Relax," Jaxon chimes in. "We're not gonna run around telling everyone you're crushing on some girl you've been sneaking around with."

Girl? I'm so stunned, it takes me a few seconds to get anything other than that word out of my head.

"You think your best friend isn't gonna recognize that you're catching *feels*?" Ty asks.

"I'm not catching feels," I spit out, earning glares from my whole crew. Suddenly, I realize what's up. "You all talking about me behind my back?"

"Only stating the obvious," Ty says. "You're terrible at keeping a secret. And you can't wipe that big-ass smile off your face every time I see you, the way you usually look after someone's given you the best night of your life."

I've been grinning more—Marty seems to have that

effect on me—to the point that some days I'll even notice my cheeks starting to hurt, especially if he got me laughing a lot that morning.

Marty McGovern making me grin and laugh… Who would've guessed?

"Also, when you survived probation and didn't collect from us," Keegan points out.

I only brought it up once I succeeded in passing the probationary period without incident. I deserved to rub it in, but I wasn't gonna take their money, especially when it feels like I got a lot more out of the deal than some cash.

"Hey, I was doing you a favor," I tell Keeg. "Didn't you tell me you were trying to save money while we're at Alpha Theta Mu?"

"Does that sound anything like the Ryan we know?" Keeg asks Ty.

"Hey!"

"It's not just that," Keegan goes on. "We never see you flirting with anyone at parties or formals anymore."

"Yeah, a lot of red flags," Ty affirms.

"Didn't realize how obsessed my friends were with—"

"Your *love* life," Jaxon teases, barely glancing up from his phone.

First feels, now *love*?

"Stop it, or I'm gonna go through that app and swipe left on the hottest people I can find."

Jaxon tugs his phone close to his chest, and Keegan rolls his eyes.

"Okay, dorks," Ty says. "All this talk about feels and love makes me miss my man, so I'm gonna get over to him before we start."

"Love?" Jaxon says, simulating vomiting.

Ty runs his hand through Jaxon's hair, playfully messing it up before heading over to his man. When he reaches Lance, he hooks his arms around him. Lance turns for a kiss, which starts off sweet before Ty takes a little more, and I see the way Lance's lips curl into a smirk. It's nice seeing my friend happy with his guy.

Although, I must admit I sense something that surprises me—a tinge of jealousy. Not that what's going on between Marty and me is anything so serious, but I enjoy how when we're alone in his room, I can put my hands all over him. Kiss him however many times I want.

However I want.

Wherever I want.

Out here, we're keeping this distance, when I'd love to go over and steal a quick kiss—hell, even a peck—before we get started. It's a weird thought that I don't have much time to sit with before something else catches my attention—or I should say, *someone* else. I doubt I would have even recognized the guy if he hadn't become infamous after the fire at Sigma Alpha.

"What the fuck is this?" I ask the guys, indicating

Miles Tanner, who heads down the drive, in sunglasses and a tank, his hands shoved into his jeans pockets.

I'm not the only one who's taken notice. There are a lot of looks shifting his way—and whispers, surely about the incident earlier in the year—but he doesn't seem affected as he beelines to an empty spot near the porta potty, pulling out his phone and giving it his undivided attention.

The guy's done what he's supposed to. He turned himself in for the incident, he's doing his time. But that doesn't change that his careless prank destroyed our home; injured Lance; and could have killed Lance, Ty, or Jaxon, who were all at Sigma Alpha when the glitter bomb malfunctioned.

Jaxon follows my gaze to Miles. "Oh, hell. You think this is the community service he was sentenced with?"

"Don't they have to wear something that indicates that?" Keegan asks.

"Don't ask me. I've never had court-ordered community service."

Before we can get into it, Troy and Atlas show up with the project coordinator, who divides us into groups. We grab our gear, safety glasses, gloves, and hard hats before getting to work. I manage some framing with Ty, Lance, and Jaxon while Marty's on laying plywood with Keegan and some other volunteers.

Dax and Miles work together to move extra two-by-fours into the kitchen area. I don't know why I'm keeping an eye on the guy. Maybe because I have a bad feeling about him and Dax is one of our own. As they finish up, Dax stumbles, throwing Miles off-balance, and the boards go crashing to the floor.

"The fuck, man?" Miles says, sounding downright hostile.

"Sorry," Dax rushes out. "I lost my footing. You okay?"

"You should watch where you're going."

Miles is in his face in no time, in a way I can't understand—did Dax say something else to get him so riled up?

Marty's only a few yards away, and he steps in. "Hey, I saw it, and it was an accident."

"Accident, my ass," Miles says. "You've been waiting to get me since we started."

Dax looks thrown, and somehow now Marty and Miles are getting into it. I'm shocked anyone would suspect Dax of doing something like that; hell, I'm much more likely to exact that kind of vengeance in the name of our house than he is.

Miles balls his fist and takes a step toward Marty.

The fuck? I know you did not just threaten my man.

I barely have time to acknowledge that I considered Marty my man before I see red, abandoning my post and hurrying over.

"What is your problem?" Marty asks as Miles takes another step toward him, as though to intimidate him.

"Why don't you mind your own damn business, prude?" Miles says.

"He's my friend, so it kind of is my business."

I shove myself in the middle of the situation, making sure I'm between Marty and Miles, so if Miles tried something, he'd be taking me on, not Mart. As I settle, I feel the heat radiating like a ball of fire in my chest, which feels like it's about to burst out and set fire to this asshole. "There a problem?" I ask.

Normally, if I were to intercept a fight, being a fucking giant, that would be enough to at least see the fear or worry in a guy's eyes as he accepts I'd easily kick his ass, but not this guy. If I didn't know better, I'd say he believes he has a chance of putting up a decent fight, which really, can't be true, since he's gotta be a foot shorter than me, not to mention that I'm stacked with enough muscle that it'd be like taking on a fucking boulder. This isn't just the kind of guy who's willing to get into a fight; this is the kind of guy who doesn't care about losing one either.

"Are you all gonna rotate who wants some from me?" Miles asks.

"Dude," Dax interjects, "I'm really sorry about that."

"Like fuck you are, you Sigma Alpha shit."

I never could have imagined someone would be going like this for Dax, of all people. I mean, really, Marty…this is definitely more something he would get.

I get in Miles's face. "Get our frat out of your damn mouth," I say through my teeth.

"Okay, okay," a voice comes from nearby, and Troy and Atlas push between us.

Atlas drapes his arm around Miles. "Let's have a quick chat, 'kay?" As he leads Miles off, I notice Ty and Lance are only a few feet away. They must've come over during the commotion.

"Everything's good," Troy assures us, and I realize how wound up I am, my chest in knots, my breathing shallow.

"Why the fuck is he even here?" I ask as my rage doesn't settle, that ball of fire feeling like it radiates up to my face.

"He only wants to help, same as you guys. He made a mistake, but he's actually a decent guy once you get to know him."

"We all know he's here because he was court-ordered to be. Does he get a prize for that?"

"This doesn't count toward his community service. Atlas has offered to sign off, but he said no. Okay?"

This news totally throws me, goes against my impression of him as being nothing but some Omega Psi asshole. Not that he's Omega Psi since the stunt he pulled.

"He has a temper, but he's a good kid," Troy says. "You're gonna have to trust me on that."

I can't imagine why Troy would align himself with this asshole. Although, as much of a dick as Miles made of himself, Troy wouldn't stick up for someone who was a total piece of shit.

"I'll definitely have to take your word on that one."

Dax glances toward Atlas and Miles, who are having a chat on the other side of the house.

"I know he started that," Troy says, "but if we can get him to cool down, you'd be okay with him staying?"

I should keep my mouth shut since the other guys have more reason to be mad at him than me.

"In his defense," Dax says, "it did seem like he really believed I did that on purpose."

Why is Dax defending this prick? From what I could tell, he's not wrong, but it doesn't change that he was the one starting all that crap.

I have to interject. "There was no reason for him to step toward Marty like he was about to throw punches."

"It wasn't that bad," Marty says, but I can see that his hands are a little shaky from the incident. Miles clearly activated his anxiety.

"He balled his fist up and stepped toward you."

"He was upset," Marty insists.

"It'll be fine," Lance says, and Ty's right behind him. "Agreed."

"Why is everyone suddenly defending this guy?"

Marty approaches and rests his hand on my shoulder, which instantly helps set me at ease. "No one got hurt, Ry. It was a misunderstanding."

I take a few breaths.

He's right.

I know it's because he was threatening Marty that I got worked up.

But even knowing I might have overreacted, it doesn't make me like that asshole. He set fire to Sigma Alpha. I don't care if it was an accident.

"Why don't we all take a minute to breathe and then get back to work?" Troy says. "How's that sound?"

Marty, Dax, and I take the opportunity, heading into the yard. Dax hits the porta potty, and Marty and I settle by the partly constructed home.

"You good?" Marty asks. He must sense how agitated I still am.

I size him up, like some part of me is checking to make sure he hasn't been harmed, which is fucking ridiculous since Miles didn't lay a finger on him.

"That dick was awfully close to getting a black eye if he tried to do something," I snap.

"I really didn't feel threatened. I've had worse exchanges with Atlas." He says that playfully, but I'm too on edge to ease up about this.

"Well, if he'd fucked around, he would have found out."

His lips curl into a smile. "It's adorable when you get really protective like that."

I glare at him, which turns that smile into a grin. The knots in my chest loosen.

"Whatever," I grunt.

He glances around quickly before moving closer and whispering, "Come on. Admit it. You were getting in the middle because you didn't want anything threatening your piece of ass."

I can tell he's joking, but maybe because of the mood Miles put me in, it bothers me. "You know you're more than that to me, right?" I'm surprised by the words myself—like when I thought of him as my man earlier—and the way he flinches, he's surprised too.

"Yeah, I was making a joke."

Warmth rushes to my face. "I know. I shouldn't have said that." Why the fuck am I being so weird?

"It's okay," he says. "Nothing's wrong."

"Something's very wrong." I don't mean it to come out as severely as it does, but it's the truth. Marty looks concerned, so I lean closer. "I'm all worked up, and there's only one thing that would set me at ease, and I'm pissed I can't just take what I want in front of all the guys right now."

"We'll just have to make up for that later, won't we?"

As much as that would normally put me in a great mood, knowing that I only have a couple more weeks with his perfect ass, his beautiful mouth…and fuck, the guy I enjoy spending so much time with, keeps me on edge.

"I guess Miles won't be coming to the graduation barbecue," Dax says as he approaches.

I step away from Marty so that I don't give Dax the wrong idea about us—or maybe the right idea…? As I look at Marty, there's an eagerness in my belly, but also frustration that I have to keep my distance from him still, assuring me of something I'm gonna have to admit sooner or later.

I'm definitely catching feels for this guy…

24

Marty

I REALLY THOUGHT Miles was about to make a *huge* mistake.

With how angry Ryan looked, I figured he might wind up with his own court-ordered community service or jail time, but it did feel nice that he gave that many shits about me to stick up for me like that.

"You know you're more than that to me, right?"

I do because he means more to me than any of the stuff we've done. If anything, I feel like I've been the frathole for all the assumptions I made about him over the years. Yeah, he can be rude, inconsiderate, and stubborn, but he can also be kind, caring, and if you're on his good side, apparently, protective as fuck. I only wish I'd seen it before the end of our senior year.

Fortunately, the anxiety Miles worked up eases as we get back to work, and a few hours into the job, we take a break and enjoy the sandwiches and drinks supplied for volunteers. Ryan and I sit with our crew, and I notice

Miles off near the woods at the end of the yard with two other Omega Psis. Seems like he's calmed down since our confrontation.

Troy talks to a group of volunteers, then approaches us. "Thanks again for coming out today. Something I'm mentioning every weekend, we're always short during the summer. I know most of you will be heading home to your families, but if anyone's interested in sticking around and helping out, we could really use the help."

My gaze shifts to Ryan so fast, I don't even think my brain has caught up with why until we just sit there staring at each other.

Maybe this doesn't have to be over in a couple of weeks, after all.

What am I saying? He probably has plans for the summer. I can't expect him to make time to stay here and fuck around with me.

"I'm down," Dax says—it doesn't seem like he's even thought twice about it. "And I'm getting my own place, if any of you want to stay with me."

Most of the people I know who aren't seniors will be staying with their families over the summer, but knowing Dax and the fun he likes to get up to, I imagine that's a lot easier to manage when you're not trying to screw around in your childhood bedroom.

And if he's staying, I guess I could…

"I can see if I could be free," Ryan suddenly tells Troy.

Is this really happening?

I try to play it cool as I add, "Yeah, I think I might be able to help out for at least part of the summer."

What am I doing?

Troy's brows pop up, obviously pleasantly surprised by his luck in finding volunteers. "Thanks, guys. Dax and Marty, we'd really appreciate it. And, Ryan, if you want, I can get you extra hours at the shop."

"That'd be great, actually. Perfect."

When Troy heads off, I glance around, waiting to see if anyone might suspect why I jumped in after Ryan agreed to help, but everyone gets back to their conversations. And why the hell would they suspect anything, given how we were at each other's throats when the Sigma Alphas first came to stay at Alpha Theta Mu.

After we wrap up for the day, I drive Ryan, Keeg, and Dax back to the frat in my car. "You sure you don't want to join in?" Dax asks Keegan.

"Can't. My family takes a vacation together every summer."

"Ah, too bad," Dax says. "I'm actually glad the opportunity came up. I was thinking I'd be the whole summer without all my guys, but guess Ryan, Marty, and me will have to create our own little frat in my house."

"I figured you'd want to keep the place all to yourself to enjoy all the action you'll be getting," Ryan says from the passenger seat.

"Eh, I don't think it'll be too different than it is now. It works that it's you two since you already know how to coordinate messing around with people. And don't worry, Marty, if he gets greedy again, we can kick him to the curb."

"I'll do my best not to be too greedy," Ryan says.

Don't look at me. Don't look at me.

With everything in me, I know he's about to shoot a look my way, and I can't help feeling we're gonna give ourselves away if we're not more careful.

As he sneaks me a glance, my cheeks warm.

Dax chats some more about the apartment he's getting over where Atlas and Troy and Brenner and Taylor live, talking up the pool and the fitness center. Meanwhile, Ryan and I are unusually quiet.

When we get back to my room, Ryan's grinning ear to ear.

"Why are you smiling like that?"

"You like me too."

"Huh?"

"When I said I could stay over the summer, you got all excited at the idea of me fucking you for a few more weeks, and that's why you volunteered too."

Why are my cheeks so damn hot?

I know the answer.

Because he's right.

"You were looking right at me," I say. "Don't act like

that's not what you were thinking."

He shrugs. "Okay, I admit it. Now you have to admit you like me."

"You already know I like you. We covered that."

He steps toward me, and I retreat until my back's against the bathroom doorframe.

"Come on," he says as his arms hook around me. Because of the sweat we worked up, I can smell his musky scent, which doesn't prick at my nose the way it once did. Now it's like a drug.

"You can tell me the truth," he says. "You're catching the feels."

"The feels? How old are we?"

"Well, if you're not catching the feels for me, then I guess I have to be the one to confess I'm catching the feels for you."

A surge of energy swirls in my belly, like butterflies. There's that warmth in my cheeks again.

"Can you be more specific?" Of course, I don't need him to be. I know exactly what he's saying, and it's a relief because I feel the same way.

Ryan moves quickly, taking a kiss. His soft lips overtake mine, minty from the Altoids we popped on the way home. His hands slide under the back of my shirt, gliding across my skin as his tongue expertly toys with mine.

He squats down and hoists me up by my thighs.

Pushing me back against the doorframe, he dominates me with kisses, his lips lingering for another moment before he pulls back and gazes at me, those bright blue eyes sparkling. He waits, as though he's unwilling to give me what I want until I give him what he wants.

"I've caught some feels for you," I finally admit. "Is that what you want to hear?"

He angles his head. "Only if you really mean it. And don't worry, I know you do."

He's got the cockiest damn expression on his face—the kind I used to want to punch off his face when his team would win a TaskFrat challenge, but now it's so fucking adorable.

"Can you stop saying feels?" I ask.

"The guys were giving me hell. Said they could tell I had the feels for someone, and I was telling them it wasn't true. Then that thing happened with Miles…fuck, how I wanted to kick his balls through his jaw."

"Not sure how that would work, but…"

"The point is that my friends do really know me, and all that made me realize just how right they were. Marty McGovern's got me feeling all the feels." He leans close, licking up my lips before offering another kiss. "Now let's get you out of these clothes, and then I'm gonna clean you off and fuck you in the shower," he whispers against my mouth, and that excitement in my belly bursts into heat throughout my body, stirring a familiar desire I have to sate.

We strip down, and while he grabs a condom and lube from the nightstand, I run the shower water and rinse off.

"Give me that," he says, snatching the loofah from me. He lathers more soap onto it and, starting at my chest, cleans me off. He's slow and deliberate with his movements, his eyes drinking me in as though he wants to make sure to cover every inch of me. He moves the loofah in circles around my abdomen, paying extra attention to the dips and grooves.

As he squats down, I reposition so the water slaps against my back as he takes his time on either leg, then once he's finished, runs his finger between them, wiping across my ass, massaging gently. He offers a low growl, which ignites a fire within me.

I step closer to the showerhead, and Ryan walks on his knees not far behind, until the water is flowing behind us. Pressing my forearm against the wall, beside the hanging shower caddy, I arch my back, serving my ass up to him. Ryan eagerly accepts my invitation, pulling my cheeks apart before offering a quick kiss, then a lick up the crease. It's such a simple move, but it's got my body aching for him again.

"Fuck," I mutter.

He rises to his feet, grabbing the soap and spreading

some more across the loofah before scrubbing himself down, the suds sliding across his chest and abs, as he whistles innocently.

"That was mean," I tell him. "Getting me hungry for it and then abandoning me." He likes to edge me like this, and I've learned I like it too.

"Just trying to make sure you're nice and horny for when I fuck you," he says before reaching out and snatching my hard-on, giving it a quick rub.

I grab the soap and collect some in my hand before rubbing down his shaft, stroking to show the same care at cleaning him as he did with me, then move out of the way of the showerhead so he can rinse it off. When I'm finished, I take the loofah from him and scrub him down, returning the favor, tending to that perfect flesh I've become so familiar with since we started fucking around. While I'm on my knees, covering his legs, with his stiff cock right in front of me, I can't help myself. I lean forward, taking him into my mouth. Because of what he did to me, I'm not as nice as I normally would be—I'm all tease, letting my tongue play on his flesh as water spills over my face, splashing against his cock.

He moans.

"Not so nice when you're on the receiving end, is it?" I ask as his cock swells.

"Just get up and let me fuck you."

Relieved my plan worked, I push to my feet.

Ryan grabs the condom he set on the shower nook and tears it open with his teeth, but it catches. "Fuck," he mutters. "That wasn't as slick as I usually am. Think I tore it."

He starts like he's about to get out of the shower, but I rest my hand on his arm. "We discussed that we've been tested since we started doing this. I haven't been with anyone else, and we'll be continuing this…"

His eyes light up, so clearly he knows what I'm getting at. "I haven't been with anyone either," he assures me.

That shouldn't make me as happy as it does, but I guess this proves I have these ridiculous feels.

"Mart, you want me to fuck you raw?"

Raw seems like such a dirty word, but it's exciting too, and the soaring sensation in my chest lets me know exactly how much I want that.

"Do you want to fuck me raw?" I ask, anxiety bubbling up in me as I worry he might say no.

He grins the broadest grin I've ever seen on that face and nods, and then his gaze shifts to my cock, which probably can't get much harder. "Mmmm. I like that you're eager for it. Turn around."

I obey, pressing my forearms against the tiled wall, arching my back again.

Ryan squats down and rests his hands against my ass cheeks. He kisses me again, this time tongue-filled, the way he'd kiss my mouth. Eagerness swells in my pelvis, rising to meet the excitement in my belly, which is nothing like the bundle of nerves I was that first time we fucked around.

He growls. "Fuck, I could rim you all day."

He nibbles against my ass cheek, then offers a gentle kiss before pushing to his feet.

As he pumps some lube, I spread my legs.

"Ready as ever for me," he observes. "Well, almost…"

He massages his fingers against me, providing me with extra lubrication. Then he lines himself up and slides in, cautious as he always is, reminding me how good he is about reading my body, waiting for my muscles to loosen up before proceeding. He feeds me inch by inch until he's touching that familiar spot. I arch my back some more and moan.

"Yeah, there you are," he says, and I can hear how victorious he feels.

He rests a hand against my abs, pulling me close, letting me adjust until he pushes back with a final thrust. The way he slides against that spot has my nerves in a frenzy, goose bumps pricking across my flesh.

"It feels so good," I confess, loving knowing that there's only a slight lube barrier between me and his flesh.

"Your ass feels amazing."

He leans close, his mouth against my neck, offering kisses. I turn my head so his lips are only a few inches from mine, and he takes a kiss while working up a decent pace. This guy knows how I need to be fucked.

When I pull away from our kiss, he's gazing at me in awe, taking in my every twitch and flinch as I revel in the pleasure he's giving me. I feel so exposed, like he can see parts of me that are only visible when I've let go of all my tension and uneasiness and it's just us having fun.

And I know what I want from him.

"Ry—Ry—"

"Yeah? What do you want me to do?"

"Would you want me to fuck you?" I'm anxious as I wait for his response.

His gaze shifts, like he's thinking about it.

"You said when we started that you'd be interested in that, but if you're not, forget I said anything."

"I said that before I knew how good it would feel to be buried in this ass."

I can't disguise my disappointment.

"But…" he adds, "you make it look so fucking sexy that I'm curious. One condition, though."

"I'll be very careful," I assure him, horrified he might think I'd be anything other than good to him after all he's done for me.

He chuckles. "I was gonna say…" He leans closer, until his mouth is millimeters from mine, so I can feel his hot breath against my face. "…you have to ask nicely."

Can't believe I was ever annoyed by Ryan's playfulness, when now I fucking live for it.

"Can I *please* fuck your ass?"

"I'd be honored to take that fat cock."

He takes his time pulling out. My body aches for him, but I remind myself it'll be worth it once I'm inside him, getting to explore this uncharted territory.

Ryan feels his ass, his gaze wandering. "You're probably really gonna have to work me up first," he warns.

"We can assess your ass and figure out if you can take me."

He glares at me. "Is that a challenge?"

"Maybe." But honestly, I'm a little nervous whether I'll be able to do for him what he does for me.

He smirks. "Trust me, one way or another, I'll get this monster cock in me." He grabs my dick and offers a quick pump.

Seeing how determined he is to take me turns me on. And helps release some of the anxiety about pleasing him. I grab his arm and urge him around so his ass is on display for me. As I drop to my knees, my mouth waters at the thought of having that all to myself.

Even though I haven't done this before, I know what feels good from what he's done to me. I use the skills he's demonstrated, all those things he's done with my ass, as I lubricate my fingers, first rimming his hole, watching his expression as he enjoys himself. I work my forefinger into him, gliding across a spot that makes his body twitch, and I know by his body's response and the way his lips twist up that I'm there.

"Fuck," he says in a breath that helps ease my concerns.

"Found you," I say with pride as I massage it, feeling his muscles loosening up for me. I figured it'd feel good, but I didn't realize how exciting it'd be to be giving him this same pleasure. I keep massaging him, offering another finger, then a third, enjoying the way his ass expands for me, assuring me he'll be able to make space for me.

He looks over his shoulder. "I'm ready, Mart."

There's something about the certainty in his expression, his eagerness to take me, that kills the anxieties building up within me. It reminds me that it's only me and Ryan. He's been there with me through my awkward discovery of my feelings for guys and my nerves about my first time. Even if I do get nervous or fumble, I know it'll be okay. I slide my fingers out and push to my feet.

My cock is about as hard as it gets, so I know it's gonna be a feat, but I'm curious to see how he takes me. Lining myself up, I steadily push the head against him before his hole opens up for me. I rub his thigh gently as he pushes his ass back, inviting me right in.

By how he's managing, I would have thought he'd done this before, but I realize he just knows what he's doing from the stuff we've done together, how my hole's responded to his dick. And as he eases back onto my girth, I get a taste of what he's been enjoying from my ass all this time.

25

Ryan

THIS IS AMBITIOUS, even for me. I've been totally into Marty's ass, but I'm sure that on some subconscious level, the reason I haven't suggested bottoming for him is because his cock is more than a little intimidating. But now that I'm pressed up against the bathroom wall, taking him, I'm putting the same dedication into this as I have when I was playing football.

I descend a little farther, and my muscles tense up.

"You good?" Marty asks. I glance over my shoulder, noticing the concern in his expression.

"I've collided with three-hundred-pound men on the field. I think I can take a dick." As I say it, I have to take a few breaths, adjusting to the slight sting. "But yeah, gonna need a second."

"Oh, wow. I didn't realize you were all talk."

"Well, as soon as I adjust, I'm gonna show you how much it's not all talk."

"I can wait. And if it's any help, it's hot seeing my dick in you like this."

I can't help but laugh. "It helps a little," I confess as the sting dulls. I breathe in and out, my ass relaxing until it allows him farther in. There's a little pressure, but it's pleasurable, and I'm waiting to experience that sensation, when he hits my prostate.

"Oh, hell." My breath hitches as his cock sticks tight to the spot, making my body vibrate.

"Nice, isn't it?"

"What the—" I roll my head back as a swirl of heat in my chest combines with a charge that shoots out to my toes and fingertips. It's so much better than just his finger, the steady pressure gliding across that sweet spot. "Wow."

When I'm able to collect myself, I look over my shoulder at Marty, who sports a grin that makes me feel like a god for how I was able to take him like that. "No wonder you couldn't get enough of my dick," I say. "I don't know that you're gonna be able to get me to top again."

It's like now that my body's aware of the pleasure this cock can give me, it loosens up even more, allowing more of his cock in me, sliding against that spot, continuing to stimulate me in all the right ways.

I figure his cock has to stop at some point, or I'll run out of room, but there's only another inch before my ass rests against his pelvis. The way he's wedged against my prostate has made most of the excitement buzz in my abdomen.

"Give me a minute," I tell him.

"Take as long as you need."

I laugh, but just as soon, another jolt of excitement ripples through me, pulling a moan right from me. As the pressure fades, I give his cock a test run, moving my hips back and forth. "See? Even with as big as that thing is, I'm moving pretty fast. Good for a virgin."

Marty laughs.

"Hey, give me that one."

"I don't think you can call yourself a virgin when I'm lodged inside you."

"You'll call me whatever I want if you want to stay in there."

"Yes, sir," he says as another surge of sensations moves through me.

"Fuckin' hell," I breathe. "Now you know why I've been so hung up on your ass."

I manage to speed my thrusts up some, and I can tell how much more give there is than when I was first trying to get his cock inside me.

"It's okay, Mart. Do it. Fuck me like you got something to prove," I tell him, bracing my hand against the wall.

His hands slide around my waist, and he begins

thrusting up into me. Like when I fuck him, we quickly find our natural rhythm. I don't slack either. He's been too good a bottom for me not to return the favor.

My movements feel controlled by my body craving the sensation of him sliding up against that sweet spot, again and again and again…and he doesn't hold back, drilling me in a way that drives me wild.

"Taking all that anxiety out on this ass?" I ask.

"You know it," he says as he wraps one arm around me, drawing me close, and with the other, grips my cock and strokes with that expert skill he has now that he's learned my body so well.

I turn so I can get a look at him. "You impressed by how good I am at taking you my first go? Come on, admit I'm good."

"Ry, you continue to impress me," he says, and it feels even better knowing he means it.

Our lips slam together before he pistons his hips, forcing himself in deep. I moan, and there's this feral desire in me, something I hadn't considered but I'm suddenly obsessed with.

"I want you to come inside me, Mart," I whisper. "I want you to be the one who claims this ass."

"Fuck, I want that too, Ry."

"I want to be dripping with you."

His cock swells, creating the perfect amount of pressure against my prostate. Between how amazing he feels, how proud I am of my own work, and the excitement of this being my first time bottoming for him, I'm overwhelmed—and I know where this is leading far too quickly.

"It's too much," I warn. "I'm gonna come."

"Give it to me, Ry."

It's like my body just needed his permission because as soon as he says the words, the rush sweeps through me, nerve networks bursting with excitement like a series of fireworks going off all over my body. This isn't like when I shoot normally. Being stimulated like this and feeling him jackhammering away inside me intensifies and prolongs the experience.

I grunt out as Marty warns, "I'm coming, Ry. I'm coming."

I'm still shooting as his hips thrust up against me. A quick series of movements follow, and it's so satisfying knowing he's shooting up inside me.

As my own climax settles, I mash my lips against his, my tongue greedy for his as he continues filling me up. I usually get to see his heavy load, but I love knowing that tonight it's pushing in deep, sliding between the crack of my ass and his cock.

Marty jerks a few more times inside me, the sort of involuntary movement he goes through after coming, like some primal instinct to make sure he gets every drop in deep.

We breathe into each other's mouths, coming down together in a mess of licks and kisses, taking our time as I enjoy his cock still being inside me.

"I can feel you slipping out," I tell him before deepening my voice to sound like a documentarian: "The Martifuckus Cummingus will breed inside the hole before leaving its burrow to return later to check on his babies."

Marty laughs. "Martifuckus, huh? What the fuck are you on?"

"Probably a few ounces of protein."

His cock slips farther before my ass helps along the process, steadily pushing him out.

As I spin back around to him, I say, "Mmmm. The Martifuckus Cummingus will return to breed this same hole hundreds more times over the course of only a few weeks."

"Hundreds?" he teases.

"Yeah, you know, I wasn't thinking that you needed to pay me back for all those good times I gave you, but now I'm greedy to collect."

He beams. "That good, huh?"

"Let's just say I don't think we'll need any extra practice for that."

The way Marty smirks assures me I've stroked his ego nearly as well as he stroked my prostate.

We kiss some more, then rinse and dry off before

returning to the bedroom.

I'm completely satisfied as I lie at his side.

I love how fucking effortless it all is—just our routine these days.

Lying in bed with him makes me appreciate why I was so eager to volunteer to help with the build over the summer. Not that I wouldn't have wanted to do it anyway. Hell, I have free time now that I'm not planning on dedicating the next few years of my life to the NFL.

"I like knowing that we get to have more of this," I tell him.

"Now that I know what I was missing out on, me too."

"Oh, that's all you get. I was just doing that to trap you, and now I got you, so…"

"Mmmm-hmmm, I could tell you weren't enjoying it at all," he says in that sarcastic way he has. "Please. I doubt I'll be able to keep you off my cock now."

"That's ridiculous. If anything, I like your cock and ass equally." Even being jokey, I can't keep from adding, "And now you know I like you too."

"I believe the phrasing was that we've got the feels for each other."

"I do have the feels. Got them real bad."

"You make it sound like something that's antibiotic resistant."

"Nah. It's viral."

We share a laugh, and he issues a playful glare.

He's quiet for a moment, then angles his head on my chest so he can look up at me.

Fuck, he's so beautiful.

We're quiet, just gazing at one another until he breaks eye contact.

"Before I say this," he adds. "I want you to know I'm comfortable with however you want to do this. I don't want to rush anything…"

I'm listening, curious where he's going with this.

"…but I don't mind anyone knowing what we're doing. Not that I want you to feel like you have to come out, but I do like spending time with you, and it was bothering me that we couldn't do anything in front of the guys today."

That's how I felt when I had to keep my distance from him.

I didn't like it.

At all.

His gaze shifts about. "But okay, there's that…so we don't have to talk about it again, and if and when you feel more comfortable… And now you're not saying anything. Why aren't you saying anything?"

"Because I like when you ramble."

He huffs out a laugh.

"I'm glad you said that," I tell him. "Because I want to be able to put my hands all over you and kiss you whenever I want. Show anyone who has any ideas that you're busy with me."

"Anyone who has any ideas? Yeah, 'cause I was getting so much action before we started doing this. I should be the one making sure everyone knows I have work to do on this ass now that I've had a piece."

"Mmmm. I like you saying you want to keep breeding my ass."

"Oh God," he says with a glare.

The glare of my Mart.

I give him a quick peck.

"So how are we doing this?" he asks. "Feel like Lance and Ty beat us to the whole heading downstairs and being out with it last semester."

"Yeah, we don't want to be accused of being a bunch of copycats."

I consider how we should break it to the guys when Marty's eyes widen. "What if we waited another week?"

"Huh?"

"I actually have a fun idea."

"I like fun ideas. What is it?" I press.

"Maybe you should have to earn it from me." He smirks.

"Oh, really?"

"Yeah, I don't know that it's fair that you got me up inside you, but my ass is empty. That's a foul or...what do they call it in football—a penalty?"

I raise my hand to my chest like I've been shot. "A penalty? Ooh, you really know how to hurt me." I roll toward him and offer a kiss.

"Does this mean I get a penalty kick?" he asks when our lips part.

"You get a penalty *dick*…and don't you dare roll your eyes at that one."

As he laughs, my lips crush against his again, and as my cock stiffens, I know I'm not gonna have any problem giving Mart exactly what he wants.

26

Marty

THOUGH WE BOTH want to be out and open with the guys, we manage another week because our surprise is just too good. The following Friday, we're at the final TaskFrat Challenge of the year. Tonight's challenge is an obstacle course on the Peach State football field, which we always secure for the final. It's a beautiful, warm April evening, which is perfect weather for the skimpy outfits we're in. Alpha Theta Mu selected G-strings and crop tops to pay homage to the prank Sigma Alpha pulled on us at the start of last semester, while Sigma Alpha wears the lingerie from when we got them back.

The stadium is packed, far beyond the usual frats and sorority attendees we're used to, which is why we always have to make sure this is like the Olympics of fratting.

There are beer-pong tables set up at the start, where one of our housemates represents Alpha Theta Mu. Each frat has to sink a pong into a Solo cup to proceed to the next part and tag their teammate. Our house makes its way through the series of tasks involving Hula-Hoops, a blindfolded potato-sack race, and a sound meter to determine whether the guys have barked at the right decibel.

Lance and I stand alongside one another on the track around the football field, at the second to last obstacle. Pairs representing each house are lined up alongside us as we all wait for our teammates to reach us so we can begin our task. As Payton approaches from his task, he passes a condom he had to fill with water so that it looks like a water balloon. I catch it, and quickly realize it's doused in lube, which is gonna make this a tricky task.

Ty and Ryan have already handed off their condom, so they're a few feet ahead of us in their own lane.

"Come on, come on, come on," Lance urges.

"Not helping," I assure him, passing it to him.

We're not allowed to hold it for more than five seconds—if we do, we'll have to restart this task—so Lance and I continue passing the slippery water-filled condom between us.

This is the second to last task, and we need to get past the slip-'n-slide and hand it off to Ash, who'll take it to the finish line.

I sneak a glance to where Ash is waiting on us, waving his hands over his head to flag us down. If we don't succeed, Sigma Alpha will, and win not only today, but the year. And Lance sure as fuck isn't having that.

En route to the slip-'n-slide, an idea springs to mind. If he can get some lubrication on himself, he might be able to zip right through the slip-'n-slide.

"Wipe some of the lube on yourself," I tell Lance.

"Huh?"

He assesses the situation before his eyes widen as he catches on. "Good idea."

After passing me the condom, he rubs his hands up and down his body. We swap a few more times before Ty's already diving onto the slip-'n-slide, which leads to Keegan, who waits for him at the end. Fortunately, we're right behind them, and I'm hoping this will give us an advantage when Lance takes his dive. As soon as he hits the plastic cover, he goes blazing past Ty, and he's practically shot out the other side like a cannonball.

"Ash, Ash, Ash!" I hear him call as he somehow manages to toss it right to our buddy.

Ash fumbles with the condom, earning *oohs* from the crowd, but quickly recovers and spins around a moment before Ty passes his condom to Keegan. It's the narrow lead we need as Ash rushes through the finish line only a few seconds before Keegan.

It's done!

Alpha Theta Mu has reclaimed our title for the TaskFrat Challenge, and the frat goes wild as the audience cheers from the stadium seats.

We really fucking did it!

I catch my breath as I jog over to Lance, who Ty raced to right after he got out of the slide. When Ty reaches his man, he helps him back onto his feet.

"You wild fuck," Ty says. "Do anything to beat my ass, wouldn't you?"

"Damn right," Lance tells him, though he still seems a little out of it from his turbulent slip-'n-slide ride.

That's my buddy.

"Nice one," I hear beside me as Ryan approaches, looking sexy as hell in the lingerie I picked out for him last semester, the lace tight against his hips, teasing by barely covering that beautiful V that emphasizes his bulge—which the guys still don't realize I've become all-too-familiar with.

Ryan smirks as he offers me a firm handshake.

Makes me think of all the other things I know he can do with that hand.

And also how sneaky we're being tonight.

As much as I want to surprise the guys, it sucks that we can't grab each other right here and enjoy a few kisses, but I remind myself it'll be worth it.

"You sexy little jerk," Ty tells Lance. My Alpha Theta Mu president barely has time to react before Ty squats down, lifts him, and takes kisses. He shoves him up against the partition before the stadium seating, and they're going at it like dogs.

"Guess despite appearances," Ryan says, "it didn't kill Ty to lose to Lance this year."

We share a laugh, sneaking each other a look, because we're both happy that our guys have so much fun together.

I regroup with Alpha Theta Mu to celebrate our victory before heading toward the stadium seating. I head up the steps to Aiden, who came to see the challenge. In all four years at Peach State, he's never missed a final. Although, he had to get me back after I had to see his weird-ass play a few weeks earlier.

He's got a huge-ass grin spread across his face, and I can tell he's proud. He knows how much these challenges mean to Alpha Theta Mu.

"Big bro kicked some ass tonight," he says as I give him a great big hug.

"Thanks for coming."

"You know I wouldn't have missed this for anything."

True. Though this year I was a little worried, considering he hasn't been the easiest to keep in touch with.

I hear some huffing behind me and turn to see Ryan jogging over in the sexy lingerie.

"Hey, I don't think we've officially met. I'm Ryan."

Ryan has seen him at some of the challenges, but given that we weren't exactly on great terms until this semester, didn't actually have a reason to make an introduction.

"You're Sigma Alpha trash?" Aiden asks, clearly trying to give him the much-needed hell that is expected of him.

"You're a real Alpha Theta Mu in training, huh?" Ryan says with a grin.

"Just looking out for my bro. Nice panties, by the way."

"Aw, this old thing?" Ryan jokes.

They chat some as we wrap things up before returning to Alpha Theta Mu.

Aiden is sticking around for the formal tonight, and he brought a change of clothes. So we all make a quick change into our formal suits, then head to the party. Even though we're not out yet, that doesn't keep Ryan or me from taking every opportunity to get a little too close…caress the backs of our hands together. There are even a few moments when I can tell he wants to sneak a kiss. I wouldn't mind, but I'm glad we're saving it for our big reveal.

We take our time, navigating our friend groups.

Aiden knows most of the guys, so he catches up with everyone, and once the place is packed, I head over to the DJ booth, where Lance, Ty, Ash, and Colin are hanging.

"Hey, mind if I get in on the set list?" I ask.

Lance shrugs.

"You're gonna hate me for, like, a minute, but you

gotta trust me."

"Now I'm offended you think I wouldn't trust one of my own."

He passes me his phone, and I input the next song.

"What are you putting on?" Ash asks suspiciously.

"You'll have to wait and see."

"I wanna know *now*." Ash starts toward me like he's gonna sneak a peek, so I tug the phone close to my chest.

"Uh-uh. You have to wait for it. Surprises are the best."

"You and Ryan have been acting weird tonight," Colin observes, his gaze narrow.

And fuck, have I already given us away?

"I'm not saying a damn thing." I slip away from the DJ booth, since I have a feeling if I stick around too long, I'm gonna blab.

The guys seem to be respecting my wishes by not picking up the phone to see what's coming. I head to the dance floor, where a bunch of fratbros and sorority sisters are enjoying a Megan Thee Stallion song, which assures me this is gonna make for a really awkward transition.

I'm kind of nervous when I see Ryan chatting with Keeg and Dax, his gaze on me. He's got that mischievous smirk playing across his lips, which he licks, like he's thinking about what he has planned for me once we're finished up for the night. And I must admit, I'm feeling extra frisky after all that adrenaline the TaskFrat win pumped me up with.

When the song that's playing comes to an end, it transitions to a tango, and the dance floor fills with audible groans while a few look around like they're waiting for Lana Del Rey to start playing.

Ryan turns to his buddies and excuses himself before making his way to me.

I'm tempted to look back at the guys, see what their reaction is at the DJ table, or maybe try to find Aiden to see if he's about to witness this, but I can't take my eyes off Ryan. He looks so damn sexy in that suit. And I know he's got his pomade to spike his hair in the front the way it is.

When he reaches me, I say, "Can I have this dance?"

"It'd be an honor." He winks.

I didn't realize how nervous I'd be about doing this in front of everyone, but it makes it easier that he's here, and as usual, doesn't give any fucks about what anyone else thinks.

We get into position.

"I'll lead," I say.

"I think I can handle it."

"No, that's how I learned it, so I feel like I'll be better that way."

He laughs. "Right."

We begin the dance, and I use those moves I've picked up and shared with him throughout the semester, and this is a lot easier than when we were just starting together.

"Kind of wish we could pro it up right now," I tell him. "Pull some moves that could really impress everyone."

"Trust me, this is enough to impress most of the guys here. And you should be impressed—I haven't stepped on your toes nearly as much as when we started."

I laugh.

He hasn't stepped on them at all for this, but, as I point out, "It's early in the song."

Ryan searches around. "Guess they don't seem to mind us interrupting their dancing."

"They'll probably give us hell later anyway."

"That's what fratbros are for, right?"

Just then, his foot catches my toe, and I stumble.

So much for it being perfect.

But Ryan moves quickly, hooking his arm around my back, dipping me, and planting a fat kiss on my lips. He repositions his free hand under my thigh, pulling it off the ground to dip me even farther.

He's such a phenomenal kisser, it's easy to get lost in the moment...to forget we're in public right now. But only for a moment before I hear the crowd losing their minds—hooting and hollering with excitement over our dance, like they did when we won the challenge earlier.

Our lips finally part, and Ryan gazes down at me

with those gorgeous blue eyes, which have me under some kind of spell, in no small part due to the energy that he left coursing through my body.

"You're really something, ya fucking party killer," he says.

"Same to you, frathole."

It reminds me of what feels like a lifetime ago, when we were at each other's throats. When a night like tonight seemed impossible. When I was oblivious to how this frathole could make me feel so good.

He grins, practically glowing with the lights hanging around the dance floor, and he pulls me back to my feet.

We finally break away, scanning our audience that's still cheering on our display.

"You little fuck," I hear behind me, and as I turn, Lance throws his arms around me as Ty tackles Ryan and says, "You just had to upstage us, didn't you, dude?" He means when he and his man came out last semester.

"You weren't kidding about us needing a whiteboard, after all," Colin chimes in as he approaches with Ash.

"How long has this been going on?" Lance demands to know.

"Pretty quickly after probation," I reply.

"Oh, so he likes a bad boy?" Ash teases, which gets us all laughing.

Soon, we've got Dax, Keegan, Jaxon, Payton all joining in, offering up the support I expect from our guys.

"I guess you're gonna be having a real fun summer at my place," Dax says, shooting us a pointed look like he's imagining how much sex we'll be having.

And I sure hope he's right.

"Bro!"

I turn to see Aiden heading to the dance floor. I knew my friends would be here for me, but tension knots in me because I'm wondering what he's gonna think about all this. When he nears, he gives me a nasty look, but then grins, and a wave of relief hits me. A combination of opening up to my friends and to one of the most important guys in my life.

"We have a lot to catch up on, *mister*," he says with a tone.

We really do.

27

Ryan

I T'S GREAT NOW that we can be ourselves around Alpha Theta Mu's house and campus, and I don't take any of it for granted. Every time I see Marty, I make sure to grab him and give him a kiss…and maybe more if he can sneak off with me for a minute.

It's a hectic couple of weeks before finals, followed shortly by graduation.

My parents come together, and of course I want them to be here for me for this big day, but also, it's another of many reminders that, regardless of what I had in mind for the future of my family, it can't ever be what it was.

On the plus side, I also get to see all my buddies again—from school, the frat, old teammates. And after, we have a huge party at Alpha Theta Mu, a final night of partying and debauchery for the senior crew. I still feel hungover by move-out a few days later. It's easy enough to deal with my stuff—deflate my air mattress and pack the bag I kept there throughout the semester—but Marty needs more assistance, so I help him get his stuff back to his parents' place.

I place the box I'm carrying next to the ones marked CLOSET—because of course Marty would be super organized with this shit.

"Whew," Marty says as he sets a box by his bed. "Done."

"You need help getting situated?" Philip asks. I met his parents at the graduation ceremony, and they seem as cool as his brother—and far more chill than Mart, that's for sure.

"Nah. We got it. I was just gonna put some things where they belong and make sure I have what I need to take to Dax's."

"You're still gonna visit, right?" Tegan says in an overdramatic way like my mom might—like she's making a joke, but really, I can tell she wants to see her son.

"I'll be back plenty," he assures her before offering a warm hug.

This is a side most of the guys don't get to see of him—one I didn't get to see until we started spending more time together. Despite how worked up he can get and, at times, be annoying, he has a big heart, and the guy adores his family and his fellow Alpha Theta Mus.

"It's great of you to help Marty out," Philip tells me.

"Hey, he was looking out for me all semester, so kind of owed it to him."

"More like keeping an eye *on* you," Philip jokes, evidently aware of our initial drama.

We haven't come out to our parents yet. Marty wants to talk to his today, and I plan to wait until my mom's back from her impromptu trip to Europe—to de-stress, I'm sure, after the year she's been having with my dad.

"Well, you should stick around for dinner," Tegan says.

"Of course he's staying," Marty says, sneaking a glance my way.

If he's trying to keep his secret, he needs to be more careful because the way he's looking at me is like a mating call I'm struggling to resist.

Philip writes down our takeout orders, and then they head out to grab food from the restaurant. Once they're gone, I go to the door and peek out to make sure the coast is clear.

"I think I deserve a smooch for that," I tell him.

"For helping me move?"

"For keeping my greedy hands off this body for the past few hours." I move close, sliding my arms around him. "I'm gonna think of a number…"

"Number?"

"Of how many smooches I deserve."

He rolls his eyes, which is why I said it like that, and the way he glares at me gets my dick twitching. Makes me wonder if part of why I enjoyed giving him hell initially was because it kinda turns me on.

"Will you settle for a *kiss*?" he asks.

I nod before reeling him in for a big one. We're both sweaty as fuck, but it's not like this would be the first time that ever happened. Or the last, with what we'll be doing on the builds for the next few weeks.

When I pull away, I study his expression. I know him well enough now to tell when he's stressed about something, and since finals are out of the way, he can't pin it on that anymore. But I have a pretty good idea what this is about.

"You sure you're ready to tell them?" I ask.

"Just stressed about initiating the conversation, but I'm fine with them knowing what we're up to."

"*Only* fine?"

"Shut it," he says, leaning close and taking another kiss.

"Mmm…" I whisper into his mouth. "How far is the restaurant they're going to?"

"About fifteen minutes."

"Oh yeah?"

I squat down, lifting him and carrying him to the bed. His arms and legs wrap around me in a way I'm used to since we've fucked around so much. I crawl across the mattress on my knees, laying his head against his pillow.

"You think your parents will be suspicious that we haven't unpacked a damn thing by the time they're back?"

"Maybe a little." Although, that doesn't keep him from kissing me again.

And again.

And again.

Soon we've got our tongues down each other's throats, making up for lost time, before a sound catches my attention. Instinctively I pull back, and my gaze shoots to the door, where Philip and Tegan stand wide-eyed, frozen in place.

"Uh…" I say, feeling awkward as fuck. "Too late to say this isn't what it looks like?"

My joke's a knife through the tension as Philip and Tegan lose it. Tegan cups her face as she howls with laughter while Philip leans on the doorframe, looking like he's about to cry.

"I thought you were going to the restaurant," Marty says in an accusatory tone.

"I wanted to stop by the store," Tegan says, "and I figured I would check to make sure you didn't need anything."

Philip grabs the doorknob and starts to close the door, Tegan retreating with him. "Do continue. Don't mind us."

Marty winces. "Mom…Dad…"

"No, please. Keep going," Tegan insists, giggling as they shut the door.

"Mom and Dad, get back in here!" Marty snaps.

"You might want to put a pillow on your lap first," I warn him, feeling his girth against my hip.

"Oh, wait. I need a minute!"

AFTER RECOVERING FROM the awkward moment, we head downstairs and chat with his parents at the kitchen table.

"So, are you two boyfriends?" Philip asks.

"We're *seeing each other*," Marty says. "We haven't really put a label on it."

"*Yet*," I find myself chiming in, which catches his attention as much as mine. We haven't had any chats about being boyfriends, but…I really like him and he likes me. Fuck, we changed our summer schedules so we could spend more time together. It's not exactly complicated.

"But I'm attracted to guys *and* girls apparently," Marty says. "So I'm bi."

"Thank you for sharing that with us," Tegan says.

"Yeah, but I'll be honest," Philip adds, "I kind of

prefer the way it happened to you coming out. It's gonna make for a much better story."

Marty grins, and I can tell he's happy with how they've taken the news. From everything he told me about them, I expected this would be their reaction, but it's nice seeing he can rely on his parents.

They talk a little more with him, offer hugs, and then head out to grab our dinner, leaving us on our own in the kitchen.

"What was that all about?" Marty asks, and at my confused expression, he adds, "When Dad asked if we were boyfriends."

Hearing him say the word activates something in me, this swirling sensation in my belly, like the excitement before playing a big game, but so much better.

"Do you want to be boyfriends?" he asks.

As excited as the idea makes me, I must admit, "I don't really even know what that means."

"I think it means we're more than fuck buddies…"

"We're definitely more than that." I know that's not what he was suggesting, but the thought that anyone would think that's all we are pisses me the fuck off.

"And more than just seeing each other…" he adds.

"Yeah, there's been a lot of seeing each other already."

Marty bites his bottom lip.

"Jesus, you make even that look sexy," I observe.

"What?"

"How am I supposed to think about this when you're biting your lip like that?"

He flinches. "I didn't even realize I was doing it."

"That's what makes it so fucking sexy."

He stops biting it. "Sorry. I was thinking that I've never had a boyfriend."

"Neither have I. Or a girlfriend, aside from high school for, like, a minute."

"What does that even mean—*boyfriends*?"

"At least that it's a long-term thing, or that we want it to be."

"I'm planning to come back here once we finish helping with the Activate Kindness builds," Marty says. "And you're planning to move to Peachtree Springs to work at the shop."

"That's a thirty-minute drive max, and you're going to grad school at Peach State, so that's not really an issue." That this would even be considered an obstacle grates on my nerves.

"I know it's not this big thing," Marty insists. "But I'm trying to be practical and make sure we're thinking this through."

"Because you don't want to be my boyfriend?" Christ, I sound as annoyed as I did when Gisele was about to kiss him. The way he's talking about this is stressing me, nerves twisting up, my jaw tense.

"Whoa, where is this coming from?" Marty asks. "I'm the one who's supposed to be freaking out over shit."

I shake my head. "You're not wrong, and I know you have no reason to not want to be my boyfriend, right? Or do you, and you want to break it to me easy? Or has this all just been fun for you? Fuck, is this what's always running through your head? This is awful!"

He laughs, approaching me. He rests his hands on my shoulders, the tension in my jaw instantly easing up.

"I'm not gonna let you suffer, Ry. I haven't even considered that until today because I've enjoyed what it's been, but I don't want this to end after the build."

There's a lightness in my chest as it feels like, for the first time since we started talking about this, I can take a decent breath of air. As though I've been holding it, worried about what he would say.

"I want to be your boyfriend," he says, a smile playing across his lips.

I'm surprised how quickly that shifts my mood, as his words assure me that he was just doing his risk-management assessment of us, not trying to talk himself out of continuing this long term. "I mean, of course you do. Who wouldn't?" I tease, pulling a laugh right from him.

"And back to your usual conceited self."

I slide my arms around his hips, cupping his sides

and reeling him close. "Hey, I'm not the guy who decided to be my boyfriend, but don't worry. I want to be your boyfriend too, so I guess you're one lucky guy."

He cringes. "I can still take it back."

I lean close, our lips millimeters apart. "Don't you dare, or you won't get to fuck me again."

"I have a feeling I could get away with saying it and you'd still fuck me."

"I hate it when you're right, but that's part of having a boyfriend now."

"See what a fast learner you are?" His grin must be about as big as mine right now, and I'm living for it.

I tilt my head back, considering what this means, now that we're boyfriends. "So…we get to do boyfriend shit now."

"Like…handholding?" Marty asks.

"Gross."

"More cuddling?"

"I'm on board with that one."

"Dates?"

I didn't think I could grin any more than I was, but I was wrong. "I like where this is going. So like going out to dinner? Or maybe the summer festival together?"

"Yeah, like that," he says. "And maybe some *smooches*."

Even as he's trying to be playful about it, I can tell by the way his brows tug closer together that he still fucking hates that word, and it's adorable.

"Of course," I say. "Plenty of smooches. Was that ever a question?"

"Shut it and give me a smooch."

I obey. He's my boyfriend now, after all.

I guide him over to the fridge, pushing him against it and sliding my hand under his shirt, fully appreciating his lips, the gentle assurance that they're all mine. When I finally pull away, I gaze into those green eyes glistening in the kitchen light. "I'm gonna enjoy fucking my boyfriend tonight," I say before seizing another kiss.

28

Marty

SAYING WE'RE BOYFRIENDS shouldn't have changed anything.

It's only a word.

But things feel different now.

We haven't even gone on a date yet, since Ryan picked up more hours at the shop and I've started a summer gig as a lifeguard at the local water park. We have the build on Thursdays and Saturdays, but that hasn't kept us from making the best of things, staying up and watching movies together or playing video games with Dax. Despite how much I'll miss being in the frat, it's nice getting a chance to just be with each other.

One day, on the housing job site, I'm working with Brenner and Taylor on drywall inside.

"See?" Taylor stands on a ladder, showing Brenner the overlap of the top drywall with the one under it.

"You can't go higher?" Brenner asks, earning a look from his boyfriend.

"This is as high as it goes." Taylor had already suggested it might've been too big. "I think Payton might've cut this one a little off."

Brenner pulls out his measuring tape, and Taylor helps him measure. "Oh yeah," Brenner says. "Look at you. Not just a finance bro after all."

"So I have a boyfriend getting his master's in architecture, and he can help me by getting out a measuring tape like any other guy here?"

"Hey, why don't you put this house on AutoCAD or Revit, and then I'll show you what I can do?"

"Ooh," Taylor says. "I like it when you talk dirty."

"Sure, it's the dirty talk you like," Brenner says as he pulls the measuring tape out and holds it by his crotch. The way Taylor's cheeks turn pink, I have a feeling it's an accurate measurement. "Let's see what you must be on this thing." He pulls the tape out near Taylor's crotch.

"Stop," Taylor says. He fights a smirk for a second, but then caves, giving his man a look, and Brenner sports a grin, as though fucking up on this drywall was worth it just so he could get that line in.

I've hung out with these guys some while they were undergrads at Peach State. Even though Brenner's still attending Peach State for his master's, we don't see them around as much as we used to, so it's been nice getting to see them some more on the builds because, yes, they're always this fun.

Brenner directs us to lay the drywall flat, and we remeasure, Brenner drawing a line where Payton needs to cut. While we're waiting for Payton at the saw, Brenner hooks his arm around Taylor, drawing him in for a fat kiss. It sucks not being able to get my hands all over Ryan right now—not because it's a secret, but because he's on the roof today.

Brenner nibbles at Taylor's bottom lip, lingering for a minute before Payton finishes sawing and says, "Are you guys trying to make me cut myself?"

We all share a laugh before Dax heads toward us with a two-by-four.

"Hey, man," Brenner says, "could you check with Miles where he put the sander?"

Today Dax and Miles are working on the same part of the house, but since their explosive exchange, they've kept their distance. Miles occasionally cuts a glance Dax's way, like he's one move away from snapping and tearing our friend a new one. Who knows what his deal is, but the way Dax's eyes bulge at Brenner's suggestion tells me that's a bad idea.

I'm wondering if no one mentioned the incident to Brenner, but then Taylor nudges his shoulder, and they sneak each other a look. "Oh, right, the whole beef thing," Brenner says. "I can ask him when I'm finished with this."

"That's probably for the best," Dax says.

When the drywall's ready, we install it, and then Brenner and Taylor head off to find the sander. Dax and I are putting nails in the drywall when a familiar scent hits my nose. Ryan hooks his arms around my waist, drawing me close, and I glance over my shoulder. "If you'd surprised me, I could have hit you with my hammer."

"All good. I got about a hundred and fifty pounds of muscle…and a hard hat." He grips the edge of his hat, tilting it like he's sporting it for a commercial.

I spin toward him. As usual, he's not wearing a shirt, so it's just flesh and sweat, making him fucking irresistible. Although, I tense up when I notice his shoulders are a little pink. "Someone needs sunscreen."

"We applied some a few hours ago. You timed, remember?"

"Yeah, and you have to reapply every two hours. Plus, you've been on the roof all day, so turn around."

"Ooh, he's getting bossy. He does that whenever he's feeling toppy," he tells the guys, and before I can admonish him, he says, "Shut it? Yeah, I know, I know."

I slip the sunscreen out of my back pocket and take his shirt out of his belt loop, using it to pat down his shoulders and back before applying.

I make sure to get his shoulders good, to ensure he won't get too red. "Still think you might get a burn here," I warn him.

"Nah. Knowing my skin, it'll be tan by tomorrow."

When Ryan turns around so I can get his chest and abs, he says, "This is totally turning Dax on, isn't it? Watching my man lube me up?"

Dax shrugs. "It's not *not* turning me on."

I laugh because really, I'm having the same issue. Slathering him up reminds me of how much muscle mass there is to cover on the guy, and it takes me a minute to finish with his abs before I make it up to that thick chest, ensuring I get in the dip between those pecs, which he flexes, and I can't keep from smiling.

"So..." Ryan says, "I know we're only starting the summer, but we haven't really discussed when we're gonna have our date."

"When were you thinking?" I ask because I can tell by that smirk he's got something on his mind.

He doesn't hesitate. "Tonight."

I tense up. As much as I want to go on a first date with Ryan, I don't think there's any way to make tonight happen. "We're gonna be messy and tired after today. We're not gonna want to go out."

"Exactly," Ryan says, and now he's really caught my interest. "What if we made something for dinner?"

"Well, we don't want to impose on—"

"I'm heading out tonight," Dax interjects. "Not planning to be back until late."

I look between them. "Did you guys talk about this already?"

Ryan wears a guilty expression, the sort he used to have when he violated some rule at Alpha Theta Mu. For a change, I'm both impressed and relieved. The idea of a night in with him, doing something more than watching TV or playing games, sounds nice. And very us.

Dax mouths, "*Go on the date. You should do it. He's cute,*" then winks, making me laugh.

"What do you say?" Ryan asks. "A fun night in with your favorite guy?"

29

Ryan

IT'S LIKE RIGHT before a big game—not the kind I'm nervous about, but the one where I feel like we're about to kill it. Excitement mixed with the dopamine rush…and this buzz. I never felt it outside of football until I started seeing Mart, and it's really going now that he agreed to have a date night with me.

When we finish at the build, I swing by the store and grab some stuff for us to make chicken parmesan. By the time I get back to Dax's place, Marty's already showered up. I put the ingredients in the fridge before hopping in the shower, and once I'm done, I head into the kitchen in only my towel.

The apartment is a one-bedroom with an open-design kitchen, so I can see Mart in the living area, chilling on the couch, which we fold out into a bed at night. As he reads a book, I think about how nice it is seeing him enjoy more leisure reading since school let out—not just with his head in a textbook to study.

As I approach him, he peeks up at me.

"Hey, *honey*," I say before crouching down and giving him the kiss I've earned after a hard day's work. He rests his hand on my shoulder, and I grit my teeth at the sting of his touch, jerking back. "Well, you weren't wrong about my shoulders. Put some lotion on after my shower. Hoping that will help."

"I should have applied more sunscreen sooner."

"Not sure you can blame yourself for the fact that *I* wasn't wearing enough sunscreen. And if you hadn't been around, it probably would have been even worse."

"I knew you shouldn't have been shirtless on that roof."

"Just 'cause you nailed me down doesn't mean you can deprive everyone of the view."

He issues his signature glare. "Deprive everyone of the view? Wow. Aren't you obnoxious?"

"Clearly, you're attracted to obnoxious."

His lips curl upward. He can't deny it any more than he can deny me. "I guess that is pretty damn clear," he says.

And now we're both smiling.

I give him another kiss. We enjoy each other's tongues for a bit before I pry away, grabbing my duffel bag for some clothes, and as I'm pulling on a pair of jeans, he says, "Okay, so how are we doing this?"

"Not sure. I'm kind of a master chef from meal

prepping for football, so I've never had to consider making it with anyone else."

I'm about to put on a shirt when he says, "No, no. You should let your shoulders heal some."

I see the panic in his expression—as if the mild irritation I might've felt when I threw my shirt back on would've been too much for a guy who's been at the bottom of more than a few dogpiles on the field. Although, that worry written all over his face gives me these little tingling sensations at the back of my neck.

"You can admit you want me shirtless when I'm cooking for you," I joke.

He doesn't fight his smile this time, and while he follows me into the kitchen, he says, "You know I can't cook for shit, right?"

"Eh, I figured as much."

"What is that supposed to mean?"

"Relax. It's only chicken parmesan. How hard can that be, on a scale of flaccid to what I know that thing can get?" I pat his crotch, earning an eye roll. "You should save those eye rolls for when we get started. Have a feeling there'll be plenty. So we have the main dish, and I got some stuff for a salad."

"*And* we're making salad? Wow. You have some high expectations for me."

We get to work. I start slicing up some onion, and Marty cuts up a garlic clove on the other side of the counter. I notice I'm cutting without much thought, but Marty's precise with his chops.

"That's really adorable, watching you cut those like you're gonna get graded after."

He sneaks me a look.

It's such a little exchange between us, but it's the kind of moment I live for with him. Just us being playful, giving hell, but now in a way that makes me feel like we're the only two people in the world.

Next, we make the marinara, then sear the chicken in a pan. I direct him on how to brown it just right.

"It's almost there," I say, inspecting his work.

"I'm not doing too bad, am I?"

"Not even a little bad. You deserve a kiss for how well you're doing it."

He's grinning ear to ear, and all I can think is what good boyfriend shit this date night is. It's a moment that allows me to fully appreciate how much I enjoy having him in my life.

"Mom comes back from Europe next week, so I was gonna see if she and Dad wanted to get together." I slide my hands around his waist and tug him close to my pelvis, rubbing my face against the side of his neck, kissing. "I was thinking that would be a good time to tell them about my new boyfriend."

He turns to me, his expression too serious for my tastes. "You sure?"

"What does that mean?"

"I don't want you to feel rushed or like you have to because my parents know."

"That's not why I'm telling them. I want to bring my boyfriend around whenever the hell I feel like it."

His lips curl into a smile.

"You know," I go on, "it's not gonna be as easy with holidays now that we're a couple. We'll have to start sorting out when to take turns with each other's parents, and then birthdays…probably get on each other's nerves because you'll want to go on a family trip without me." I kiss his neck some more, and while I enjoy the scent of his cologne, he tilts his head, stretching his neck so I have more to cover.

"You keep doing that," he says, "and I'm not gonna be able to spend many vacations away from you."

"That's the plan."

He snickers. "And you know we have to finish this chicken at some point, right?"

"Give me a kiss, and I'll let you go," I say like it's a stick-up.

He offers the kiss, and I grunt, prying free of him, when I detect a smell that isn't his cologne.

And suddenly I realize we might have been kissing for a little too long.

I glance over at the chicken. "Uh-oh…"

So my great date-night idea goes south real fast, and

despite attempting to save the chicken, we wind up with only a salad, which we enjoy before lying on the couch, rewatching *Alien* while we wait for pizza.

Mart uses my chest as a pillow, the way he usually does. He stirs before angling his head to look up at me. "Should have known I would mess up date night."

But with my boyfriend pressed up against me, gazing up at me with that beautiful smirk across his lips, I know there's nothing else I'd rather be doing right now. "It was actually a *perfect* date night."

THESE PAST FEW weeks—staying with Mart at Dax's and working with him on the build—have been amazing. And I'm having a great time down at the shop with Troy and my coworkers, working on cars and goofing off.

If I'd gone on to the NFL, this wouldn't be my life. I'd be too busy training, gearing up for the season. Not goofing around, enjoying a carefree date night, and having lengthy fuck-and-cuddle sessions. I'm sure other guys would trade it all for the NFL—hell, at one time, I would've done the same. But today, this is right where I want to be. Living a much more relaxed life with my guy.

My guy?

Something I never thought I'd be thinking. I never could have imagined I'd be so hung up on anyone, let alone a dude, but I'm totally fine with admitting he's got me.

And I've got him.

Now I want to share this guy with my parents, who I have no doubt will be happy I've found someone who makes me as happy as he does.

My parents meet me halfway between Peachtree Springs and our hometown, at a restaurant where we've had brunch before. As soon as I spot Mom, she's already on her feet, hurrying to me. She has a bounce in her step that takes me by surprise, and when she gets close, I catch the bronze tones in her usually fair complexion, how the highlights in her hair are a little lighter.

"Wow, someone got some sun in Europe," I say as I draw her in for a hug.

"It was a great time to be in Lisbon. The beaches are absolutely incredible. Don't worry, I have plenty of pictures to bore you with."

"You won't bore me," I assure her.

As she pulls away, she wears a tooth-filled grin, and while I want her to be happy, I can't help but know it's because of the time she's spent away from Dad.

"Come on. Sit down, champ," Dad says as he tackles me for a hug. "Feels like it's been forever. I'm fine with you walking away from the NFL, but I'm not fine with not seeing you for this long."

He's trying, I can tell, but I know he's not fine. Hard

to blame him either. When he releases me, I observe how he looks completely different from Mom. His eyes are red, like he's on the verge of tears. He looks as tired as he used to get when we'd be out training through the day or when he'd have to wake up before dawn after a busy day at work to haul me across town for a game.

We settle at our table on the restaurant balcony, overlooking the lake. It's a gorgeous view, and Mom practically glows in the afternoon light while Dad looks like the life has been sucked right out of him.

I'm trying not to think too much about it, but the way he keeps eyeing her, it's like he knows the woman he fell in love with all those years ago is getting away from him. And how can I blame her when I don't think I've ever seen her looking this happy since I was a kid.

I ask Mom about her trip, and she displays some photos in her phone for me. From London, she shares Buckingham Palace, Westminster Abbey, and Big Ben. From Paris, the Eiffel Tower, Arc de Triomphe, and the Louvre. Then sites from Vienna, Rome, Barcelona, Lisbon.

"Wow, you didn't get any rest the past month, did you?"

"You have no idea," she says with a laugh. "And this is a gorgeous beach that's about forty miles north of Lisbon." She shows me another photo.

It's taken from farther away, and when I zoom in, I

accidentally swipe to the next image, where Mom stands with a man who's got his arm hooked around her, his hand resting on her hip. The blood in my face drains, and my stomach churns.

"Sounds like it was a great time," Dad says through his teeth. By the frustration in his tone, I can't help wondering if he knows about whoever the hell is in these pictures with Mom.

"Sorry, I guess I swiped," I tell her, and when she sees the picture, her grin softens. And then she looks to Dad in a way that suggests he knows about this. Of course. I'm the only one who doesn't, just like I was the only one who didn't know about the divorce.

"This is Enzo," Mom says.

"Carrie," Dad chimes in. "We agreed not to say anything."

"Well, he's seen now."

It's a simple exchange, but it reminds me of the way they would pick at each other the past few years. The sort of thing I imagine wore them both down.

"I would like to know what's going on," I say as the heat in my chest intensifies. "Or were you both gonna wait and tell me when you decided to have another kid?"

The light in Mom's expression diminishes, and I hate that I did that to her, but I'm also pissed as hell since I'm always the last to know about these things.

"That's not fair," she says.

"None of this is fair," I say through my teeth. "First there was that stuff going on for over a year, and now there are all these other secrets. How long have you even been seeing this guy…Enzo?"

"Can we talk about something else?" Dad asks.

"I *want* to discuss it." My words are harsher than intended, but I can feel the resentment in me mounting.

"If he wants to know…" Mom says.

They start getting into it, back and forth, back and forth. Here I was hoping to enjoy brunch with my parents, tell them about my boyfriend and how amazing he is, and instead, this is what I get? And it reminds me of plenty of tense moments between them. The steady erosion of what was once love.

I sit in silence, feeling this ball of tension radiating through me, steadily growing until it feels like it's so big, it might tear right through me. "Please stop," I spit out, my face red, taking deep breaths as I try to remain calm. I don't know how it came out, though, because they quiet and turn to me with stiff expressions. "How long have you been seeing Enzo?"

"It's been about eight months," she reveals.

Eight months when they've only been separated for a year. It seems fast, but if anything, it assures me that it was over between Mom and Dad long before they agreed to a divorce.

"He's a nice guy," she says. "I've told him all about

you, and he's excited to meet you when he gets a chance. We were thinking about doing a cruise for Christmas. Maybe you could come with us."

"He might want to spend Christmas with me," Dad rushes out.

She searches around uncomfortably. I'm sure she only mentioned Christmas to push through the awkward tension, but it's only amplified it. She must realize that it's too much for me because she says, "We can sort all that out later. We can manage with whatever you want to do."

Even though there are no plans set, between Enzo and this tension about my hypothetical Christmas plans, it's overwhelming. Fortunately, the waiter arrives, as though the universe realizes I need a mental break. I rush through the menu, flustered as my mind swirls. I swear I might throw up. When the waiter finally walks away, I say, "You know, maybe it's too soon to talk about this stuff. Can we put a pin in it?"

"Of course," Dad says.

"Sure, sweetie."

Feels like some mercy knowing they're willing to set it aside, but that can't erase what's going on inside me. And I feel like shit because even though I haven't seen either of them in a month, after that pic on Mom's phone, this awkwardness between us lingers, spoiling what could have been a lovely brunch by the lake.

Fortunately, there are other subjects. Dad catches me up on his job, and I tell them about mine, but I don't tell them about Marty. I care about him so much, but I don't want to share him with them when I'm in a mood.

By the time I head home, I'm stressed as fuck. When I arrive at the apartment, I'm relieved to find my boyfriend sitting on the couch, his MacBook Pro on his lap desk. He glances up, bright-eyed, clearly about to ask me how it went. But his expression shifts in an instant as he picks up on my mood. He sets his lap desk on the coffee table and pushes to his feet.

"Ryan?"

I start to say something, but it catches in my throat.

He moves closer, his arms finding their way around me.

"Fuck," I mutter, batting at my eyes with the backs of my hands.

He doesn't push, gives me time to recover.

Having him here, knowing I can lean on him, means everything. Gives me the strength to finally get it out. "It was hard when they first shared the news, but it still didn't feel real because things were normal. I think a part of me wanted to pretend it wasn't really gonna happen. That they still had time to make up or make things work. Not that that would have happened, but it's something I wanted to believe, but then I saw this picture on her phone with another guy, and it's like my world came crashing down all over again. And next thing, Mom and Dad were already getting into it about who I'd spend Christmas with. I think Mom was just trying to keep things from being awkward, but it reminded me that nothing's ever gonna be the same now."

Marty's quiet, just listens to my pain.

"I'm so sorry, Ry."

His words are reassuring, offer that familiar soothing sensation. He pulls me in for a hug I eagerly accept, and the tears roll down my cheeks.

"I don't know what to do, Mart."

"We'll figure it out."

Of course, I know he's not gonna have some magic answer to fix all this. Nothing can fix what's been broken. I have to accept that now.

30

Marty

RYAN'S BEEN IN a funk since his visit with his parents. He's not the smiley, friendly guy I'm used to seeing, the guy who doesn't give a shit about anything. He's not eating as much. He's quieter. Even his kisses don't feel as sincere. And we definitely haven't been fucking as much.

Not that I expect him to be a fuck-machine all the time now that we're boyfriends, but it only plays on my insecurities. I've tried to give him his space, not push, but I hate how it's eating away at him.

It's the same today, but at least he's taking some of his frustration out on the build, hammering away like he's got a grudge against the roof, while Lance and I toss chunks of debris into the dumpster in the driveway.

It's been a few weeks since we've seen Lance and Ty here, so I'm glad they were able to make some time to help this weekend.

Lance chucks a piece cut off a two-by-four into the

dumpster, then bows forward. "Oh…I think Ty and I might've gone on a little long last night. Really got him to hammer me."

I cringe. "I really would prefer not to think about the two of you fucking."

"What's the point of you being queer if we can't talk about stuff like this? Like, did you ever think that bottoming in missionary would be such a good core workout?"

I have to laugh because it's true and not something I would've considered before fucking around with Ryan, but now I know how well it works the abs, something I can tell some of the people at the pool notice these days.

"Topping apparently works out the glutes more than you'd think too," I observe.

"Not something I'd know anything about," he points out.

He's mentioned he prefers to bottom, but now I have to ask, "So you two never like…trade off?"

He shrugs. "Nah. He's very happy to give me that dick, and I'm happy to give him this ass. Seems to work out. But if he wanted to try, I'd be down to give it a go. I bet I'd be a good top." At my cringe, he says, "Okay, you don't get to ask questions like that and then be grossed out when I answer."

He's got a point there.

"Speaking of knowing too much about each other's

sex lives, you heard from Ash and Colin?"

"Yeah, they're having a blast in Chicago. They keep going out to this place…Steamworks. Sounds like they enjoy it."

"I'm sure a lot of people are enjoying watching them enjoy it."

We share a laugh.

"What about you guys?" he asks. "How's this new relationship thing going?"

The way he drags out the question, I can tell he's pressing cautiously, like he knows something's up. And I doubt I'm hiding it very well. "Why would you ask it like that?"

Lance's brows tug closer together. "Um…A: you're one of my best friends and you seem off. And B: the way you just answered me sounds like you're hiding a body under these boards." He smirks playfully, clearly trying to cheer me up. Not while Ryan's still this on edge. "Is this about the stuff with his parents?" he presses.

Ryan talked to Ty and Lance about his conversation with his parents, but I still feel like talking to Lance about this might be betraying his confidence.

"It's healthy to talk to your friends about stuff that's bothering you," he reminds me. "But if we can't talk about that, I can talk to you about how Ty prefers to fuck me."

His attempt at cheering me up finally cracks through

my armor. "I'll pass on the latter. And as for Ryan, it's been rough for him. I honestly don't know how to cheer him up. He's in a lot of pain, and it's hard to see, you know?"

We glance over at Ryan, still hammering away on the roof. Seems like Dax is trying to tell him a joke, but Ryan forces a halfhearted smile. Such a simple thing, but it tears at my fucking soul.

Ryan finishes up on the panel he's nailing into the frame before moving on to the other side of the roof, out of sight.

Lance turns to me with a sympathetic expression. "He just needs some time."

I know, but saying that to myself a million times isn't going to get rid of the anxiety that's all twisted up inside me.

"He'll be fine," I say, surely sounding as fake as Ryan looked when he smiled at Dax. "Anyway, we're heading over to see my parents after this. You and Ty wanna join us?"

"Aw, we already made plans with my parents tonight, but give me a heads-up next time, and we'll make sure of it."

I'm relieved to hear him say that because even though we've graduated, I wanna keep hanging with my guys.

Lance and I finish up with the debris in the wheelbarrow, and we're about to start back to the house to help the other guys when a loud *clang* fills the air, followed by, "Holy fuck!" from Ryan.

A primal instinct kicks in, and one moment I'm standing next to Lance, and the next I'm running, searching for Ryan. I can't get a good view of him yet, but I hear him grunting. He's hurt. The walk around the house, to the ladder, feels like an eternity.

"Ry?" I call out for the tenth time to no response.

I finally reach the ladder and climb up. He's surrounded by the guys, even Miles, whose face is locked in a concerned expression. And it sure as fuck can't be good if that guy gives a flying fuck about what happened to my boyfriend.

"Ry?"

The other volunteers move out of the way so I can see him. He's on his ass, Atlas on his knees at his side. Ry's face is tense as he grits his teeth. He grips his hand, his thumb red and swollen.

"Okay," Atlas says, "let's get you off the roof and get some ice on this. Come on."

"Jesus fucking Christ," Ryan says through his teeth before hissing.

And all I care about is making sure he's okay.

SINCE HE CAN'T use his hand, it takes a little time to get Ryan off the roof, but we manage. Then Troy takes us to the nearest urgent care, where they assess the damage and tend to his injury—a hairline fracture, which they set in a splint. I don't leave his side the entire time, and finally we're alone again in the patient room, since Troy's calling Atlas to assure him everything's okay.

"How's the pain?" I stand beside the examination table where he sits.

He huffs. "This really was too much drama. I've had less care after having ten two-hundred-plus-pound guys stacked on top of me." He says that in a particularly frustrated tone before glancing at me. He assesses my expression, then takes a breath. "But it's better. Thank you for caring." He takes my hand with his good one. "Sorry, Mart. I'm just frustrated with myself. I should have been paying attention. I was…" He trails off, but I know what's been distressing him.

His eyes bulge. "Wait. What time is it?"

"What?"

"We were supposed to meet up with your family."

After what happened, it totally slipped my mind, and I haven't been keeping track of the time. As I'm pulling out my phone, I tell him, "Don't worry. I'll call and let them know that's not happening. I would rather stay at home with you anyway."

"Don't do that, Mart. Go hang with your parents.

Honestly, I could use some time to myself."

His words catch me by surprise, and I tense up.

Time to himself?

Since we started messing around, the only times we haven't been around each other have been when we were working, and even during my shift, I was absorbed with thinking how great it was gonna be when I got off so I could…well, get off. Sure, we spend time with our friends and family, but outside of that, we're practically on top of each other.

He must notice how uneasy I am because he says, "I'm not saying I need time away *from* you. I…"

But I don't know how else to take it, and my anxiety-prone mind's already spinning with theories. Have I spent too much time with him? Is he getting bored with me already? Now that he's seen his parents' relationship implode, is he thinking we might not work out either and it's not worth it?

Ryan releases my hand and rests his hand against my cheek, caressing with his thumb. So gentle, so reassuring.

"Hey," he says, like he's trying to pull me out of my head. "This is not the part where you get all anxious and insecure thinking I'm gonna break up with you over the shit I'm going through."

"Why did you have to use the B-word, then?" I spit out.

He sighs. "Because I may not have been your boyfriend for long, but I know how you get all twisted up in that sexy head of yours…and I'm not going to let you have a moment where you think any of this stuff is coming between us. Got it?"

That cuts through my fear before I've had a chance to sit with it for long, and I appreciate that he understands my anxiety enough to make sure my mind doesn't go there. Of course, it will anyway, but it was thoughtful of him to give it his best effort.

Ry moves in quickly for a kiss, and I hadn't realized just how much I needed one until I feel his lips against mine, releasing me from all that hot tension that rose up after he got injured.

It's the sort of kiss that makes it easier to remind myself: He's fine. We're fine.

The past few days, we haven't kissed like this. They've felt forced, like he was going through the motions, trying to say things are fine when they're not. But this one offers me assurance that despite wanting some space, he still cares about me.

When he pulls away, he says, "So…this is not an I'm-so-frustrated-and-confused-about-us moment. This is an I care about you. I want you in my life. And I-could-use-a-night-to-sulk moment."

I get that. But I hate it too. Not for myself, but because he has a reason to sulk. And because there's nothing I can do to cheer him up.

"We'll get back to the apartment," he says, "and then you go spend time with your family. I'll probably order in, and when you get back, we'll cuddle the fuck out of each other. How's that?"

Another assurance that any concern I may have is ridiculous.

"That sounds good," I lie because really, all I want is to be here for him right now, especially with how worked up I got over his injury.

But maybe he's right. He does need some space. Since that uncomfortable conversation with his parents, he hasn't had a chance to sit with it on his own. Maybe it'll be good for him.

Then why doesn't that make me feel any better?

31

Marty

I TELL MOM, Dad, and Aiden about Ryan's injury and why he couldn't make it to dinner, assuring them he'll be fine. But it's evident they can tell something's off, that I'm not myself, which sucks because now they're probably worrying about me the way I've been worrying about Ryan since he found out his mom was seeing someone new.

I catch them up about what's been going on otherwise, and after dinner, Aiden insists I throw the ball around with him out back.

"This is why I wanted Ryan to come over," Aiden gripes. "I need a real throw, give me some distance."

"Fuck, Aiden, I'm giving it the best I can."

He backs up much farther. "If you don't make it, you have to stay out here for another thirty minutes."

As much as today sucks, it's nice being back to the way things were when we were kids.

"It's not even gonna be light out then!" I call to him.

"So it's really gonna suck, isn't it? Just give it to me."

I put my all into the next throw, tossing a ball I wish we could have recorded for Ryan. It's even got that perfect spin on it that Aiden taught me how to do. He catches it like it's nothing, hamming it up like it was such a breeze, though I know he's just as impressed with himself.

"There we go!" he calls out. "You'll do anything to get out of a good time, right?"

I can't stifle my laugh as he hurries toward me. I meet him halfway, and as I notice the sweat on his brow, I realize I'm sweating too.

"That was pretty good, right?" I ask.

He cocks a brow. "Eh, it was aight."

"Whatever." I nudge his chair, and he smirks.

We head over to the pool deck, where I settle on the swinging chair, and he pulls up beside me.

"So…" he drags out. "Now you gonna tell me what's up?"

"Huh?" I'm hoping I can bluff my way out of this one, but his glare suggests it's not gonna work.

"Don't play with your brother. I know you better than anyone."

"I told you Ryan got hurt today."

His glare intensifies. "Yeah, you're real worried about your linebacker boyfriend's boo-boo on his thumb. I'm sure."

Fuck, I'm not getting out of this one.

"He's not a linebacker anymore." I'm trying to deflect, but Aiden isn't having it.

"Well, let me know how that bottling it all up and letting it eat you alive is working for you."

He can't realize, but that really strikes a nerve since I know it's what Ryan's doing, and it definitely isn't working for him.

"This have anything to do with his parents getting a divorce?" he presses.

I take a breath. "He got some more news from his mom." I leave it at that. Even though I don't feel like Ryan would be upset about my sharing this with my bro, I don't feel it's my news to share. "It was a lot, and it's catching up with him how much things are gonna change for his family. And he has all this other stuff going on too. He's not playing football anymore, which used to be how he worked out stress. That path was pretty set for him, and he's like…what does the future look like? On top of that, we aren't seeing all our friends, and our lives are changing completely." Just saying it makes my anxiety flare up, twisting in my chest.

"Sounds tough," Aiden says, and he's not being jokey or playful—a rare thing for him. "I get it since I'm feeling similarly about high school. I'm gonna be heading off to Peach State next year, and everything will be changing from here on."

"Yeah...and I keep trying to think of a way to reach him, to help him, but I can't think of anything right to say, or what to do to make this better. Like...it's not the kind of thing you can make better."

"Trust me, I know what that's like too."

My chest constricts even more. I wasn't considering what I was saying, and given Aiden's sorrowful expression, I know he's thinking about the other thing I couldn't change. That no one could change after his accident.

"I'm so sorry." Tears stir in my eyes. Because like I told Ryan, deep down I feel this is something I've done to him.

"You have nothing to be sorry about, Mart."

I try to keep it down like I always do, but the stress of everything that's happening, my worry about Ryan, makes it bubble to the surface. "I should have been there."

His forehead creases. "It's just a shitty thing that happened." He says it so matter-of-factly, like it's never even crossed his mind.

"I would have made sure you didn't get on that ATV." As soon as I get the words out, I fucking lose it. The tears break free, rolling down my cheeks.

It's all too much. My powerlessness against what's going on with Ryan has prodded something so dark within me, this guilt I carry over the past. "I'm so sorry,"

I blurt out, my words barely audible with how much my voice cracks as I bow my head to keep him from seeing his big bro crumbling like this.

I don't know how I'm expecting him to respond, but suddenly, his hand is on my shoulder. "Hey, you," he says, the way Dad used to whenever we would get worked up like this, and it pulls me out of my dark thoughts long enough to look his way.

I'm expecting to see judgment, to see this side that's always blamed me, that maybe that's why he hasn't spent as much time with me this past year, but his expression is soft, sympathetic.

"It took me a long time not to blame myself even," he says. "But we were kids. Plenty of kids do dangerous things, and nothing ever happens to them. Everything that's happened to me has made me realize how deeply unfair life is…and you know what? It is unfair, and I don't give a fuck that it's unfair because that's not gonna keep me from doing all the things I want to do. It's changed things for me, but as you can see, I'm perfectly capable of living a fulfilling, meaningful life. Just different than we thought it would be."

I snicker uneasily. "That's the Aideniest thing you could have said."

His lips curl into his dimples. "I don't blame myself for an accident. I don't blame our cousins. So I sure as hell don't blame you."

"Yeah, well, I'm not gonna magically shake away the guilt anytime soon."

"I can't do much about that in a quick chat, but I know what I can do."

I can't tell where he's going with that.

"Do you remember *after* the accident? When I finally got back from the hospital, you, Mom, and Dad were all over me. Taking care of whatever I needed. Getting me to specialists and helping me get around town. You were basically my personal servant for a while there, and I needed it because I was in such a dark headspace. Wasn't ready to deal with the fact that this could be my forever."

I remember it all too well. The despair. The depression. It was hard, not only because of what happened, but because of how difficult it was to see the light in his eyes fade to the point where I thought I might never see the real him again…or at least the version of him I'd known up until that point.

Although, I don't get why he's bringing it up now.

"I knew if I let you," he says, "you would have been there like that for the rest of my life."

"If you said you wanted me to do it again, I would. You know that, right?" I don't ever want him to question that. Ever feel like he needed to do this on his own.

He grins, a warm glint in his eyes. "I've got a good big bro, but one day you were getting dinner ready for me because Mom and Dad were on vacation, and it really locked in for me. That I would never get to really live. Maybe I'd have fewer struggles, but I'd also never have success or accomplishments…or anything to enjoy again. That wasn't the life I wanted. I wanted to be my own person. I still had dreams. You had your own dreams, and I know I was hard on you because you wouldn't leave me alone right away, but it was the right thing to do…to push you away."

Even hearing him talk about how he pushed me away breaks my heart because all I wanted was to be there for him, to take care of any issue he might have.

"Clearly, you were right," I confess. "Now you're killing it and making it all look so easy."

"It's not easy, that's for sure. Some days I do fucking hate it because I can't not compare myself to my friends, but then some days, I can appreciate aspects of it all." He grips my shoulder tighter. "But all that aside, you know what made it easier to do all this? Having you as my bro."

I'm not following, especially since the whole point of his story was to remind me of when he pushed me away. Surely, my confusion's written all over my face since he adds, "It was scary, Mart. And I didn't know how things were going to work out, but I knew I was gonna be okay because, even if something happened, even if I couldn't figure it all out on my own, I had someone who would catch me when I fell. No matter what happened, you'd be right there."

I'm shocked to hear that because he sure as hell never talked like this when we were younger.

"Knowing you had my back made me fearless."

Relief washes through me. Assurance that he really gets how much I love him. That I would have done anything in the world for him.

"I'm glad you know that, but sometimes I wish you needed me more."

He angles his head, issuing a glare so much like my own. Must be genetic.

"You're missing the point, Mart. You can't fix some things, and sometimes the most you can do is be there for someone when they're having a hard time. Because knowing I wasn't alone at the hardest time in my life was what was important." And it hits me like a brick before he says, "I know it sucks that you can't magically fix Ryan's problems, but being there for him is enough. It's always been enough."

A warm sensation stirs in my chest where all that tension had been bundled up, partly because I'm so touched by what he shared, and partly because I know that's something I can do for Ryan right now. What I must do for him.

"Now give your little brother a hug, and then let's go inside and I'll give you hell like this conversation never happened."

I chuckle as his sense of humor cuts right through the seriousness of the moment. I give him a big hug, holding him close, appreciating the warmth of his hold, remembering times when we used to hug like this.

"You're a really great guy, Aiden."

"I know I am," he says in a conceited way that gets me laughing.

"You'd make a good Alpha Theta Mu."

"Actually, I'm too cool for them. I was planning to pledge Sigma Alpha."

The fuck?

I pull away, giving him a nasty look, and he laughs.

"Sorry, I shouldn't have made a joke while you're all vulnerable like this. You know I'm Alpha Theta Mu, just like my big bro."

"Damn right you are."

"Gotta get to the frat, show all those guys that there's at least one cool guy in this family."

"You little prick."

He grins, and as much as I may have helped him by being there for him when he was younger, it's nice having this moment where he's doing that for me.

"You really like him, don't you?" he says.

Like? That doesn't even cover it. Not even a little.

"It's much more than that," I confess.

Because I think I might be in love with him.

32

Ryan

SITTING ON THE couch at Dax's apartment, I scroll through old pics and videos on Instagram.

Mom, Dad, and me at the Grand Canyon.

Six Flags.

Universal Studios.

Westminster Abbey.

I search through these reminders of our past, analyzing my parents' expressions, scrutinizing every one to see if I can tell when things went so wrong that they couldn't be fixed.

I settle on a video from a hike in Cape Town. Well, Dad told Mom it would be a hike, but it became more like a climb, which annoyed the hell out of her because she wasn't wearing the shoes for it. But as I watch the video of us, celebrating reaching the top of the mountain, she's smiling as much as ever. She and Dad kiss behind me as I hold my phone, keeping us all in the frame. *"Get a room,"* I tease them before the video comes to an end.

I scroll back in my profile feed. We look happy, but maybe I'm wrong. Maybe things weren't working for even longer than they've shared with me. After all, they've been keeping this secret. It's hard to tell when they started hiding their drifting apart.

I want to go back to the way things were, yet I also wouldn't want them to do that if it meant Mom wouldn't have that bright smile on her face again.

This sucks.

And something about this internal turmoil makes pain flare in my goddamn thumb, which is still giving me hell. To think that working out the stress on the builds was really helping me, and then I went and fucked it up by hurting myself. And now, as I'm sitting here, alone, I'm regretting letting Marty go to his parents' place without me because I want to be with him.

He was so good when I got injured. Taking me to urgent care, right at my side. Just like he's been through all this shit since I found out about Mom's new boy-friend. Or really, not so new.

What I hate most about this is I've put up a wall. I know he feels it too, but it's not about him. It's this part of me that fears, if the two people I was most open with about my life can wind up doing something that hurts like this, then why let anybody in? And that makes me hate myself even more because if anyone has shown me that I can be vulnerable with him, it's Mart.

I grab a bag of peas from the freezer to soothe my thumb, and as I wrap it up, the doorknob rattles. Relief pulses through me, but when the door opens, it's Dax.

"Oh…" I can't help the disappointment in my tone.

"Ouch." He presses his hand to his heart, as though signifying the figurative bullet he just took.

"Sorry. I thought it'd be…"

"I'm offended, not stupid. And really not *that* offended. I get it. How's the thumb?"

I head into the living area. "Doesn't feel like it's about to fall off anymore."

"Well, that's progress. Troy caught us up on the urgent care visit. Glad you're doing okay. Where's Mart? Getting food? You think if I text him, he can grab me something?"

As he plops down on the couch, I tell him, "He went to his parents'. I insisted. I just…needed some space."

"Considering how eager you looked when I came in, I'd say you wished he was here right now."

"Anyone accuse you of being too perceptive?" I joke, since that seems to be his thing.

"Sometimes," he says in this cocky but charming way he has.

Maybe it's his cool attitude or the fact that he's always easy to talk to. Or maybe I just need to get this out of my system, because I go for it. "I've got a lot going on with my parents, and it feels like being buried under a dogpile right now. It's hard because I care about Marty so much, but I hate that he knows how much this is hitting me. Makes me feel like I'm ruining his summer."

His brows tug together. "Okay, you're worried *you* might be ruining Marty's summer? I'm sure most people would assume it'd be the opposite."

"Hey, he's more fun than any of you give him credit for." I'm surprised by how defensive that comes out, and the way Dax's eyes widen, he is too.

"You know that was a joke, right? You used to be good at those. And also, you were the one who always gave Marty hell about his attitude. The rest of us knew he was cool."

Now I feel guilty for snapping at my friend. "I know, sorry." I settle beside him on the couch. "Between life and my thumb, I'm in a grumpy mood."

Dax angles his head, giving me a pointed look like he knows something I don't. "Is that what you really think it is?"

"What do you mean?"

"You think you jumped all over me when I said that about Marty because you're in a mood?"

"What else would it be?"

I take a moment to work out if I missed something, and he grins.

"Oh, wow…" he drags out. "You really can be oblivious sometimes."

I guess I am because I don't know what the fuck he's on about, maybe because my brain's so scrambled with all this other crap.

"You want to play a video game?" he asks before noticing my hand. "Oops. Right. Maybe a movie?"

I'm surprised by how quickly he changed the subject, but given that moping about isn't doing much for me, maybe it's not a bad idea to chill with a buddy. "I'd like that."

"Cool. You mind if I shower up first? Still smell like sweat and work, and not in the fun, sexy way."

I chuckle. "Yeah, go for it."

He hops up and heads to the bathroom.

I rewatch the last video I pulled up from my vacation with my parents. There's still that sting in my chest, like a knife digging into my heart. I force myself to set my phone on the side table, when there's another rattle at the door.

This time it has to be Mart.

I guess it could be a burglar, but it's probably Mart.

The door opens, and he heads in. Funny how something as simple as seeing my boyfriend sends a rush of adrenaline right through me, like scoring a touchdown. I want to push to my feet and rush to him, but that mental heaviness keeps me from having the strength to stand. Like a part of me is forcing me to stay on this side of that figurative wall.

"Hey," I manage.

As I adjust the peas on my thumb, I notice Marty's eyeing me strangely. He has a hand behind his back, like he's hiding something.

"What is it?" I ask.

He closes the door behind him, licking his lips. "I got you something on my way back," he reveals, and my first thought is to wonder if I've missed some kind of anniversary, but of course, we haven't been together that long. "It's nothing major. Just…" He starts toward me, presenting this secret item—a protein bar. And not just any protein bar, but my favorite—the peanut butter and chocolate one I was notorious for borrowing from Payton whenever I'd run low. "I was hoping to come back with a whole box of them, but you were right about them being hard to get in the store. I stopped by, like, four before I found one."

The heaviness weighing me down lifts, like the guys steadily leaving the dogpile. I set the peas aside and push to my feet, approaching him as he fiddles with the bar, which looks a little dented.

"It was the last one, and it's not in great shape. I was debating whether to even give it to you, but…I wanted to get you something to cheer you up." He holds the bar out, looking so shy about it.

I take it and study the glistening wrapping. It's only a

protein bar. Such a simple gesture. But it's not. It's a testament to the kind of guy Marty is—always has been. The guy who notices the little things. Who in a moment, when I was at my lowest, wanted to do something to cheer me up. The guy who's been surprising the shit out of me since we both let our guard down with one another.

Now my eyes are welling with tears. Fucking tears.

"Ry?" He puts his arm around me, sliding his hand along the small of my back. The ease it elicits is enough to subdue the stinging in my thumb. "Is everything okay?"

He's so caring. So thoughtful. And he can't realize what such a simple gesture means to me.

Wrapping my arms around him, I draw him close, feeling the full reassurance of his hold, appreciating it more than I ever have before, when a realization hits me.

Now I know what Dax was giving me hell about when he said I was oblivious. I wasn't just jumping down his throat when I thought he was insulting Marty. I care about this guy so fucking much…but it's more than that. And it took a fucking protein bar to figure out just how much. And why I've been pushing him away.

I pull back, looking into his beautiful green eyes. "Mart, I'm sorry I've been keeping you at a distance. I've never felt like this for anyone before, and with everything going on with my parents, I've been scared to let someone else in, trust them when I know how much it could hurt if they betrayed me."

"I can understand that," he says, sounding so much more empathetic than I ever would have guessed during our initial animosity.

"I want to get through this, though," I tell him. "I don't want this shit to stand in the way of what we have. Because I love you." I say that without hesitation, and as the words pass my lips, I know their truth. "Like…in love with you *love you*."

My heart swells as he smiles.

"I love you too, Ry."

There was relief in revealing it to him, but even more when he said it back. It's hard to believe this is real, but I'm too appreciative to question it. I pull him against my chest, keeping him close, enjoying how these sensations are so much better than the ones I was struggling with while he was visiting his family.

I kiss the side of his face, then make my way to his mouth. I've kissed this guy so many times, I know how it feels, but our confession has deepened the sensation, and I worship his lips and tongue for all the pleasure they have to offer.

"I want you," I whisper. "I need you, Mart."

"I'm right here," he assures me, meaning so much more than right now.

And as long as I have my guy with me, I know I'll be okay.

33

Marty

IT'S WILD TO think about how this all started.

From annoying the hell out of each other, to fucking, to exchanging *I-love-yous*.

On my way back to the apartment, I knew I'd wind up confessing my feelings for him, so it was a shock to hear him say those words first. Maybe he's not the only one who can be an oblivious fuck sometimes.

There's no question or doubt in my mind. I love this man.

We make our way to the couch. Ryan's always been skilled, but all that talent is on full display once we're out of our clothes. He scoops me up by my thighs and rests me on my back on the sofa cushions. His mouth travels down my throat, probing and exploring like this is the first time he's ever tasted my flesh. I roll my head back and moan, fully embracing the moment, reveling in how my nerves still perk up when they feel his warm, wet tongue grazing across my skin.

Suddenly he groans, which is hot as fuck until he whispers, "Dax is still here."

Fuck.

He pulls away and eyes the hall. "Let me put the door hanger up in the bathroom so we don't get interrupted."

Technically, we've already been interrupted, but I bite my tongue as he hops up, his fully hard cock shaking about with his swole muscles as he rushes to give our friend a fair warning, and as he returns in a jog, I'm sort of annoyed.

"Look who's gotten better about the rules."

"Just worried he might try to join in." He winks before grabbing lube from the duffel bag by the couch. "Now...where the fuck...were we?" he asks between kisses.

I don't even hear him pump the lube before I feel his slick cock against my crack, and he's pushing in steadily, my body welcoming him. All the tension and uneasiness of the past week fade as he glides into me. This is so much easier than that first fuck—as though all this time we've been fucking has been to train my ass to take him.

He hits that familiar spot, the one he first introduced me to, the one he's pleasured for me so many times since we first realized the power of this chemistry between us. My body bursts with excitement, my nerves hypersensitive to the touch, making each tongue-filled kiss, each caress of his hand that much more satisfying. As he thrusts, he leans back, gazing down at me, and I bask in the attention from his blue eyes as he looks more exposed than ever before. It's not only his body that's naked, but his soul too, like he knows I see all the pain he's going through, and he's not hiding any of it from me. Trusting me with this part of him. There's something so satisfying about sharing this moment with him, knowing for at least this time, I'm able to pull him from the darkness looming over him.

He rests his hand against the side of my face, trailing his thumb across my cheek as he offers some more thrusts. As stressed as I've been the past week, I find it so easy to let go and embrace everything he gives me.

"Never thought this ass would be giving you so much pleasure, did you?" I ask.

"Just like you never thought you'd be hungry for my dick."

With another thrust, I arch my back as sensations pool through me. "Jesus Christ, Ry," I say, moaning.

He moves closer, offering a few more kisses before he whispers, "Do you want me to come inside you?"

"Yes."

"Beg for it."

"Please," I say immediately, since I'm not above begging.

He growls. "Now that we've said I love you, you

know when I come inside you, that means you're all mine."

Heat builds in my face as this powerful urgency overtakes me. I grip his ass, pulling him with each thrust, encouraging his hard work. I want to be all his. "Is that what it means?" I ask. "So when I come in you next time, you're all mine."

He hesitates, though I notice he's smirking as he says, "Nah. You already got me."

Before I can tell him he clearly already has me too, his lips mash down against mine and he really fucks me good. My body trembles as his quick pace sends spirals of sensation through me, forcing moans past my lips. Considering we haven't messed around much lately, it's such a beautiful reminder of how good it feels when we share moments like these. Of why my body was struggling so much without it.

I'm so accustomed to his movements now, it's easy to tell when he's close, and I know how he is about wanting me to come first, so I tell him, "Do it, Ryan. Come inside me."

"But you need to come too."

"I want to come after you mark me."

His smile curls against my face before he leans back, hooking his arms in the crooks of my legs. His muscles expand and contract as he offers slow, deliberate pumps, the pumps of a man who knows how to satisfy me. He bites his bottom lip and frees one of his arms, positioning his hand behind my neck to keep me in place as he continues his work, gazing into my eyes until his expression twists up in that familiar way.

"I'm coming," he warns. "I'm fucking coming."

A quick series of thrusts lets me know we've reached the end and he's filling me up. And with one more thrust, it's too much for me. As that intense urgency takes over, I reach out, gripping the sides of the couch to keep my hands from reaching down to my cock, but he slows his movements.

"Not quite yet," he warns.

Fuck him and his goddamn edging.

"I'm right there," I tell him, sneaking a peek and seeing his wicked expression. My body trembles, alive with sensation, trapped in this suspended bliss that feels so electric, it might kill me.

"Almost," Ryan whispers as he strokes my abs, which twitch at his touch. "You like how I've learned your body so well that I know exactly how to work it?"

"Please, Ry…"

I feel everything. His palm. Each breath I take. The sweat gliding down the side of my face. Every nerve in my goddamn body is ready to erupt when he forces in again, moving in quick succession. The urgency shifts to an explosive release, and I moan as the warmth rushes across my abs, up to my chest.

"Holy fuck," Ryan mutters as another rush pushes out, settling near my navel. He doesn't let up, hitting that tender spot until I'm empty, like he's making up for delaying my release. His expression is lit up, his smile back as he seems to marvel at what he can do to me.

And it's everything. I'm high, delirious with pleasure.

He strokes my abs, and when I look at him, he's scooping some of my cum with his thumb, raising it to his face for a quick taste. "Mmm." He leans down, close to me. "Tastes better when you're mine."

I can't help laughing, and a shift of his cock against my prostate sends another powerful sensation through me. I roll my eyes back, moaning.

"I like this expression much better than the glares," he teases, making me laugh.

Then we lock gazes before he moves close, nuzzling his nose against mine.

"I'll be okay, Mart," he whispers, and it sounds like a promise. For the first time since all this stuff with his parents came up, I really believe it.

We exchange another kiss before there's a knock from farther back in the apartment. Dax's muffled voice comes from the bathroom. "Uh…I don't want to ruin anything, but you guys finished? I'm really hungry, and I'd like to get into some clean clothes."

Dax couldn't have had better timing, and Ryan and I burst into a fit of laughs, his cock still buried inside me.

He slides his arms under mine, tugging me close.

"What do you say? Wanna get some dinner with Dax, I'll watch you both play video games, then maybe recreate this once he gets to bed?"

"Depends," I say, playing coy. "We gonna put on a movie?"

He winces. "Okay, but no horror right before bed."

We snicker again before there's another knock from the bathroom. "Uh…guys?"

"Yeah, we're good," Ryan calls out.

"Ry, you're still inside me," I remind him, since apparently he's forgotten we're naked and he's still got his cock against my prostate.

"Oh fuck. One minute!"

That really gets me laughing. "I can't believe you just did that."

"Well, at least you know I'm still the same old oblivious Ryan. Who really doesn't want to pull out right now." He pouts.

And honestly, I don't want him to take his cock out either.

He presses some of his weight against me, then nestles his face against my cheek, offering the gentlest of kisses.

It's a moment that's so perfect. A moment I want to keep him in for as long as I can before real life intrudes again. I wrap my arms around him, keeping him close.

Stealing a few more seconds, but knowing this is really only the beginning of many more sweet moments with Ryan, who hasn't just claimed my body, but my heart.

34

Ryan

A WEEK AFTER my thumb injury, I pull up to the driveway of my parents' place. I asked if they could meet me at the house, though from what I gather, Mom isn't staying there anymore.

As I park alongside the curb, Marty glances over from the passenger seat. "You sure you want me to come in with you right away?"

He's giving me one last chance to bail.

"Why? You worried they're not gonna like you?"

"You know damn well that's not what I'm worried about."

"Maybe you should start worrying."

Marty enjoys a laugh before resting his hand on my thigh, offering a gentle rub. As the knot in my gut loosens, I rest my hand on top of his.

"How do you do that?" I ask him.

"What?"

"How does the most anxiety-prone guy in Alpha

Theta Mu know how to set me right at ease?"

"Not the most anxiety-prone guy in Alpha Theta Mu anymore. I mean, not technically."

He got me there.

"Well, I want *this* anxiety-ridden guy to come with me," I assure him. As much as I struggled with the news of Mom seeing a guy, I know it's time to have this conversation. "I want them to meet you. You're my guy now, and I'm tired of secrets. We've all been keeping too many of those."

"Okay," he says, "but should we have a code word in case things get awkward and I need to bail?"

"What kind of conversation do you think this is gonna be?"

He shrugs. "I don't know. I haven't met them yet."

"It'll be great."

Not only because I expect my parents will be fine with me having a boyfriend, but because I know, no matter what happens in there, I have him. It reassures me that however this evening goes, things will be just fine. It's something I've really let sink in since Marty bought me that silly protein bar. Since I realized this is my guy.

"How about…Xenomorph?" he asks.

"Huh?"

"For the code word in case things get awkward. It's not likely to come up on its own."

I chuckle. "Sure, why not?" It's a funny word to use,

but it does make what we're about to do feel less heavy.

I brace myself, and we get out of my car, head up the drive together. He doesn't seem to know what to do with his hands. Keeps them in his pockets one second, pulls them out the next, scratches at his shoulders. I've learned this is one of the ways he shows he's uncomfortable. And I love noticing little things like that about him. Things I've picked up because of how much time we spend together, and I'm sure he's noticed similar things about me. I move close, resting my hand on the small of his back, and he seems to relax.

When we reach the door, I key in the code and head inside. "Knock, knock," I say to announce our entrance.

Some shuffling comes from the kitchen before my parents appear, greeting us in the short hall to the foyer. Their eyes go right to Marty.

I told them I was bringing someone with me but didn't qualify it, and they didn't ask. Maybe they just think I brought a mediator with me.

"Marty, this is my dad and my mom. Mom and Dad, this is my boyfriend."

No hesitation. No awkward pause. Only me claiming my guy with my parents.

Marty's lips curl upward, like he's pleased I don't have an ounce of uneasiness about letting them know whom he belongs to.

Mom's jaw drops as Dad tilts his head. They stand

there stunned, and Marty rubs a hand against his arm. "Nice to meet you," he says with wide eyes and a smile.

Mom snaps out of her daze first. "Yes, wonderful." When he extends his hand for a shake, Mom says, "If you do hugs, you might as well start now."

He breathes a sigh of relief. "I'm fine with that."

"But make sure you have one for me too," Dad adds, making eye contact with me, grinning in a way that assures me he's cool. I never imagined my parents would be dicks about this, but it's still a relief because fuck, that would have been awkward if his parents had been cool and mine had been a bunch of d-bags.

With the introductions out of the way, I say, "I wanted to bring him here because I wished I'd introduced him to you both sooner, but also because we all need to start sharing more about what's going on in our lives. Mom, if you have a guy you're seeing, I don't want you to feel like you have to hide that. But I don't like the fact that I was the last to know everything. I'm not saying I want a blow by blow of the divorce proceedings, but I do want my parents to be my parents and to be a part of my life, whatever that looks like now."

Their frowns suggest their sorrow about everything that's happened, which makes me feel like crap. "I'm not saying I blame you. It was a tricky thing to navigate, but now that things are out in the open, can we make an effort to be more transparent? And no more surprises, at least for a while?"

They exchange a look. "We can do that," Mom says. "We're sorry. We know this must have been a lot. It's been a lot for us too."

"Now, come on in," Dad says. "The delivery guy brought extra meatballs. So I hope you came with an appetite, Mart. I can call you Mart, right?"

"Sure thing, and I love meatballs," Marty replies.

"And I brought over a trivia game," Mom adds. "So I hope you like games."

"Oh, not a game," I groan.

That's my mom for you.

"Can you just let me know whose team to be on so I can beat him?" Marty asks. "This is one of the few things I think I could win against him with, and I want to really impress my boyfriend."

He sneaks me a look as they burst into a laugh, cutting through any lingering tension.

"You stick with me when it comes to trivia," Mom says, guiding him into the kitchen, and Dad sidles up beside me. "I like him already, champ." He hooks his arm around me, tugging me close, as though to remind me he's my dad and he cares.

We enjoy dinner, then play trivia, with Mom and Marty stomping Dad and me out. When Mom and Marty get to chatting about her trip to Europe, Dad invites me to go out on the back porch with him.

"You're full of surprises this year, aren't you?" he says. "I'm just happy my son's happy, you know that, right?"

It's not only his words, but his gentle expression that tells me the same.

"That means a lot to me, Dad."

"I shouldn't have pressured you so much. I did really want you to go pro, partly because I couldn't make the cut. But I never wanted it at the expense of your happiness."

"I knew that would be how you felt. I hesitated because I didn't want you to feel like all those years and that money went down the drain. Like I wasted your time. Because I did want it, really bad. But things change."

His gaze shifts, and he looks out to the yard. "Speaking of things changing, it's time for a confession. I did pressure your mom to keep these secrets—the divorce and Enzo—so please don't put any of that on her. When we first told you, I didn't mean to be so obvious about not wanting this. Just…the way it all played out, and I couldn't keep my mouth shut, but I do think you should keep in mind that since we agreed to this, your mom's been really happy. I mean, happy in a way I've never seen her before, which also makes this hard for me."

It's a tough thing to hear, and I can see the heartbreak as his lip twists down, a deep sadness in his eyes.

"But," he adds, "just because I wish things had been different doesn't mean I don't want that happiness for her. Knowing she fell out of love, it's better this way, even if it's hard. I don't want anything I've said or done to make you feel any way about her or us other than we had a beautiful marriage together. We were lucky enough to have an amazing kid, and it breaks my heart that you would think I would see all the time and money I spent on football with you as a waste."

This catches me by surprise.

"A waste of what?" he says. "How many dads can say they spent that much time with their kid? That we'd even happen to have a similar interest that would allow us to share that time? I got to see every game and every practice. I got to coach when you were a kid. I got to practice with you. I will *never* see a moment of that as a waste."

He tears up, and now he's got me all choked up, really appreciating all that time we had together. Both my parents knew how much it meant to me, and they moved heaven and earth every time an emergency or schedule change came up so that I wouldn't miss any of it.

"I love you, champ. And in the same way that I want your mom to be happy, if football isn't what makes you happy anymore, then you have to move on with your life, regardless of the dreams your dad was living out through you. You get that?"

Now he's got my eyes watering.

Dammit.

"Sorry, I didn't mean to get all emotional like this." He pats my shoulder.

"It's good. It's been an emotional year. And a lot of surprises, clearly." I indicate Marty through the French doors.

Dad glances at him and then back at me. "Speaking of your new man, I do wonder about this thing they say about queer people and genetics."

Given what we've been talking about, this one really throws me. "Huh?"

"Something I've been thinking about myself recently too. Before your mother, there was a guy in college…and we had some fun. I don't know."

Now I'm the one stunned into silence. Dad messed around with a guy in college?

"Wait, what?" Questions race through my brain. "How much did you mess around with this guy in college?"

His gaze wanders. "Maybe six or seven months. Just fun stuff."

"Oh my God." I can't believe I'm only hearing about this now, but also, guess it's not the kind of thing to tell your kid either.

"I'm only telling you because I might be keeping my

options open now that I'm a single man. I've been thinking about downloading one of those apps…"

"Gross. You're not supposed to say that to your son."

"I thought I was supposed to be more honest."

By the wicked glint in his gaze, he knew damn well what he was doing, but it's definitely nice that he felt comfortable enough to share that part of himself with me. And it makes me even happier that I brought Marty over tonight.

He pulls me in for a hug. "I love you, kid. Nothing will ever change that. And when I do stupid things, just give me a kick in the ass."

"Won't, now that I know you might like it."

We share another laugh before he says, "Come on. Let's go spend some time with your man."

We head back inside, and I settle beside Marty, resting my hand on his thigh. As he looks at me with that tender expression, the relief I'm feeling about tonight, and the conversation I had with Dad assure me that even though things might be messy for a while, I'm gonna be okay.

EPILOGUE

Marty

Late summer

"SHOTS, SHOTS, SHOTS!" Jaxon shouts, raising his shot glass high.

Colin, Ash, Ty, Lance, and I hang by the bar in the Sigma Alpha backyard. Construction is complete, and it's official: their house will be up and running for fall. In the meantime, they've managed to secure the place for one last hurrah before the start of the semester, inviting alums and members, including Alpha Theta Mus because of our solidarity after the fire. Tonight's theme is Rome was Rebuilt in a Semester—any excuse to wear a toga. But considering the oppressive humidity of August, it's perfect.

Our crew cheers, and we down our shots before Keegan says, "Hey, we still have an extra one because Ryan didn't come back."

Payton and Dax dragged him off for a game of beer pong, and I figured I'd finish catching up with my buddies, some of whom I haven't seen in months.

"I'll take it," Colin says. Keegan's about to pass it to him, but Colin says, "One sec."

He scoops Ash off the ground and lays him across the bar. Ash has already let the shoulder of his toga fall, so the cloth is only hanging from his waist. Colin takes the shot from Keegan, then pours it across his man, most of it pooling into Ash's navel. Colin takes his time, lapping it all up, his tongue traveling up until he kisses his man.

Keegan laughs uncomfortably, though he doesn't take his eyes off the show, kind of making me wonder if we might need to revisit the whiteboard idea.

"Oh my God," Jaxon tells him. "You're acting like that's the first time you've ever seen them do that."

Keegan's brows knit together. "That seemed longer than usual."

"It did seem a little long," Lance chimes in, all smiles, sneaking a look to Ty, who grabs his boyfriend's ass, giving it a good squeeze, but then doesn't let go.

Fuck, everyone is little horndogs tonight, but I must admit I'm wishing my guy were around so I could get some action too. I search the yard, finding Ry over at the table for beer pong.

Ry and I helped on the builds until early July, when we both headed home to our parents, though we've been swapping whose parents' place we stayed at. His mom officially moved out, and his dad's been doing better since he started dating again, which has helped Ryan feel less like shit about the whole situation. It hasn't been easy, but he's adjusting, and this kind of thing takes time. I'm here for him, however long that may take.

Ryan's beer-pong team includes some of his old teammates and Angie. As he loses a round, he downs a beer, some of it dripping onto his chest, sliding under his toga. And now I'm realizing it might be better not to watch him if I don't want to have a raging boner in front of everyone.

"What was I saying?" Lance asks me. "Before we were interrupted by shots?"

"Your internship."

"Oh yeah. I'll be interning at Peachstar Biomed, and Ty's got a job with a tech startup not far from there, so we were thinking we'll get our own place."

"Like moving in together?" I ask, genuinely surprised. "I mean, maybe that's not weird. You've been sleeping in the same bed since the fire."

"Kind of since before then," Ty says, and they exchange a knowing look.

"Okay, whatever. It does seem like the next logical step. But you guys will have to make time to come out here and see us."

"We'll have to," Lance says. "You, Ash, and Payton are in grad programs for the next few years. Troy and Ryan work at the shop. A lot of guys have graduated but are still floating around Peachtree Springs."

"Um, Ty," Keegan pipes up, "don't forget you still have friends here too."

"Nah, these losers can take care of themselves," Ty insists.

"Fuck you!" Jaxon says with a smile, nudging his shoulder against Ty's.

I continue catching up with my guys, and at some point, Ash and Colin sneak off.

Eventually, boos and shouting alert me to the end of the beer-pong game, so I excuse myself from the gang. While heading across the yard, I admire the way the white cloth drapes across Ry's body, exposing his sculpted pec and that perfect nipple. It's difficult to imagine having ever seen anything other than perfection when I started getting to know this guy.

As he notices me, his eyes light up in a way I've learned is just for me, and he approaches. He leans close, his hot breath tickling my ear as he whispers, "Now that I kicked their asses, you mind if I abduct you?"

"You can do anything you want to me in that," I admit, and he practically glows.

He takes my hand, interlocking our fingers, and guides me through our half-dressed peers. He takes me through the living area, where plenty of people are gathered, and I see Aiden chatting with a group of Alpha Theta Mus.

"Looks like he's not gonna have any issues adjusting to frat life," Ryan notes, and I never had a doubt.

Since our chat, Aiden's made sure to spend more time with me this summer, but I've been giving him his space tonight so he could make connections with the guys he'll be spending time with next year, when he hopefully earns his place at the frat.

"Hey, you two," a voice comes from nearby, and we turn to see Dax. Along with his toga, he sports a chaplet of leaves. "I think the place looks even better than before the fire."

"It does," Ryan agrees. "Some Omega Psi prick can light the place up, but we'll build it right back up, huh? Sucks that you'll still have to see that guy around campus."

Dax's lip twists into his dimple, like he's thinking about something, maybe their confrontation. Although, I remember that weird moment when we were talking about Miles after. Dax seemed to have something on his mind then too, as if the subject confused him for some reason. And confusion isn't really Dax's thing.

"Uh…yeah, you know it," he finally says. "Anyway, you two looked like you were up to no good, so I'll let you get back to it. I'll be grabbing a refill."

We hug it out, and then Ryan guides me upstairs.

"Where are we going?"

He sneaks a look over his shoulder, his lips curling

into a mischievous smirk. "You'll see," he practically hums, and the way he's eyeing me, I don't press because I have a feeling I'm gonna like wherever this is going.

We start down the hallway on the second floor, when we hear sounds coming from one of the rooms, both of us recognizing the voices even before hearing, "Fuck me, Ash. Fuck me harder."

I cringe but can't fight a smile. We exchange a look, and I can tell Ryan's thinking the same thing I am.

"Maybe one last time?" he says, as though reading my mind.

We approach the door, and Ryan presses his knuckle against it, cracking it open. I close my eyes, unsure I can follow through with it, but then I force myself to peek. With their togas on the floor, Colin lies on his back on the desk with Ash holding his legs, drilling him like it's his job.

"This looks familiar," Ryan whispers before Colin turns and catches us.

"Oh, hey, guys!"

Ash spins around, offering a half-wave and a " 'sup," which doesn't seem to affect his thrusts.

I can't look long, though. It's too weird, so I pull back, and Ryan starts to close the door.

I stop him. "I think they'll enjoy it more if it's cracked open."

"Such a good friend," Ryan teases before we continue

down the hall.

"Never thought I'd say this, but I'm gonna miss potentially running into them."

"I have a feeling that's still a real possibility with those guys."

"Yeah, I think if we head to the fourth floor of the library, we'll still have plenty of opportunities."

As Ryan approaches another room, he checks the knob—it isn't locked. He guides me inside the space, empty except for the basics—bed, dresser, desk.

"I'm guessing this was your room?"

He grins. "Yeah. I never had a chance to show it to you."

"I assume it's a lot tidier than it was when you were living in it." It's an intentional dig at the mess I learned he was when he moved into my room, and really, he hasn't changed much since.

He places his hand over his heart. "Ow. I'm not that bad."

"I think you're back to gaslighting me," I joke.

He's all teeth as he pulls his phone out of a pocket in his toga.

"What are you doing?" I ask, but he doesn't respond, just keys away before setting his phone on his desk.

It takes a moment for the music to start playing. I recognize it because it's the song I used when I was first teaching him how to tango. Tango classes ended a few weeks ago, but Ryan and I have kept up our lessons, getting even better.

"My turn to lead," he says, taking my hand and resting the other against my back. I don't resist him, and we start to move through the basics.

It surprises me at first how easily I go along with him, especially considering the reason why I preferred to lead was because of how I wanted to be in control, but Ryan's helped me loosen the reins on that a bit.

But only a bit.

As we travel in a circle, I get lost in the sparkle in his blue irises, wondering if they were always this blue or if I only see them this way because of how my feelings for him have changed.

"You know Ty and Lance are moving in together," he says.

"I do."

"I was thinking…we should discuss the possibility of moving in together too."

I can't fight back the smile that stretches across my face as a flurry of sensations shifts in my belly. But… "I don't know… We do have to sort out your being a mess."

He angles his head, shooting me a dirty look. "You've got to be kidding."

"You think you're gonna live with me without any rules?"

He rolls his eyes.

"And another thing we need to settle: when the red light starts blinking on the water-filter lid..." It's something I've given him hell about when we were at Dax's or when he's come over to stay at my parents' place.

"That's not a set rule. You can use it through another gallon."

"And you can also take a minute to swap it out," I say with a tone, and Ryan's eyebrow pops up.

"Honey, are we really gonna fight right now?"

"Don't you *honey* me right now." But he's still smiling because he knows that always calms me down, even when we have a minor disagreement like this.

"I think you're trying to start a fight because you think it's hotter when we have makeup sex."

"Well, we can only do that after you agree to change out the water filter when the light turns red."

"After I finish up the pitcher?"

I groan, and he leans forward, planting a kiss.

I wish I could stay annoyed, but I submit too quickly as he shoves me back and guides me onto the bed, until soon we're making out.

As he pulls away, he glances around. "This reminds me of that first time in your room. Making out, wondering what was going on." He presses his crotch against me.

"No question what that's about now," I say, and he shakes his head.

"Not even a little."

He licks up my lips as one hand slides under the cloth draped across my torso, gliding his fingers up my abs. My body prickles with life, my thoughts scattering as we get lost in another kiss.

Though it's similar to that first night, it's not even close to the same. There's no confusion. No worry. No anxiety—not about these kisses, at least.

His lips pull away, and he whispers, "Was that enough to convince you to move in with me?"

"I think you're gonna have to really up your game to convince me of that."

He leans back, glancing at me with a familiar cocky expression. "Up my game, huh? Well, I can do that." He lunges at me, his mouth at my throat as he nibbles, going feral.

And as he forces my toga down my shoulder so he's free to kiss down my body, I already know...

We're definitely getting an apartment together.

THE END

Preorder Dax and Miles's story today!
mybook.to/PeachStateFratbros

If you enjoy the *Peach State Fratbros*, check out the
Peach State Stepbros!
mybook.to/ForFratsSakePSF3

Follow Devon on Social Media
linktr.ee/devonmccormack

BONUS CONTENT

The following deleted scene takes place during Ryan and Marty's first date.

Marty

SO APPARENTLY, I fucked up the chicken.

Because of course I did. I wouldn't be Marty McGovern if I hadn't.

Ryan did his best to salvage it, insisting, "Should be fine. Yeah, it'll be good," but said it in that way that made me real skeptical. Still, we managed to put everything together and keep our hands off each other to finish the rest of the chicken-parmesan recipe. Okay, maybe there were a few slips and a handful of kisses, but overall, we did good, and somehow got the job done.

It's still anyone's guess if it's a success.

We sit at the dining table, across from one another, with our finished dish and salad. Each of us has a breast on our plates, topped with marinara and parmesan, resting on a bed of noodles.

"It looks good." I use the tongs to collect some salad for Ryan's plate, then mine.

"Oh, such great service," Ryan says. "We'll have to come to this place more often."

"Whatever happened with the chicken parmesan, we can at least say the salad's probably okay."

"It might be a little dry," Ryan warns. "But it should be edible."

He grabs his fork and knife, cutting a piece. I do the same, and he waits for me.

"Hold up," he says. "Let's cheers."

With his fork in one hand, he grabs his beer with the other, and I have my White Claw.

"To our first date night," he says. "May there be many more, and may they be just as good."

We tap our cans together, and then he scoots from his chair, leaning across the table. "A little kiss for luck?"

I give him a—cringe—smooch, and then we settle back in and take our first bite. I'm hopeful as I chew…and chew… The chicken's tough, like rubber.

"Mmmm," Ryan says, his eyes widening as he fights to chew too.

I can't last anymore, so I grab my paper towel and spit it out. "Ugh," I say reflexively, but Ryan's still going.

"Mmmm-hmmmm," he hums, rubbing his belly like he's satisfied, though he looks like he's about to cry.

"I definitely burned that," I tell him before he grabs his paper towel and spits it out too.

His face is bunched up as he moves his mouth, like

that's gonna get the unsettling texture and taste out. Then he glances at me and says, "Pizza?"

So…we have salad and decide to rewatch *Alien* while we wait for pizza. Meat-lovers with beef instead of sausage, which is our go-to because he'll eat anything and I'm not a fan of Italian sausage. After it arrives, we're even hungrier than normal, so we both devour slices. With Ryan's size, he should be the one tearing it up, but I'm doing an impressive job myself.

After I swallow the last of the slice I'm on, I take a breath, like I need to recover from the pizza-eating workout.

"You think the garbage disposal enjoyed our attempt?" I ask.

"It didn't sound like it was having an easier time stomaching it."

He's not wrong.

"I knew I'd fuck it up."

"Hey, I'm just as guilty, but admittedly, I'm not used to being distracted when I cook."

But really, I enjoy being the one distracting him.

I lie across the couch, resting my head in his lap, and his hand relaxes on my stomach, which feels bloated with all the pizza I've scarfed down.

"Is the baby kicking?" I ask.

He slides his hand under my tee, feeling carefully, like he's playing doctor.

"Nah, I think you're good…" His hand slides up toward my chest. "Oh, wait. What's this?" He feels between my pecs. "Oh no. Oh fuck."

He pumps his hand up and down, balling it into a fist so it looks like a Xenomorph from the movie is trying to pound its way out of my rib cage, which really gets me laughing. He glances down at me, beaming, like he's just happy he could pull that laugh from me.

"Can't believe I agreed to watch this for date night," he says.

"It's a good movie."

"It's okay. You can hold your boyfriend real close when he's having nightmares about Xenomorphs latching to his face and breeding him with their alien eggs."

"You're not talking about the Xenomorphs," I explain.

"What?"

I snicker at his rookie mistake. "You'd be having a nightmare about face huggers. The Xenomorphs are what burst out of people's chests."

He winces, grinning. "Oh, 'scuse me. You never told me you were an expert in this franchise."

I laugh. "If Lance could hear you say that…I think I've seen one or two others with him, but this is the only one I know. Are you suggesting I ruined date night?"

"Couldn't if you tried," he assures me. "But this was

a great date night. I don't mind losing out on chicken parmesan for a chance to grope my man a little more."

"Me too," I admit.

"So it's settled, then. We'll have date night once a week and try out different recipes."

"It's a deal. But how about we aim for something easier next time?"

His brows tug together. "Mart, I don't know how much easier we're gonna get than chicken parmesan."

I can't stop smiling. Ryan has that effect on me, and he gazes down at me with those perfect blue eyes of his.

Never imagined being around him could feel like this.

Or that he'd be eager to tell his parents about me.

"I'm glad we stayed with Dax to help out on the build," I admit.

"Me too." He rests his hand against my face, stroking his thumb across my flesh.

He leans down and offers a gentle kiss against my forehead. I close my eyes, appreciating the sensation it stirs. When he pulls away, I take his hand in mine, rubbing his fingers.

Despite the lovely date, I detect some discomfort in his expression, so I probe. "What is it?"

"Huh? Nothing."

I glare at him. "Come on. I'm your boyfriend. Add to the rules that we talk about shit when it comes up."

A soft smile plays across his lips. "I was just thinking it's a lot of change all at once. Don't have football to dive into. My parents are divorcing. And now we've graduated and most of our friends are moving on with their lives."

His words touch something bittersweet within me. "Right? As happy as I am to get on with my life, being with those guys at Alpha Theta Mu was incredible. It's wild to think there won't be any more committee meetings or parties or TaskFrat challenges. That I can't just walk down the hall to see Lance or Ash."

"At least Ash will be going to grad school at Peach State," Ryan says. "And Lance and Ty are sticking around. You'll still get to see them, but I'm definitely bracing myself for the change. It's gonna be different, and not always fun not getting to see the guys all the time, but I didn't want to bring it up because there's one guy I'm glad I still get to see."

"Same," I assure him, earning a sweet smile that makes me chuckle.

"What?" he asks.

"Just thinking how many times I used to want to deck you in that sexy-ass face of yours."

"You would never," he insists.

"No, I'm not a violent person. Surely, you've picked up on that."

He wears a sneaky expression before he says, "I

meant because you'd never want to bruise this impressive jawline—and there's my glare."

Fuck, I didn't realize I was even doing it, but he's beaming over it, practically glowing.

I don't know that I can feel much better than I do right now, my head in his lap, his eyes on me as I drink in his beautiful flesh, even tainted by the pink marks on his shoulders.

"Okay," he says, "you're gonna need to scooch. Time for cuddles."

We reposition so he can spoon me. On the screen, Ripley suits up, so I know it's not much longer before the Xenomorph gets sucked out of the ship.

Hooking an arm around me, Ryan buries his face against my neck, offering gentle kisses, and I tuck my ass back against his pelvis.

"Good date night, huh?" he asks.

"Kind of perfect." I rest my eyes, appreciating that, really, I don't know that it could have gone better.

ABOUT THE AUTHOR

Devon McCormack

Devon McCormack grew up in the Georgia suburbs with his two younger brothers and an older sister. At a very young age, he spun tales the old-fashioned way, lying to anyone and everyone he encountered. He claimed he was an orphan. He claimed to be a king from another planet. He claimed to have supernatural powers. He has since harnessed this penchant for tall tales by crafting worlds and characters that allow him to live out whatever fantasy he chooses. Devon is an out and proud queer man living in Atlanta, Georgia.

Find Devon:

www.devonmccormack.com